The Bridge

By

Jesse Myrow

Jesse Myrow

Acknowledgements

Special thanks to Elena Pintilii the founder of "Ana's Stories" for the attention to detail And creativity to produce a perfect and beautiful book cover.

Jesse Myrow

The Bridge

Jesse Myrow

Prologue

Ana stared up at the street at the bright yellow mailbox Jesse had described to her. She remembered thinking it would stand out more, like a beacon of color amidst drab and gray houses surrounding it, but the neighbor had a red one. The house next to her was blue. She might not even have the right house.

She stepped forward, one click of her heeled boots at a time, and kept the mailbox in her sights, vision tunneling so heavily she was reminded of when she was a kid. She used to collect the cardboard tubes of paper towel rolls and color them with markers and stickers—a box in her closet held all of her "telescopes"—and she would use them almost daily. She'd close one eye and let the other focus on the one distant item small enough to fit in the scope of her cardboard toy. Her neighbor's door, a stop sign, a cat.

A mailbox.

Her feet stopped before she made a conscious decision to do so. The mailbox stood before her, the address meticulously stenciled on.

This time, she stared at the door of the house. There wasn't anything unique about it. It was wooden, painted creme with a rectangular window, but she found herself putting significance to the choices despite that. Jesse never wore white, so maybe it was too bright. He was straightforward, so maybe he preferred the straight lines over an arched window.

Or maybe, more than likely, he didn't choose it at all and it was already there when he moved in.

With a deep inhale, she moved forward to stand on the porch, the two steps of the stairs creaking underneath her. She knocked. Ana expected to wait, perhaps have more time to overanalyze the type of wood next, but within only a couple of seconds, it swung open—and there was Sarah.

"Oh," Sarah breathed out. Her straight hair was coiled in a tight bun, but a couple of strands fell to frame her surprised face unevenly. "Ana."

She inclined her head. "Sarah."

The sound of her name seemed to jolt Sarah into activity, and she stepped back, the door jerking open wider.

"S-Sorry. Come in. Please."

The shift from cool weather to central heating made the entrance into Jesse's old home feel like stepping into another world—and, in a way, it was. Her life in Germany was notably different from the ranch-style American home surrounding her.

Sarah kept a tidy home, the exceptions being children's shoes thrown near the door and a few toys scattered around the living room floor off of the front hallway. Sarah directed her to sit on the gray couch, while she fetched some coffee. Ana sunk into the plush cushion. It seemed newer, likely bought within the last couple of years, and matched the other cushioned pieces. The chair next to Sarah's was empty. The rest of the furniture, as with any house, was a mismatch. One was probably from Sarah, one from her husband, one bought together at the store. Ana wondered if any were from Jesse.

Sarah brought in a large silver tray in with a collection of bowls and containers: sugar, cream, creamers, spoons, and, of course, the coffee. The mugs Sarah presented were hefty pieces with melted glaze dripping down the sides, and Ana ran her thumb over the uneven bumps of green and blue. A spoon tinging against ceramic drifted her gaze up to the woman across from her on the chair, who was nervously stirring sugar into her drink. Ana brought her own tea to her mouth, trying not to wince at the temperature.

The silence was heavy, weighing them down so they sunk further into the cushions, until Ana set her cup down with a decided thump.

"I don't want this to be awkward," she said.

"Neither do I." Sarah sighed, also setting her mug down. "But you can understand why it is."

Ana nodded, and she watched Sarah copy the motion as the older woman tapped her fingers against the armrest. Cleared her throat.

"Is, uh, Simon here?" Sarah asked.

"He's still at home. I was unsure how long my business in America would take, so I thought..." She interlocked her fingers, swelling them white and red. "I thought...I'd bring him next time?"

Ana didn't mean for the questioning inflection to leak into her tone, but to make up for it, she held the other woman's gaze and waited for her response, pointedly ignoring the steady beat of her heart.

Sarah didn't pull her eyes away either, seeming to scrutinize her.

Finally, her eyes softened. "Next time." She smiled and leaned back in the chair. "Jake would love to see his—uh..."

"Uncle?"

Sarah seemed to freeze, mouth held open and expression pinched. "R-Right. His uncle, or half-uncle?" A bubble of laughter escaped her, and Ana tried to ignore the manic tone of it. "Jake's Uncle Simon."

Ana tapped her fingers against her knuckles. "I think...just Simon's fine."

"Yes, that would be—that would be better." Sarah shook her head. "Anyway, Jake would love to see Simon and play with him."

Relief settled over Ana, and she smiled. "Good." The empty chair next to Sarah stuck out, a gaping gray with navy blue stripes. She licked her lips before asking, "And...your sisters?"

"Ah." Sarah shifted in her seat. "Well, they're...not here. Obviously. Monica and Kaylee just need...time."

"I see."

"All of this, you and Simon, it's a lot."

"You don't have to explain."

"I don't want you to feel like you don't belong."

"Sarah—"

"Because you *do*. You're family now, Simon especially. And I promised that you would be welcome." She swiped up her mug to cradle in her palms. "I promised."

Not knowing what to say in return, Ana followed Sarah's movement, then took a drink of cooling liquid. She didn't notice before, but there was a taste of hazelnut. She wondered if Jesse passed on his favorite kind of coffee to his daughter or vice versa.

Her eyes drifted around the room, but she didn't find many family pictures. It wasn't unexpected. Jesse didn't like his picture taken, and from what Ana had heart about Sarah, she wasn't particularly sentimental.

But she did find one photo. It was a simple little thing; the frame was wooden with clean edges, varnished with a light stain, and it held a standard five-by-seven photo. Jesse stood in front of an armored truck, directing men to their positions. It was a candid shot, so he wasn't smiling, but Ana thought she preferred that.

Sarah must have noticed where she was looking. She said, "He sent that a year before you two met, I think it was." She chuckled. "Well, his co-worker did. Dad would never have sent it himself."

Ana huffed out a laugh. "Very unlikely, yes." She stood and walked over to it. "Do you mind if I...?"

"Oh, feel free!"

The frame was lighter than she was expecting, the photo a little blurrier. She brought a finger up to touch Jesse's head. Though peppered with gray, he had the same hair color as his daughter.

From Jake's picture to the right, he also appeared to have the same.

Though it took Ana longer than she told herself it would, she finally made it to their home. She'd made the mistake of delaying things in the past—career, love life, friendships, family—but she wouldn't waste any more time. Not again. Ana swore it to herself as her finger drifted down to his chest.

Chapter One

The sun was rising.

It was a dim realization, like noticing a leaf had fallen onto his sleeve through a thick sweater. He knew because his eyes were tracing the shadows of the hotel ceiling fan instead of the red light of the smoke detector, the color duller as the slow brightness seeped through the curtains.

Jesse sighed, casting the sheets off with a tired pull. When he first started traveling, back in his twenties, he could sleep at any time, any place, but at fifty, he had trouble just sleeping through the night, let alone jetlagged and six hours ahead in Ludwigshafen.

"I'm gonna need some coffee," he said.

His lips turned up in a wry smile as the heat turned off; he thought the room might be pitying him with some sort of audible response.

"Yeah, I know. I say that practically every day."

The empty room stayed silent.

With a groan, he lifted himself up and stumbled to the bathroom to splash some water on his face. The cold water certainly helped, but he would definitely need the coffee. It wasn't a light work day, so he'd be busy, though—thankfully—not for a couple of hours. He could treat himself to some caffeinated monstrosity with sugar—something better than hotel packets of instant coffee, anyway. There was a small cafe on the way to the office he'd noticed yesterday, so he figured he may as well try it out. It wasn't as though he was getting any sleep.

After shrugging on a T-shirt and throwing on some jeans, Jesse grabbed his sweatshirt and headed out the door, down the elevator, and into the crisp air of the barely there morning. It was still a tad early for the cafe to open, he assumed, so he moseyed around, eventually making it to a small park. He preferred it to the busier, touristy *Englischer Garten* in Munich even though that one was much more beautiful. Jesse liked the quiet more.

The most notable feature was the river slicing steadily through the trees; a combination wood-and-stone bridge connected the opposite areas of the park. Squinting either way, Jesse couldn't see an end to the water feature, one end curved around a thicket of foliage, while the other end moved forward and out of sight.

Jesse stood a safe few feet away from its bank, just off the path, and watched leaves and a few twigs chug by him. He blinked in surprise when something smacked into the rock near his feet, halting its steady pace down the river only long enough for him to notice it was a stuffed bear. It tumbled further down the river, a dark brown mass of matted fur. Through the glaring sun shining through the trees, he couldn't tell if the bear became so waterlogged it had sunk, or if it had drifted away even farther.

Either way, the child who lost it wasn't getting it back, and he felt a pang of sympathy.

Jake had a toy like it, he thought. Pepper, Jake called it, after upturning a shaker of the stuff into its fur. His grandson would be three in a few months, so maybe

13

Jesse'd buy him another, give the lonely stuffed bear a friend. He could name him Salt.

Unfortunately, he'd need to wait until he returned to America, which wouldn't be for a couple of months. He sighed. *Just a couple of months longer.*

Shaking his head, Jesse turned from the bank and made his way back to town. By the time he walked there, the cafe was finally open. Dark clouds rolled in as he pushed open the wooden door, accompanied by a faint chime from a bell, which sounded like it might need a new clapper.

The inside of the cafe was quiet, and the only other patrons were a businessman with his briefcase and suit, and, judging by the green scrubs, someone in the medical field. Despite so few customers, there were two workers—one behind the counter, the other waiting tables and cleaning the main area, and Jesse's eyes unconsciously followed the colorful pattern of the barista's skirt before turning to order.

"*Hallo. Ein mittlerer kaffee, bitte, mit...*uh..." He pursed his lips, wracking his brain for the right, crucial-for-his-morning word.

Seeming to take pity on his struggle, the barista offered, "I speak English if that helps."

Relieved, Jesse smiled. "It does, yes. I'd like a shot of espresso."

"Coming right up, sir." Before she turned, she said, "The word is *espresso* in German."

He snorted. "Of course. Thanks." He waved to her as he waited at the pickup counter for her to whip up his drink, casting his eyes around the room. None of the sparse decorations were particularly interesting; his eyes wandered instead to the only source of movement in the room, the waitress.

He couldn't look away, barely blinking.

Gliding—that was the right word, he thought. She was gliding across the floor, elegant and smooth. The long, flowing skirt cinched at the bend of her waist with a belt rippled like water disturbed by a lone skipping stone. Even the movement of her legs, her head, her smile, were delicate yet exact, like the way a ballerina's arms would float as she drifted across the stage.

After being in and working for the military twenty-seven years, strong movements and plodding boots were what he was used to. He was conscious of his own heavy footsteps as he made his way to a corner table, so unlike the feather-dusted shuffle of her flats against the floor. Jesse had clobbered right over the floor when he entered, but she sidestepped the loud creaks of the old paneling as she gathered used cups.

The woman turned her attention to the scrubs customer, her back to Jesse, but he managed to hear her laugh, something louder than he was expecting, though it didn't seem out of place.

When she continued to chat with the woman, Jesse was suddenly aware of how long he'd been watching her. Shifting uncomfortably in his seat, he turned his gaze to the opposite end, already feeling his cheeks warm. Evidently, he was alone in his hotel room too much if he was gaping at a woman multiple years his junior like a prepubescent boy.

She had a magnetic quality about her, though, and he almost scoffed at how much that sounded like it belonged in a romance novel—but it was true. Even after looking away, he could feel his eyes wanting to pull up from their locked position on the floor.

Instead, he purposely cataloged what he had to accomplish at work, and he absorbed himself in his checklist, determining which tasks he could push until tomorrow if he didn't have enough time. A few could be delegated to his men. Inventory of the base could go to Jackson, filing through emails to Yates, and Ramales could page through the applicants. That left Jesse with some time to make a few phone calls.

Then fabric, curled over the tips of black flats, settled in the middle of his gaze.

"Can I get you anything?"

When Jesse flicked his eyes up, his heart stuttered. There she was. Outside of her general appearance (a long face with green eyes), the first thing he noticed was how genuine her smile seemed. It wasn't stretched wide or a barely-there quirk; it curled up evenly on both sides, something soft and pleasant. In America, the waitresses tended to be overly friendly, hungry for tips to add to their low wage, and perhaps the lack of tipping in Germany contributed to the woman's different attitude, but he suspected not. She smiled and waited for his answer like an old acquaintance wondering how he'd been.

She blinked a couple of times, and Jesse realized he hadn't said anything yet.

"Oh, right." He gestured to his full coffee. "I'm fine, Miss...?"

"Ana."

"Thank you, Ana. I'm fine for now."

She smiled once more, inclining her head. "Then just let me know if you need anything. I'm sure I'll hear you if you call."

He cast his eyes from one end of the opposite wall to the other. "Yes, it is a bit...small."

"Cozy," she corrected, a lightness to her eyes, and Ana waved over her shoulder as she continued with her duties.

He didn't realize his heart was beating quickly until it quieted down once she left with a swish of her skirt. She drifted over to her coworker, and they conversed quietly, though their giggles filled the small space with lightness.

Her name was Ana. A pretty name, he thought.

Jesse turned back to his coffee, drinking it despite the temperature. If he waited long enough, it would be iced coffee, and by that point, he would be late to work and have even more to catch up on.

As he heard their chatter in the corner, he realized they were speaking in German. It wasn't a shattering discovery, considering which country he was in, but playing back the conversation he just had, it was in English. The barista at the counter must have told her. He ran a hand across the back of his neck. He hadn't even noticed...

A faint ting against the glass made him glance toward the window. The rain had started, which seemed to displease the scrubs woman; she cursed and stood. Grabbing her bag, she called out her thanks as she hurried through the door, and through the window, Jesse watched her scurry down the street.

He was the only customer in the café. It was an odd feeling, both intrusive and comfortable. When a much younger Jesse had worked in customer service, he had always wanted the customers to finish quickly. Directing them to the item they were looking for took all of two minutes, but when the store was empty, he was allowed to fiddle with personal projects or even lounge on the counter.

He doubted Ana would sit on the countertop. If she did, Jesse imagined her with a straight back, crossed legs, and hands folded in her lap. Though maybe she'd surprise him and plop down after he'd left, slurping up her own drink.

Rivulets of water streaked down the glass window, and the awning above the door waterfalled the heavy downpour onto the concrete. Jesse may have to kill a little more time before he left. He didn't think to bring a raincoat, only a sweatshirt that didn't offer him much protection, and he didn't have a change of clothes at the base.

"It's really coming down."

He startled at Ana's voice near him. Her hands held a tray of empty plates and cups as she watched the storm. She'd picked up the scrubs woman's mug and empty muffin plate, the crumpled-up wrapper still wadded up in the middle. The businessman's larger plate was stacked beneath it.

"Yeah, I wasn't exactly prepared." Jesse pointed to his clothes, and Ana turned, scanning his attire, ratty compared to hers.

"At least you have the hood." She mimed pulling it up, and he smiled.

"True. I may still wait it out a few minutes anyway."

"Probably a good idea." The plates clinked when she stepped toward him. "Finished with that?" She lowered the tray a little.

"Oh, sure." It only had a few cold sips left, so he set it down. "I will probably order another, though."

"What would you like? Same as you had, or something new?"

As Ana straightened, he noticed a small braid near her ear, held at the end by a blue bead. It suited her, framing her face and tapping her collarbone when she moved. Her dark hair and bead contrasted against her ivory skin.

Watching as the bead rolled to rest at the edge of her collar, he found himself muttering, "Something new."

Nothing sounded from her, and he tore his eyes away to see her waiting expectantly for his answer. He flushed; she hadn't heard him. Maybe it was for the best.

"Ah, right. How about something sweet?"

She laughed. "Well, that's not very specific. A surprise, then."

"I guess so." His lips curled up.

"Anything you *don't* like?"

"Uh," he said, "I don't think so. Peppermint, maybe?"

"Okay, I can work with that."

With one last smile, Ana trotted to the counter and set the empty dishes on atop it. The other worker stared at the pile before sighing, picking them up to take in back. Ana, on the other hand, got to work on his drink. Jesse, admittedly, had never really paid much attention to the process of making coffee. As he watched her, he realized there were more steps than he was expecting. She skipped between a couple different machines which let loose a variety of whirring and sputtering noises, and a pump of some syrup dripped into the cup.

There was clatter as she grabbed a metal container, and Jesse raised his eyebrow at the stick she pulled out to poke at the drink after she'd poured what looked like milk. Finally, she placed the lid on with a click he could hear from his table, then sheathed the cup in a cardboard sleeve.

When she turned around, he acted as though he hadn't been fascinated by her, but he didn't know how successful he was. She placed the drink on his table and clasped her hands in front of her.

"Hopefully you enjoy it."

Curious, Jesse took a delicate sip, still piping hot, and his eyes widened.

"That's delicious! What is it?"

A pleased smile lit her face. "Cherry almond latte."

"Huh." He took a heftier sip this time. "Never would've chosen that combo, but glad you did."

"It's a favorite of mine around the holidays. Tastes like the shortbread jam cookies my family makes."

"Oh, I'm terrible at baking."

"Me too," she admitted. "My family makes them, not me. I provide the caffeine."

He laughed, his grin wider than it was at the beginning of the conversation. "A good contribution, I'd say. I definitely appreciate it." He nodded his head and lifted the cup as if in cheers. "Thank you, Ana."

"You're welcome, Mister…?"

"Jesse. My name's Jesse."

She pinched the sides of her skirt with just a finger and thumb then shifted into a small curtsy, a teasing glint to her eyes. "Then you are very welcome, Jesse. I'm glad I could give a little holiday cheer this gloomy fall day."

He agreed, but before she could say anything further, a distraught voice called from the back, "Ana! The sink's clogged again!"

A flicker of exasperation pulled at her face, but it was gone as quickly as it came, and she gestured to the back.

"It appears I'm needed."

Disappointment sunk Jesse's heart.

With a smile, Ana turned to leave, but something about the way her skirt flared out, maybe the way her hair covered her face at that angle, made regret already simmer in his heart—like if he didn't say anything at that moment, he would never see her again. He blurted his next words.

"Would you like to go to dinner?"

Visible surprise flickered across her face as his own flushed.

"I mean—" Jesse took a sip of his coffee, burning his tongue on the careless drink. "I didn't mean to ask that."

She raised an eyebrow. "What *did* you mean to ask?"

"Well, I should say I *did* mean to ask it. Just not yet."

Her face shifted, and he already knew the type of response she'd give, though he couldn't help the pang of disappointment.

"I'm flattered, but—"

He held up a hand. "Ah, that's okay. Enough said." He chuckled. "I imagined this going differently, I have to say. Should've asked you after *two* conversations instead of just one," he joked, which seemed to work; she chuckled.

"Well, to put your mind at ease, I doubt my answer would've been different then, either." She shrugged. "I'm not looking to date anyone at the moment."

"Neither am I."

Ana tilted her head, but her eyes sparkled with amusement. "Then this conversation is certainly not what either of us expected."

"Guess not." Jesse's expression was sheepish as he lifted his cup. "Thanks for the coffee and company anyway."

She hesitated a moment, and one hand fiddled with the seam of her skirt. Then, "You're welcome."

Ana turned away, retreating to the kitchen, and Jesse was left to sip his drink in silence. Muffled conversation seeped through the cracks, but he didn't feel the urge to strain his ears to hear them. He looked at the clock and hefted himself up from the chair. Rain still pelted the window, so he flipped his hood up. He glanced back at the kitchen door, solid and shut, and jogged out the shop, already feeling his clothes getting soaked.

Jesse wondered if Ana glided back out when the bell chimed, wondered if she noticed he was gone.

Probably not.

He ducked into the first available cab, preemptively apologizing for a wet seat. His coffee was still hot, and he could feel the uncomfortable tingle of a burnt tongue, so he carefully lifted the lid, but he paused at what he saw.

There was a misshapen drawing of some sort of animal. He could make out an ear and the long pull of a whisker. He thought some part of it looked like a little heart, and his lip lifted at the corner.

Maybe she would notice.

Chapter Two

That man was sitting at the corner table again.

Garbed in his tennis shoes and baggy sweatshirts, he was quickly becoming part of her morning routine. In a week, he'd been to the café every day Ana worked, and from what her coworkers told her, every day she wasn't, as well. He was there for no longer than an hour before work, and he'd quietly order his coffee, smile to her, then sit down at the same table, same chair every day.

She had regulars, of course. Sabine skipped in at eleven every morning before her afternoon shift at the daycare, and Ana always wondered why she thought she needed the caffeine in the first place with how bubbly she was. She had Klaus, who stumbled in before his calculus classes on Tuesdays and Thursdays, claiming he'd never look at another number again once he passed.

Then there was Jesse.

Ana expected never to see him again after he'd left that first day. Then, she expected their encounter to be awkward when he did return.

It wasn't.

Jesse acted as though she hadn't rejected his date, for lack of a better word (considering he claimed to not want to date). And, even more surprising, Ana talked to him as if he hadn't asked. It was…odd. She even found herself waiting for him to walk through the door, habitually shuffling his feet on the mat at the entrance before making his way to the counter.

That morning, he had on a plain red sweatshirt zipped up halfway to cover a symbol she didn't recognize in a clashing shade of purple. She may have had to squint looking at him if he'd worn colorful pants too, but they were faded jeans, nothing outrageous. She'd already greeted him when he came in, so Jesse bid his time sipping from his mug, leaned back in the chair, ankles crossed. She found herself stepping toward him without a conscious decision.

His smile was a soft one as he lifted his brown eyes to her. "Hello, Ana."

"Jesse." She nodded to his cup. "What do you have today?"

He took a sip of the drink, and a look of puzzlement tilted his lips. "You know, I'm not entirely sure. I told Elaine to surprise me, and I think she gave me something…floral?" He shrugged. "I like it, actually."

"Lavender vanilla, I'd say then. She's been quite obsessed with it the past few days."

"I have no idea what lavender tastes like."

Her lips curled up, and she pointed to the drink. "Presumably that."

"Ah, well—"

The bell above the door rang, accompanied by a flustered woman stumbling inside, arms filled with paperwork. She apologized for the noise and scurried over to claim a table, plopping her folders down with an audible thud.

Ana watched her, saw her flip through some pages, probably ten of them before Ana realized she wasn't moving toward the woman, and her cheeks flushed. She was waiting for Jesse to finish his thought, but of course, he didn't. He was probably wondering why she wasn't helping her customer, raising his eyebrow the way she'd noticed he did often.

Shaking her head, she cursed her uncooperative legs, then strode forward to take the overwhelmed woman's order. Caramel, Ana guessed. She found the day more fun when she played her little game. Otherwise, she got bored, so she was pleased when the woman ordered just what she expected.

She would've guessed black with cream for Jesse, but he surprised her by getting something different every time. Yesterday, he'd gotten a pump of butterscotch flavoring, and she had laughed at the unrestrained disgust on his face.

Since the only two patrons were Jesse and another woman, Elaine could whip up the drink quickly. She tilted her head toward the man when she handed over the latte.

"How'd he like it?" she asked eagerly, and Ana chuckled.

"Are you going to ask that of everyone you give that drink to?"

"Of course." Elaine spoke like it was a stupid question to even ask. When Ana didn't speak further, she poked her shoulder. "*So*, how'd he like it?"

"He likes it just fine, don't worry."

She wiggled a little dance in excitement. "Beautiful! I have to say, it's been *real* nice having a new regular to try out my drinks." She patted Ana's shoulder. "Just make sure to keep flirting with him so he can continue to be my guinea pig."

Ana leveled her with an unamused glower, and Elaine rolled her eyes.

"Oh, you know I'm *kidding*." She elbowed her lightly with a teasing lift to her lips. "Mostly."

In response, Ana turned around to hand the frazzled woman her coffee, who looked as if Ana had given her holy water.

Then, she realized she didn't have anything to do, and she pointedly ignored Elaine's snickers as she headed toward Jesse's table. She was checking to see if he needed anything.

He didn't, but he offered to order something when he realized she didn't even have a dish to clean or a window to wipe; she'd already done all that.

She resisted the urge to sigh. "No, that's alright."

"Tell me what you'd rather be doing, then—other than this."

Her mouth opened in surprise.

"This isn't the first time you've been bored," he added as explanation.

After a moment's hesitation, Ana asked, "At this moment?"

"Sure," he said. "Or down the line."

The fabric of her sweater, never something she was interested in staring at, drew her attention to her sleeve, and she fiddled with the cuff. She'd been asked questions like that before; of course she had. Friends had asked, mentors had asked, family had asked. The same answer always came out of her mouth.

"I'm happy as I am."

But, for some reason, the words wouldn't leave, sticking to the honey-coated lining of her mouth, finally too weighted down to fly out. The only way to speak was to swallow them back down.

Jesse merely sipped his drink, waiting.

The words that left her were soft, quiet, and tiny like a gnat.

"I...don't want to work here anymore."

She expected something to happen in response, something like a coffee cup crashing or Elaine gasping, maybe even her mother calling, but he merely nodded like he expected that—then waited again.

The silence seemed much more intimidating than the question, and she pressed her lips together, spreading the already thin layer of lipstick.

"I love art. I went to school for it." Her eyes drifted away from him, around at the store. "I like this job, too, but…"

"You don't want to be here the rest of your life. I get it."

He nodded again, casually shrugging his shoulders like it was no big deal. But it was to Jesse, wasn't it? It was a simple matter that his barista didn't want to work at the café for the rest of her life. She didn't own it; it wasn't a family business. It was an easy, conversational fact.

"Well," he said when she didn't respond, "I hope your career in art works out." He smiled.

"Thank you," she breathed out. If it wasn't for those kind, attentive eyes, Ana would've claimed the conversation to be distant small talk. But his eyes never left hers, and her heartbeat soundly in her chest.

"I—" She cleared her throat, stepping back. "I have a couple of things to do."

He waved a hand. "Don't let me keep you."

Ana turned away into the kitchen, bypassing Elaine who was filling out an order for a customer she hadn't noticed come in. She wiped the countertop. She rearranged some cups. She rechecked their inventory of muffins and breads.

She poked her head out of the door. Jesse still sat at the table, this time typing something on his phone. Texting someone, maybe. Forcibly pulling her attention from him, she found the frazzled folder woman casting her eyes around, likely looking for service.

Ana set aside the conversation and worked. She found things to do, kept busy. Without her realizing, one hour passed, and she only knew because of the scrape of Jesse's chair.

He was leaving.

Her feet took her forward, following him. Another logo Ana didn't recognize stretched across the back of the sweatshirt, waving her goodbye as he moved to the door.

"Off to work?" she asked his retreating form, and when Jesse turned his head back, he seemed surprised she had stopped him.

"Yeah, uh," he said, "last day of the week, though."

"Start of the weekend, then," she said and immediately felt the need to cringe at the awkwardness of her reply. She didn't really know what possessed her to call him back, not really.

"Uh, yeah, yeah it is." Jesse shifted his feet. "Do you work tomorrow?"

"Just until noon. Then the weekend."

He stared at her for a few moments, scrutinizing her, and if Ana was wont to blush, she would have. Instead, she purposely stood straight, waiting, not entirely sure what she was hoping he'd say. Did she want him to ask another question, talk about his coffee, or explain what was on his T-shirt and hoodies?

She didn't know.

Finally, he turned fully toward her. "There's a park not too far from here. It's not too busy, and...I'll be there at one, regardless of company." He shrugged, trying to appear casual, but she had noticed the way he tapped his finger against his pant leg, his thumb hooked in his belt loop. "If you're interested in a walk."

Her lips curled up. "Is this another not-date?"

"Just a nice stroll between acquaintances." He grinned. "So, what do you say?"

Her answer came easy: "Where should I meet you?"

***

A swan flapped its wings, pebbling the water with droplets from its spot on the river's bank. It cleaned under the left wing, its feathers a stark white against the dark stones and green grass. Ana had arrived about a half an hour early, waiting for Jesse in the middle of the bridge. Stone gave the bridge a solid base, and she tapped her shoe on the wooden boards that lined the top. She leaned her elbows over the railing and watched a couple of kids chase each other around a crooked tree.

One child shrieked with laughter as he hung from a branch, while the other much shorter child attempted to leap up as well. She laughed at the younger's screech of triumph when she finally grabbed on to the bark.

"Rambunctious little things, huh?"

Turning to the voice, it was Jesse, dressed — again — in a sweatshirt, though it was a hoodie this time. It looked to be a restaurant logo, a diner of some sort.

"Kids usually are," Ana said as he settled next to her.

"Do you have any?"

At the familiar question, she mechanically shook her head.

"I have three little girls." He laughed. "Well, three *big* girls now. One's married and has her own kid. Probably about that little girl's age."

There was no hiding the pride in his voice, and she smiled, though she noted his expression was tinged with a hint of sadness. His fingers were threaded before him as he leaned on the railing, and his eyes followed the kids as they swung from the tree.

"You miss them."

Jesse took the observation in stride, merely tilting his head toward her. And he answered simply with, "Yeah. I do."

"I hope you see them soon then."

Smiling at that, he said, "Not too much longer. I'll be back in America in a few weeks."

He went on to explain how he was a defense contractor—the general manager of the company, in fact, so he had to drift between offices, the two largest branches being the one in Germany and the one in America. With a hint of amusement, Ana thought that explained his loose attire; he didn't exactly have to dress up for bases which held training and hulking Humvees.

They drifted from the bridge and followed along a dirt trail dotted with wooden benches, and they only ran across one woman sitting with a book. The rest of the trail was empty, probably because of the day's chilly winds. Ana herself was in a thick sweater, a wool scarf wrapped around her neck.

She was surprised at how well they conversed with each other. There never seemed to be much of a lull, and even by the time they made it to the end of the trail, they were deep in the middle of a conversation, so they looped back around.

"Do you ever work nights?" he joked at one point. "You're always there in the mornings."

She chuckled. "Oh, yes, I've worked both. I'll close the lights and lock the doors in the evening..."

At the uptick of amusement on his face, she paused.

"What?" she asked.

"Ah, sorry. It's just—shut the lights off. Not close the lights."

"Oh." She huffed and looked away. "There are so many expressions. It's hard to keep track of."

"I would imagine so. I can barely speak the one language."

He laughed at his self-deprecating dig, and she waved a hand. "Your German was fine. Besides, I speak more than two."

Ana enjoyed the look of interest on his face.

"I'm Romanian," she explained, then she pointed to the swan moseying down the river through the gap in the trees. "*Lebădă*."

"And that means...swan?"

She smiled. "Yes, it does. *Lebădă pod*. Swan bridge."

When Jesse repeated, his A was a tad nasally, but the pronunciation wasn't too bad. He smiled. "I like it. Sounds like it should be in a play. Or just in *Swan Lake*."

She laughed. "Naming the lake after the swan isn't enough?"

"So maybe it's a little on the nose."

"And there's another odd English expression."

"Maybe I should have beat around the bush a little then."

Ana didn't think she could've rolled her eyes with such amusement, but she managed quite easily, especially with the enjoyment creasing Jesse's face.

"I love going to the theater," she said. "Art in motion. Everything: the lighting, the costumes, the sets, and dance routines—all is designed to show us something. A mood, the time period, color. It's so beautiful to watch."

She could imagine *Swan Lake* and how she leaned forward in her seat when she first saw it—from the stunning painted ballroom in the beginning to the dark, enchanting forest where the swans flew. The ballerina drifted across the stage like a bird, fluttering her arms like wings as the collection of other dancers swarmed around her like the formations Ana noticed in the sky.

The swan next to the river... Ana could see the ballerina there, leaning her body to one side so she could pluck at her feathered tutu draped across the rocks as weightless as fabric. From there, she may extend herself, craning her arms out to fly toward her lover, Prince Siegfried. Though, maybe it was before she'd met him, alone with the other swans by her deep lake.

River, she amended, hearing the one trickling beside her and Jesse.

When Ana turned to him, his eyes were soft, and her heart fluttered like the swan's wings.

"That's a beautiful way to think of it."

She flicked her eyes away, a nervous giggle escaping her, and she pinned some hair behind her ear. "O-Oh, I wouldn't say that. I just appreciate the craftsmanship."

"I can tell. You really do love art — in all forms."

The rightness of his words was a warm hum in her chest, and she smiled. "I do."

There was a moment of hesitation from him before he spoke.

"If you don't mind me saying," he said, "the conversation about work earlier seemed...difficult for you."

Her stride stuttered, but she merely let out a small laugh. "Yes, I suppose it was." She wasn't surprised he'd noticed. "I couldn't find it in myself to lie to a kind stranger."

"Sometimes, those are the easiest people to talk to."

Ana hummed. "So, should I expect our conversations to get more difficult?"

"I hope not." Jesse pulled his hand from the warmth of his pocket, rotating his wrist with expectation to hurry her along, and she wrinkled her nose.

"Fine." She sighed. "I started working at the café a year or so after school. My father was ill at the time, so I needed to be near, and I needed something with flexible hours. Then, he got better, and my mom needed help with her commissions to help with medical bills. She sews from home, and she taught me how when I was young. So, there I stay at the café again." Her hand drifted up to twiddle her braid. "After that…well, I'm still there."

"And you don't want to be."

"Not particularly, but…"

The pause settled into the ground like pieces of gravel, which Ana kicked with her shoe.

"Family," he said after a moment.

She nodded.

"Jake hates when I have to leave for work," Jesse supplied, and she raised a puzzled brow. "My grandson." He shrugged. "So, I get it. The two don't always mix. But, maybe someday."

"Yeah," she said, voice soft as they approached the end of the trail once more. "Maybe someday."

Their shoes sounded against the wooden boards over the bridge, and when she looked toward the tree from earlier, the kids had gone. Ana and Jesse stopped once they made it across the bridge and turned toward each other.

Jesse squinted against the sun poking through the clouds, the wrinkles around his eyes more pronounced as he did, and her eyes were drawn to them. Ana blinked her attention away, though, when he brought a hand up to his brow, giving her a cockeyed salute, and she smiled.

"This was nice," she said.

"It was."

The wind rustled through their beats of silence, bringing with it a few tumbleweeds of leaves. One touched her ankle as it skittered away, and Ana watched it go.

"I guess I'll see you tomor…" Her lips pulled down. "Right. Still the weekend tomorrow. My day off, too."

"Right."

"Right," she echoed much quieter, unsure if he even heard her.

They stood, and when the wind blew again, she realized she was standing closer than she thought. Ana wasn't sure if it was cologne or not, but she smelled a clean, fresh scent coming from him. She liked it.

A snort from him startled her, and Ana darted her eyes up. Those wrinkles crinkled his eyes, and Jesse shook his head.

"I feel like one of those kids," he mumbled then addressed her with a bit more volume—or maybe it was confidence. "Do you want to walk tomorrow?"

A swell of happiness she wasn't expecting made her nod. "Same time?"

"Same place?"

"Then see you tomorrow at *lebădă pod.*"

"Swan Bridge it is." He saluted her with the hand still over his eyes, moving toward the diverging path from her own behind her. "See you later."

Ana waved. "Tomorrow."

As she retreated back her own way, she noticed the swan was gone.

Chapter Three

Jesse tapped his fingers on the table, menu in the other hand. The woman across from him was browsing through as well—for quite a while now. He'd only picked the menu back up because she was taking so long. He'd already decided on the risotto, but she was debating between...what did she say? She considered five different meals so far.

He imagined that Ana would know before they even made it to the restaurant what she wanted to order—and quite aggressively squashed that thought beneath his mental boot. The whole reason he was on a date in the first place was because he was trying *not* to think of her, so when he met Katerina at the coffee shop, he accepted her offer for dinner—a sharp contrast to his own offer to Ana.

He groaned internally, smacking that thought away as well.

Shaking his head, Jesse put the menu down and smiled at the woman in front of him when she glanced over. The laugh lines on her face stretched.

Divorced for a couple of years, she was looking to date again, she told him, and being widowed for more than a decade himself, he saw no reason to say no. She had a kind smile he couldn't help but return.

Ana was also absent from the café the day he accepted.

He was relieved when Katerina finally set the menu down, hunger bubbling in his stomach, and the waiter came shortly after, probably eyeing their table for the last few minutes. A light conversation picked up, but Jesse found it difficult for the topics to hold, like the two were throwing paper at each other rather than playing catch with a ball. She'd toss out a subject about her greenhouse and it would flutter, arch back to her, and he'd have to lunge to grab it.

He didn't remember having to try so hard with Ana.

Just a few days ago, they found themselves deep in discussion about museum presentation, a subject he'd never really considered to even think about, let alone mention.

"It has to *flow*," she'd said. "You have to account for where people will stop. You can't just have things evenly spaced apart."

"That just seems wasteful if you have to redo the layout every time."

She shook her head. "It doesn't matter where a painting was last year. If I have to stand here," she pushed herself into his side, almost making him trip, "to read something over a stranger's shoulder, I'm not stopping to read the information."

Her breath tickled his neck, and he shivered, laughing to cover up the loud beat of his heart. "Okay, okay, fair point."

She nodded, satisfied, and leaned away. But she kept a hand in the crook of his elbow, which warmed something in his chest.

Then they were off talking about the most crowded places they'd been to, Ana claiming her middle school fundraiser was the worst she'd ever experienced. Her description of her schoolmates still made him chuckle.

But at the table with Katerina, Jesse sighed, not even bothering to shoo memories away. Talking with Ana was easy. It had been a couple of weeks since their walk in the park, and pretty much every day since, they'd seen each other either at the bridge or the café.

Well, except that evening.

He concentrated on Katerina's story about her son to alleviate the sting of guilt for canceling their walk, trying not to remember the way Ana's face fell when he said he couldn't go—though she tried to cover it up, transferring her disappointment into the way her hands tightened around her drink tray rather than show on her face.

Katerina said she liked to sketch, and Jesse perked up.

"Oh, I don't really do anything special." Katerina waved her hand, but she reached for a clean paper napkin and used the pen from her purse. Katerina inked her drawing in short strokes, overlapping each other, and leaving the elephant rather feathered and blurry. He'd seen people draw the way she had before; his middle daughter, Monica, used a similar technique.

Ana drew with sure lines, pausing long enough beforehand to know what she wanted to put down on paper—or on the ground as was the case a few days ago. She was waiting for him on a bench, a stick in hand, and she scraped it along a patch of dirt next to her. A long, curved line appeared first, followed by a second, which mirrored it a tad crookedly. When she spotted him, she didn't stop, just waved her free hand and continued.

Jesse had watched in fascination as the tree in front of him formed, carved into the dirt with precision. She'd giggled when he contributed two blobby stick figures sitting underneath, and his hands tingled from where she guided his to color in the bark of the tree.

The elephant in front of him was good, and Katerina blushed at his compliment, tucking a stray strand of hair behind her ear, her dangling earrings chiming against her finger.

Jesse expected to see a bead, and he pursed his lips. His brain felt like a child's in the car. No, they weren't there yet. No, they *still* weren't there yet.

No, Jesse, not Ana. No, still not Ana.

Even though he told himself that, his mind imagined the braid hanging from Katerina's temple.

Ana wore hers every day. He'd noticed the habit after the first few times he'd seen her, and it was always the same ear—her left—so Jesse finally asked her.

They'd been sitting on a bench nestled between two trees on their usual trail, arms pressed together in the chill of the evening, and she'd curled a finger around her usual braid.

"It's from my mother." Ana flicked the bead attached to the end. "Something her mother did as well. I put it in my hair every day."

"A nice tradition." Jesse reached up to touch it, following the bumps of her braid until he made it to the bead, which he let rest on the pads of his fingers. The blue swirled with various hues, but the base color was a rich cobalt. It was cold against his skin—unlike her breath, which ghosted over the back of his wrist.

His eyes trailed back up to her face, and his heart stuttered at the way Ana watched him silently. His knuckle touched her cheek, and she tensed at the temperature but relaxed and turned her face into his hand. Her green irises didn't leave his.

"Beautiful," he breathed, and her eyes widened slightly, enough for him to notice. The breath that hit his skin came out harder than the ones before. He swallowed thickly and, with slow movements, brushed her braid behind her ear. It wasn't meant to be there, bubbling up at the base, but Ana didn't correct him.

"The bead," he said, running his thumb over it once more before letting go. "Beautiful."

When Jesse leaned back, her eyelids fluttered, then she turned away, quickly enough to release the braid from her ear.

"R-Right," Ana said, smoothing our nonexistent wrinkles in her dress. "Thank you."

Though her hair covered half of her face, he could still peek at the flush on her cheeks, but the sight didn't make his face warm, too. Instead, it made him feel colder, and he had shoved his hands in his pockets.

Ana was thirty-two.

He repeated that to himself the rest of their walk. He repeated it the next day.

It became a mantra in Jesse's head when he felt himself wanting to say no to Katerina's date.

Ana was thirty-two.

Katerina, the woman growing exotic flowers in greenhouses he should be interested in, was his age, only four years older at fifty-four. So, Jesse smiled at her, laughed at her jokes, forced himself to have a good time and ignore the ever-present flash of Ana's smile, her floral skirts and silky tops, her distinctive hair.

It was like when he'd visit his daughter, Sarah, when Jake was at daycare. Though he wasn't there, no matter what room Jesse stepped into, there was Jake's favorite animal—a bear drawing in the kitchen, a bear cartoon character action figure on the couch, a stuffed bear on the floor. Even if they were out of Jesse's eyesight, there they'd be in his peripherals, and all he'd have to do was tilt his head, and he'd see it again.

He barely had to tilt his head to be reminded of Ana.

Katerina mentioned how close she was to retirement; he thought of how Ana was about to explore the possibilities of her own career. Katerina moaned about getting more tired than she used to when she was young; Ana had so much energy, especially when she spoke of something she was passionate about. Katerina found art galleries boring; Ana would live in one if she could.

He laughed a little too loud at one of Katerina's jokes to make up for the comparison.

Finally, though, with only two bites left of their tiramisu between them, she said, "There's someone else, isn't there?"

And all he could really do was sigh, feeling a tug of guilt in his stomach which made him regret eating that last bite of dessert. Jesse wasn't much of an actor.

"There shouldn't be," he confessed. "There is, though."

She nodded. "I understand." Then her mouth curled up at the end a little. "My husband was a 'shouldn't be.'"

He raised an eyebrow. "And aren't you divorced?"

"After twenty years of happy marriage."

"You were married for twenty-eight."

Katerina laughed. "Well, think of it this way: in twenty years, you'll be in your seventies and probably be too exhausted to bother fighting over the types of things my ex and I did."

"I guess that's one way to look at it." His face fell into seriousness. "I'm sorry this didn't work out."

"That's alright." She patted his hand. "Honestly, this helped me out more than anything. I feel a little less nervous about the next first date. It was a nice meal besides."

"Glad it wasn't a total waste, then."

Jesse tilted his head and allowed his peripherals to jump into the foreground.

His eyes drifted to their wine glasses. *Ana didn't drink.* Katerina's orange top. *He'd never seen Ana in orange.* Their waiter jumped between tables. his steps seemed to find the noisiest parts of the floor; a dark wood like in the café. The painting on the wall. *Ana would know who painted it.*

Katerina—her features, her smile, her voice.

The whole night, the mantra of Ana's age had gotten quieter and quieter in favor of wanting her there instead.

Besides, Jesse thought, *I should've started the mantra as soon as I talked to her.*

***

The café was busy that morning. Why, Jesse wasn't sure, but he had to find another table than his usual. He chose one next to the window, where he sipped on his cinnamon-drenched concoction. He smacked his lips together. It wasn't one of his favorites, but he appreciated Elaine's delight at serving him something new each day.

He didn't need to be in the office for another hour, so he settled in, extending his legs under the table. With the sun out, not a cloud in sight, the streets seemed busier as well. A woman laughed, a child skipped, a dog lapped his tongue.

"Hello."

Jesse turned to the greeting, blinking hard as his eyes adjusted to the darkened lighting of the café. As the person behind the voice came into focus, he smiled—both at Ana and the thumbprint cookie sitting on a plate.

"Elaine's baking, but my mom's recipe," she explained before he could say anything. "Don't worry, I didn't bake."

Jesse accepted the plate from her, setting in on the table next to him. What looked like raspberry jam pooled in the center of the cookie just like warmth in his chest at the thoughtful gesture.

"I'd have tried it anyway," he said, his voice becoming softer as he continued, "You would've made it after all."

Her answering smile was soft. "That's very sweet." Her hands folded in front of her. "I thought I might follow through and give you the cookie I based your coffee on."

"And *that's* very sweet."

Ana merely shook her head in response, amusement in her eyes, and Jesse expected her to get back to work, considering how crowded it was. He even turned back to his coffee and the cookie in front of him. Her long black skirt didn't move from the corner of his eyes, and he tilted his head to look at her.

Ana was biting her lip, gaze turned to the window, and she seemed to be debating something, so he waited. She took a few more seconds before she cleared her throat.

"Elaine told me you had a date. You met her here?"

Jesse almost jolted in his seat; his mouth certainly parted in surprise.

"Uh…" His cheek flushed. "Uh, yes, yes, I did have a date. Yesterday…"

"I wondered." She shrugged, a purposely nonchalant motion. "Since we didn't go for a walk, that is. I simply wondered." Ana paused. "Did you…have fun?"

Jesse had a thought then. It followed quite closely behind the number thirty-two, and he considered it enough to start constructing the words like sandcastles. He could lie. He could tell her it went well, that he was going out with Katerina again, maybe even mention her name. He'd smile and tell Ana a story of their dinner, and she'd laugh at all the right points. Then Elaine or a customer would call her, and he'd be left with that same regretful feeling the first day he'd met her, like he'd never see her again, watching as her skirt waved to him. Jesse wouldn't call her back.

His mouth dried, and the sand sculptures of his sentences crumbled before they could even form, obliterating into dust, coarse on the inside of his cheek.

Jesse took a sip of his coffee, and the words washed down his throat, muddying up his stomach at the idea of saying them aloud.

"It didn't work out."

"Oh," Ana said, and he didn't know what to make of that as a first response, but her face soon shifted to one of sympathy. "I'm sorry."

"That's okay." He caught her eye. "I just didn't connect with her like...well, like other people."

Ana was silent for a moment. Then, with a slight smile, she said, "A walk tonight to cheer you up?"

His chest lightened. "I'd like that very much, Ana."

"Good." She nodded her head to the side. "I have to get back, but pick me up after work?"

"I can do that."

Her lips stretched wide, and she waved to him before gliding between tables. Her skirt did, too, a light movement which seemed to flutter with his own excitement.

The past couple days, her age beat along to the drum of his heart, a constant reminder like a ticking clock, and it still clicked, but it was the faint sound of a wristwatch, only noticeable if Jesse bothered to lift it to his ear. It was the same noise that had accompanied her as soon as his heart stuttered at her smile. He *liked* Ana. There was nothing he could do to change that. And she seemed to like him—at the very least as a walking companion to talk to. There was nothing she could do to change that, either.

He lifted the cookie to his lips; being as small as it was, Jesse popped the whole thing in. As he chewed, he caught Ana's attention, and she lifted her thumb up then down, an expectant look on her face. With cheeks filled, Jesse gave it a thumbs up, and he barely even tasted it as he watched her smile.

Chapter Four

Jesse nodded to a passing couple as they headed into the museum, hands in his pockets as he stood in front of the building next to the notable circular sculpture near the entrance. Being a weekday, he could tell it wasn't going to be too crowded, for which he was grateful. He didn't particularly enjoy museums when it was shoulder-to-shoulder people inside, so it was convenient Ana worked somewhere with inconsistent hours, and he was able to rearrange his schedule for a day trip on a Wednesday.

Ana was supposed to arrive any minute now. During a rainy set of days, he asked if she wanted to get together somewhere *not* exposed to the elements, and he was pleased she accepted his offer to take her to the museum. He shouldn't have been surprised, though; Ana perked up the moment he said the word "art."

It was nice, he thought, being able to spend time with her. His hotel room seemed so cavernously empty some days and talking to his daughters only helped so much. Having a friend like Ana helped keep the days interesting, and he enjoyed her company.

Jesse sighed.

He just wished he could remind himself enough times of the *friend* title for him to embrace it.

The click of heels caught his attention, and he lifted his gaze to see Ana walking toward him with a flowery dress and dark jacket combo. She ran a hand through her loose, wavy hair and smiled as she walked right past him.

She paused long enough to ask, "Coming?"

He laughed. "Yes, ma'am."

In a few strides, he had caught up to her, and they only waited in line to enter for a few minutes before they were free to explore. He unfolded the pamphlet with the map in it, but he didn't have time to look at it before Ana was pulling him along.

"Oh, you don't need that," she said. "I know my way around."

He shoved the laminated paper into his back pocket and trailed behind her. "How many times have you been here?"

She paused to consider. "You know, I'm not entirely sure. But I haven't been here in a while—not since they opened up the new exhibit."

"That was the...local artist?"

She beamed, nodding, and took him down a hallway with a line of paintings. "We'll save that for last. I've been following him for a couple of years now, so I was thrilled when I saw he got such a lovely exhibition."

"I'm sure," Jesse said, smiling at her enthusiasm.

Her face, lit up in a way he only ever saw when she spoke about brushstrokes and the characteristics of one era's work over another, barely turned away from each frame on the wall. Jesse had no need for the automated tour when he had Ana pointing out the various artists or techniques. Most of it, admittedly, went a bit over his head as she fell into terminology he wasn't particularly familiar with, but it was warming to watch the excitement sparkle in her eyes.

They went from one piece to the other—from the nineteenth century to contemporary—and though she spent equal time on each of the paintings, he could tell Ana was casting her attention more toward the back of their current wing.

"Here," she said when they finally stopped at a small painting highlighted by the overhead bulbs. He found himself squinting, but not because of the brightness. As with most expressionist or abstract pieces, he based whether he liked them on how they made him feel, not by if it was done well. (But maybe that was the point of that style in the first place.)

The one in front of him was a clouded red bleeding over the majority of the canvas. Dark purples and cool grays added water to the macabre landscape, and two blurry sailboats floated in the tide. The white sails were stark against the darkness, and the reflections spread over both colors. He wondered what they could be sailing into...or if they were sailing away from the ominous crimson.

It reminded him of something he'd find in a haunted house, the way the inside of the room would glow red as the fog spilled out from the seams of the door. With the painting, the door was completely open, and the fools entering did so knowing exactly what would be on the other side. Over the ocean, he didn't know what that would be, whether the danger was a storm or Moby Dick. Perhaps it was the sailor's wife, watching as the boat disappeared into the distance with only the possibility of safe return as her solace.

And, perhaps he was looking too much into it, and they weren't even boats to begin with.

Regardless, it was grave coloring, so he had to blink away the harsh glare of ruby when he saw the soft expression on Ana's face. The two occupying the same space didn't seem to fit together, like watching a butterfly sit on nose of a snarling wolf.

"Beautiful, isn't it?" Ana asked. At his hesitation, she laughed. "Ignoring the deadly omen, this encapsulates what art can *be*, the spectrum of it. Of course, there's the painstaking detail of landscapes, but there's the simplicity of color and shape. This painting strips away everything unneeded, and we still understand what he means."

"A cursed journey."

She didn't look away from the picture, merely tilted her head. "But there's something lovely about that, don't you think?"

He turned back to it, wondering.

"Those sailors are willing to risk something," she continued, "whether they know what's to come or not."

"And if they don't think they're risking anything?"

"Then I suppose…" Ana shrugged. "Then I suppose they will leave doing something they love."

"Go out," he said, and she furrowed her brow in confusion. "You *go out* doing something you love." His lip twitched up, already anticipating her huff of frustration, and she didn't disappoint, even wrinkling her nose as she did.

"*Regardless*," she said, "I think the message is nice."

"It is." He knew she was Romanian, having left there when she was twenty-one years old, and he wondered if she'd traveled outside of her home country and Germany. "What would *you* sail off to do?"

She raised an eyebrow. "Why is it I always get asked these probing questions?"

"Hey," he said with a shrug, "feel free."

Ana grinned. "Then I'll ask you the same question."

He snorted but considered. With his job, he'd been to so many corners of the globe, had sailed and flown toward one conflict after another, but he'd never really *chosen* the spot. Sure, he chose which countries housed his company, but that was due to demand more than a genuine love for the city. Where would he travel? What would he travel *to*?

"You know," he finally said, "I'm not really sure. But I think I'd like to take my girls with me. I think the last time we all traveled together was when Sarah was in high school."

Ana smiled. "I'd say that's a fine answer. You're a very cute dad."

His cheeks reddened, and he rubbed the back of his neck. "Well, I don't know if I'd say *cute*."

At his embarrassment, she laughed and made her way to the next painting. He trailed behind her and said, "What about your answer?"

She turned her head for a teasing wink, then continued forward, hands clasped behind her back. His eyes softened as he followed her, wading through the people.

A mass of light color against the dark-colored hallways, Ana sailed in front of him, but he didn't think she was moving toward the crimson skies—no, that was Jesse. With every crinkling smile, every giggle that caressed his heart, and every silken word from Ana's lips, his peripheries filled with the color of her blush. It snuck up his arm as he placed a gentle hand on her back, guiding her around a group of students. Every moment was one the paintbrush stroked against the walls, the floor, the ceiling.

He did nothing to stop it. His eyes trailed the lines of the bristles with a dawning realization. Jesse knew the base of this feeling well, knew the blue waters more than the red—but still, he knew it.

When Jesse met his wife, they floated alongside each other, and it was simple. They loved each other, they married, had children, and all was well. Nothing hovered over them until the end when she got sick. And when they realized she wasn't getting better, the encroaching red came to them despite being moored as they were. There really wasn't much of a choice to run from it or go toward the warning. It swelled beneath their boats, and he watched as Linda's filled with water.

Then he was left to bob alone in the simple blue-gray water.

His daughters paddled around him when they were younger, always within his sights, but they ventured out on their own, leaving just a ripple in their wake — as they should have. They couldn't be tied to Jesse forever, but he hadn't expected to be left by himself in the middle of the ocean.

Then Ana drifted by him, a steady crawl, and his sails opened without conscious thought to accept the gust of wind trailing behind her. The closer he got to her, the more he noticed the pink on the horizon wasn't just the sunrise, and it seeped into the water like a shark had chomped down on its prey. He continued forward, just as he was now, a hand placed yet again on the small of her back as they entered the wing of the local artist's exhibit. Jonas, his name was.

And Jesse gaped. The room was flooded with myriad of color, lights fixed to the backs of stained-glass panes to leak rippled blue on the floor like he was stepping into a swimming pool on a sunny day. Even more impressive was the design of a fish on the floor from where the patterns of the glass merged.

"Wow," he couldn't help but say. When he shifted his attention to Ana, her face bathed in light, she was practically giddy.

"Isn't it *amazing*?"

Jesse smiled. "It is. Feels like I'm submerged."

Her laugh startled him; Ana pointed to a plaque behind him in answer.

"Ah," he said. "It's called 'Submersion.'" His eyes took in each of the panes dotted around the room. "How did you know about this guy before he came here?"

"Oh, well—he was at an art fair I attended a couple years back. I talked with him for quite a white, and he showed me some of his work." Ana flicked her eyes from one piece to another. "I remember being impressed by his attention to color. He outfits homes and restaurants with stained glass, but he makes a point to choose colors and designs that work well with the direction of the sun and the interior." She laughed. "He said he would *never* use purple if there are dark wood floors." Ana shrugged in amusement. "Very adamant."

"Guess I can't get purple for my hotel room, then. The carpets are dark."

She giggled. "What a shame."

Jesse smiled and watched as she studied each piece before her, taking it in with a much more knowledgeable eye than him. While he made a point to visit museums and art galleries when he traveled abroad, fascinated by other countries' histories and cultures, he approached them as a novice. His appreciation felt rather superficial standing next to Ana.

As she tilted her head, he considered her for a moment.

"You should be a curator," he said in a moment of pause, and her mouth dropped open cutely when she turned back to him. "You obviously have an eye for talent."

"I—" Her throat flexed, and there was something about her eyes that made him feel the significance of the moment. He'd thought he'd just mentioned something off-hand, like she had nice clothes, but he realized too late the comment held weight.

Finally, Ana looked away, but his own eyes couldn't seem to stray from her face, so Jesse watched as she collected her thoughts. The corner of her lips inched up.

"I think I only told my professor back in school I wanted to be a curator. Not even my parents know *exactly* what I want. They think I just want to work in an art gallery."

"Really?"

She hummed. "Honestly, after I started helping out with Mom's commissions, the subject of my degree kind of...fell away." Her smiled widened, and she turned to him fully. "Thank you. I appreciate you indulging my interests. This has been nice."

Warmth flooded his chest. "It has."

Her crème-colored skirt flickered with blue, and he was struck by the overwhelming hue surrounding them, so unlike the painting. Even the bead in her hair was a saturated blue. He could imagine they were those two little boats chugging along, the cool, crisp water just a touch beneath them. Wind would shuffle Ana's hair around her shoulders, and he'd pass one of his sweatshirts to her to warm herself. Their boats' anchors would twine together, so where one went, the other would follow forever.

He stepped toward her, and not a pigment of red encroached on his peripherals.

What was the harm, really? And with another step forward without her stepping back, every nagging thought that made him accept Katerina's date drifted away like seafoam, fizzled distantly in favor of Ana's beautiful eyes and the way her enthusiasm lit them like sea glass in the sun.

With no one around, Jesse was grateful for the solitude as he drifted completely in front of her, and she tilted her head up to meet his attention. He felt as though his heart was shaking through his bones, but he didn't falter. If anything, the steady beat spurned him on as he leaned forward. Her eyes were locked on his as his face inched infinitesimally closer and closer. Her breaths caressed his jaw.

Then he dipped down, and his lips touched hers. The contact was brief, just a few moments, but it was long enough for Jesse to bask in the joyous flutters skipping in his chest.

As he pulled back, he felt Ana's eyelashes tickling his cheek, and he opened his eyes at the same time she did. Her brow was knitted, and he swallowed thickly at the sight. Jesse didn't dare name what caused the wrinkles in his expression, so he took one step back from her.

"Very nice," he said, voice rough.

His words startled her out of whatever she was thinking, and she blinked out of her stupor, cheeks covered with a dusting of pink. "Y-Yeah." Her finger came up to twiddle with her braid.

Ana didn't move, so he took the initiative and made a point to let his shoe hit the floor loudly enough for her to hear he was moving on to the next room. The sound of her footsteps trailed behind him.

As they took in the last of Jonas's art pieces, they only traded a few quick mumbles. Jesse shoved his hands in his pockets. He didn't regret kissing her, but he certainly regretted forcing an awkwardness into their day that never would've been there if he hadn't.

Most times he looked over at her, her lips were pressed together like she was spreading her lipstick around, her expression divided between her interest and whatever was spinning through her head.

His own thoughts cycled, but they always lingered on the feeling of her lips against his. He couldn't help the pleased hum of his heart as he relived the moment, but it dimmed every time he turned his attention to Ana.

Mouth pursed, he fiddled with the inside of his pocket as she avoided his gaze, and before he knew it, they were heading back to the exit. The setting sun cast the horizon in an amber glow, painting the sky something familiar to him.

Jesse sighed and stopped. If he'd truly messed everything up—as evidenced by Ana's steadfast efforts to never look at him again—he thought he may as well just say what he'd come to realize these past weeks.

"I care for you," he said, and the confession was easier than he thought it would be. "More than a friend," he added.

He risked a glance over to Ana, and her eyes were wide as she twiddled her fingers together. Words seemed to stick to the inside of her throat; he could see her neck flexing and her jaw working.

Lifting a hand, he saved her from whatever heartbreaking thing she was going to say.

"It's alright," he said. "I...Well, I just thought you should know, is all. Especially after the kiss." His chuckle was wry. "I seem to always do everything out of order with you, don't I?"

During his little speech, her face had evened out, and he didn't have any clue as to what she was thinking. Jesse didn't know if he preferred that or not.

"I guess we should get back," he said when she continued to stand in silence.

He turned and walked further into the cloudy day, and echoing footsteps indicated she was behind him, following at a sedate pace—until the sound stopped.

"Jesse." Ana's voice made him turn around. Her hands were clasped in front of her, delicately interlocked over her high-waisted skirt, and her face cast down. He waited.

But he almost jumped in surprise when she took one lunging step toward him and laid a kiss on his cheek, stuttering his heart more than the first kiss. Jesse imagined his mouth was gaping stupidly, but he didn't care when he saw the light blush on her face as she stepped back.

"I had fun." Her voice was quiet, but it was like she'd yelled it, the way he caught every dip to her voice, every emphasis, every vowel.

She nodded to herself, then turned, walking down the opposite way he was going—but before she was out of earshot, she called, "I'll see you at the café!"

With a hand touching his fingers to where her lips had skated across his cheek, he watched in a daze at her retreating form.

Then he grinned, the wind pushing him forward to get ready to see her another day.

Chapter Five

Ana brushed a nervous hand down the front of her emerald dress, her fingers tapping against the ribbing underneath her chest. The evening sun was chilly; her thick, long sweater wrapped around her arms, keeping her warm while she waited for a taxi. She clutched her small, matching bag in front of her and kept her eyes trained on the road to her apartment complex.

Jesse was on his way to pick her up for an evening at the theater, and she chuckled at the memory of his cheeky smile as he presented her with a ticket to *Swan Lake*. She could hardly say no to the offer, could she, especially when he attempted the name of the ballet in Romanian. With the few phrases she'd taught him, he was getting better.

The wind blew across her, and she clasped the sweater closer to her body as she waited. Jesse was due in just a couple of minutes, insisting he should pick her up for something he invited her to. Admittedly, when he asked, she was…reluctant. The one time they'd extended their friendship to somewhere outside of the café or park, the nature of their relationship had shifted ever so slightly.

But perhaps, with that kiss, it shifted more than she was willing to look at. So, after a bit of coaxing, she agreed to attend the performance—as long as it *wasn't* a date. Ana couldn't determine what he was thinking when she said that, but he'd agreed.

And here they were.

Thankfully, she didn't have to wait much longer. Not two minutes later, a cab pulled up, and Jesse stepped out. Ana had to stop herself from gaping as she noticed what he was wearing. Gone were the floppy sweatshirts and old jeans; in their places were black trousers and a plum button-up with a sleek, black tie.

She didn't have time to say anything before he gently grasped her hand, pulling it to his lips for a quick kiss against her knuckles.

"You look lovely," he said with a soft smile, and she returned it in kind.

"Thank you." Her eyes drifted to the tie. "You're quite dashing yourself. I wasn't aware you even owned clothing like this."

He snorted. "Yeah, yeah. I can actually clean myself up. But only for the right company." The wink he sent her had her laughing as she followed him into the car. Jesse must've already told the driver where they were going, because he took off without any further instruction once they were both settled.

"Really," she said after a beat of silence, "you look like a completely different person in those clothes."

He blinked down at his attire. "You think?"

She raised an eyebrow. "Normally, you dress like a sloppy college student."

Jesse shrugged, though he made a point to loosen his tie a smidge. "Sweats are comfortable."

"That's how you describe night clothes."

"Those are comfortable, too."

She let out a snort, something which somehow managed to take her by surprise. So far, Jesse had managed to get every type of laugh out of her, even silent guffaws when he'd gotten his hood stuck on a branch trying to retrieve a kid's balloon, and the more he tried to free himself, the more he got stuck and pricked by twigs until he finally huffed in defeat, sagging against the trunk. He was already bemoaning the loss of his hoodie as he retrieved his utility knife from his pocket. Thankfully for him, she was able to free him as well as the balloon.

Now, shaking her head at his devotion to his style—if one could call it that—Ana said, "I pity the woman you date."

Ana expected a steady quip in reply, but the car was silent except for the light whir of the engine and the mumbling radio up front. Frowning, she turned to Jesse from the window she had been looking through and found his attention on her, head tilted and scrutinizing her—for what, she didn't know. But it made her heart thud.

Finally, after the chorus on the radio was finished, he said, voice soft, "Would you?"

No, of course not, she wanted to say, but the response, like the question, was more than the surface words. There was a weight there—not because he was offended or concerned—because the kiss at the museum added weight to his question. And, just like then, she was left wide-eyed and silent, words not finding enough substance to form. Some bubbled up, but like the carbonation of a soda, they popped as soon as they hit the surface of her tongue.

All that managed to leave her was, "I..."

Jesse took mercy on her, and the corner of his lip quirked up as he said, "I'd pity her, too."

This time, the tone was joking, so she followed his lead. "With those clothes, she certainly wouldn't be expecting a date at a five-star restaurant."

"I don't really think I'd have the right amount of clout to get in in the first place."

"Or the amount of time needed for a reservation. You're never in one place long, right?" she recalled.

His eyes caught hers a moment before he turned toward the window. "Yeah, uh, I'm usually on the move pretty often." He paused. "And I've been here quite a while."

"Oh." Ana didn't want to ask the obvious follow-up— *when are you leaving?*—so she didn't, and they lapsed into silence for the few remaining minutes of the drive.

They were in time with a few other audience members, so the taxi driver parked his car behind the three other vehicles. While Jesse paid the driver, Ana slid out of the back; she was next to the curb, so she didn't have to wait for any cars as they passed. When Jesse emerged, she was puzzled to find he actually seemed a tad disappointed.

At her questioning glance, he explained, a little sheepish, "I was going to open the door for you."

Ana smiled, then extended her hand. "You could still give me your arm."

"That I can do."

She settled her hand in the crook of his elbow, and they went forward into the theater as Jesse fetched the tickets from his inside pocket. Considering they weren't just printed on a piece of paper, he must have come to the box office directly to purchase them. Or perhaps he got them from the hotel. Regardless, Ana held out a hand for hers after they'd been scanned by the attendant.

"I like to collect them," she explained, tucking hers away into a pocket of her purse. "I have a scrapbook I keep all of my tickets in, even from when I was a child."

"I bet you have a pretty steady collection then."

She smiled. "I have a fair amount."

"I don't really have anything I've collected," he said as they shuffled into their seats on the mezzanine layer, which Ana was pleased to see. The mezzanine section was her favorite because the better line of sight let her watch the background characters in addition to the actors up front.

"Your sweatshirts aren't a collection?" she asked.

"Oh." He chuckled. "Okay, I guess you're right."

"I've noticed they all have logos on them."

His smile brightened. "They're all businesses I like. If I go to a restaurant or store, I try to get merchandise from them if it's available."

"Perhaps I should get you one for the café then," Ana said, voice playful.

Jesse leaned closer, his elbow on the armrest touching her arm, and her head tilted, angled toward him. "If you have one. Will I get a discount as a regular?"

"Oh, I'm sure we could figure out something."

"Elaine will probably give it to me for free if I keep being her taste tester."

She giggled. "Very likely."

With only a soft hum in reply, she realized how close their faces were, and she bit her lip, turning her eyes down. Her hand came up to fiddle with her braid.

Jesse readjusted himself in the seat, feet solidly planted on the ground, posture straight. Ana had noticed that about him, the way his back was firm with his shoulders back, even in baggy clothes. The lines of his body were more prevalent in the purple shirt, and Ana could see the lines of muscles, the shapes of his arms. He wasn't rock solid in his stature, but he was defined, something she could appreciate more with the new outfit.

Clearing her throat, she tapped her heel on the ground and watched the stage for movement. They were only a minute or two away from the performance, and she was looking forward to it. She hadn't seen *Swan Lake* since she was a freshman in college. Such a long time ago, she thought.

Some days, her childhood felt so far away; she was far beyond the days when she was eager to face the world, but the longer she was at the café, those days seemed even farther past. Some of her college friends had gotten married, others had kids or successful careers, and one even moved to Ireland. And what was she doing?

Shaking her head, she was grateful for the dimming lights and zeroed her attention in on the opening curtain. Entertainers and servants filed in across the stage, ready for the guests, as well as Prince Siegfried, to appear in the park near the castle. One by one, more people appeared, emerging from the side of the painted green and orange trees surrounding the party as they overlooked the grand castle atop the rocky cliffside.

Ana tracked the graceful movements across the stage, watching as the prince's tutor appeared, followed shortly by the prince himself. The women spun and pointed their legs out, their skirts swinging around, pink and orange wisps around the white tights of their dance partners.

As a child, Ana would twirl around like that—though with much less athleticism—so her skirts would hoop around her legs and wrap around her knees. Though, remembering that usually brought a tinge of embarrassment; her mother used to mortify her with the story of how she'd cyclone around so spectacularly when she was a kid that she showed her underwear to the entirety of the market. Now, she could look at the anecdote with humor, but when she fourteen, she was certain a solitary fate living in a cave was a better destiny for her than the torture of listening to her mother recollect the event to her friends.

Regardless, the dancers on stage were much better than she was at six, and, as always, she was mesmerized by their movements. Ana let herself enjoy the stage, the dancing, and the music. If she hadn't been so captivated by the dance itself, she might have thought to close her eyes to the accompanying violins, flutes, and drums. But she couldn't shutter them for a moment, not when the story of Prince Siegfried played before her.

Act One dazzled her in no time at all, and she was barely aware of Jesse's presence next to her—but she was indeed aware of it. He'd shift in his seat, and her ears would perk up. His elbow on the armrest next to her would brush up against her arm, and prickles of electricity would spark over her skin.

Each time he distracted her, she felt a simultaneous urge to both purse her lips and do so to him in kind, but she refrained, waiting for each time he pulled her attention away from the stage. She marked the scenes by him. Jesse cleared his throat when Siegfried stepped on stage with his crossbow. He tapped her wrist to ask who the dark wizard was. She heard a hum of appreciation when the Little Swans lined up on stage and all ducked down as the prince's love interest, Odette, emerged.

There was silence for the remainder of the act until the intermission.

"Wow," Jesse said, standing so a couple could slip by him into the aisle. "This is great so far."

Ana blinked in surprise. "Oh, you haven't seen it?"

"Nah, just heard of it—as most people have, I guess."

"You'll have to let me know what you think when it's finished."

He chuckled. "I don't doubt you'll hound me for my opinion."

"I won't *hound*." She blushed, and he laughed.

"Sorry, I don't mean to tease you."

Ana raised an eyebrow. "I think you do quite often."

"No, I don't."

"Oh, yes you do. Usually about silly English idioms."

He snorted. "Okay, I'll give you that."

"When I teach you Romanian, I hope you know I won't let a single awkward turn of phrase escape me."

There was a pause, one she didn't anticipate being so significant, but when she looked over to Jesse, she saw his expression, and it almost seemed…touched.

"*When* you teach me?"

"Oh." She swallowed thickly. She hadn't realized she'd said that. Tucking a strand of hair behind her ear, she nodded. "I—yes, when. You said you wanted to learn, didn't you?"

"I did." His voice was soft, and she would've startled at how his fingers touched the back of her hand if it hadn't felt so right for the moment.

"You know," he continued, "I'm a pretty slow learner." His palm found hers, and she unconsciously linked her fingers with his, the calluses on his hand brands of pressure against her own. Ana vaguely wondered what he felt on her hand.

"I'd like to think I'm a patient teacher," she said, voice low enough that he had to lean forward to hear her, and she stared into his blue eyes, like the curtains of the theater. She also wondered what he compared her eyes to.

"Good," Jesse breathed. "The lessons may take a while."

His breath seeped into her skin, her lips, and licked them. Those theater eyes darted down then back up.

A throat clearing made her jump a little in her seat, and her face flushed at the impatiently waiting couple who had returned to their seats. Ana and Jesse stood, allowing them to pass, and without her realizing, her hand had retracted back to her front; she interlocked her own fingers, resting them in her lap as they sat back down.

"W-Well," Jesse said, and Ana was surprised at the slight stutter; she'd never heard him stutter before, "it's going to start back up soon, right?"

Ana nodded, checking the small watch on her wrist. "Only two minutes left."

"Right." He adjusted his tie. "So, uh, what were you going to say?"

Her eyes flicked to his then back to the empty stage. "Just that I'll make you some notecards."

"I see." She pointedly ignored the note of disappointment in his voice—and how she leaned her body toward his chair.

Talking with Jesse, she realized she'd missed the warning flash of lights to hurry people along back to their seats because when they darkened completely, she thought the intermission seemed a little short.

As soon as the ballet started up once more, she was back to how she'd been from the start. Perhaps it was the dim lighting that made her so in tune with Jesse, like how many say the other senses heighten when one goes away. With her sight trained fully on the stage, her peripheral senses grabbed on to Jesse, assuring her he was there.

Truthfully, she felt like a teenager, that fourteen-year-old girl who was covering her face at her mother's story when her crush sat two seats away from her on the couch.

The set was brighter, back to the daytime scenery as opposed to the darkened lake of Scene Two. This time, she kept track of his movements as she did the performers, feeling him shift toward her, and his face was right next to her ear.

"Beautiful, huh?" Jesse's breath tickled her ear, and a shiver traveled through her. She was grateful for the dark lighting, sure her face was stained red. His shoulder slid across hers, his sleeve brushing the thicker sweater, and she was overly conscious of the contact. Ana could barely concentrate on the dancers or the music, not when his warmth seeped into her clothing. Not when she could smell his cologne or soap; she couldn't tell which it was. She remembered smelling it at the park, and she licked her lips again.

Realizing she hadn't answered him when he tilted his head, Ana hummed an affirmative, and her heart skipped when he turned a smile to her, face so very close to hers. Her breath came out shaky, and she saw how his eyes flicked down to her lips then back up. The déjà vu of the moment hit her, and her own eyes darted down to his lips. But then he leaned back, and Ana felt like she could breathe again.

She also felt slightly disappointed, but she stamped that down and focused on the performance in Prince Siegfried's ballroom. Ana had always liked the jester character as he flitted between groups of dancers, first the rose-gold maidens, then to greet the royalty as they entered. Soon, the false Swan Queen would make her entrance, tricking Siegfried into marriage, leaving Odette, the actual Swan Queen, cursed to forever be a swan. Ana didn't understand the story when she was a child, enraptured as she was with the costumes and dancing, the music and presentation. It wasn't until later, when her father explained the story, that she understood the weight of their movements.

Swan Lake used to make her cry, but she still came back to watch it.

Her father understood more than her mother. Her mother usually rolled her eyes if she asked to see a play again or a movie.

"Once is enough," she'd say, even as Ana's father would flash the VHS tape from behind her mom's back. Her mother could be a little *overbearing*, so she was grateful for those small hidden pleasures.

Ana should probably visit soon. It had been about two weeks since the last time she'd been there, so her mom likely had a new sewing pattern for her to work on—Ana could start it over the weekend, perhaps when she got home from her and Jesse's walk in the park. She could pick it up in the morning before they met, leaving a little after lunchtime, and if her mother wasn't there, her father could find which pattern she needed. Maybe Ana could even pick which one she wanted for once.

She furrowed her brow, then reeled a little in surprise.

Ana had just planned around her walk with Jesse. She...usually planned around her mother. At that, Ana's brain halted, and she didn't really know what to think about the realization.

It was a convenient place for her active thoughts to recede into the background, and once more, she let herself just enjoy the show—the way Prince Siegfried impressively jumped and twirled, and how the false Odette spun and spun in place to the timing of the song. This performance, she noticed how Siegfried and Odette, false or otherwise, were in opposite colors. Black to her white when they first met, white to fake Odette's black in the ballroom, but they both had white at the end.

And the finale was always so beautiful and tragic. When Ana's father had told her, she'd recoiled back, tissue in hand.

"They *die*?" she'd despaired.

"In some versions. Not all are the same. Depends on the showrunners."

"But why would you have them *die*?"

He poked her on her sniveling nose. "Watch all of them and see which is your favorite."

"It won't be them *dying*."

Ana never did talk to her dad about her favorite after she'd seen a couple of versions, but he'd probably nod when she didn't agree with her younger self. She could admit to liking a kinder version of Odette and Siegfried standing triumphant over the evil wizard, but it didn't quite have that same poeticism. It would be odd, after all, if Juliet woke to find her lover dead only to merely mourn and walk away.

As the play came to end, she followed the dancers, wondering which ending they would get, and she found herself a little disappointed when it was the happiest out of all of them. But she couldn't complain; everything was a treat to watch, and she clapped along with the rest of the audience as the performers bowed at the end, standing at the first performer. (She cheered loudest for the court jester.)

Ana's wide grin couldn't be taken off her face as they filed out of the theater, especially when she noticed how much Jesse enjoyed the performance.

"What a ride!" he said, waving his arm up to hail a cab. "So, what, was she still a swan in the end?"

"You know, it was a little unclear," she admitted, shrugging. "But the music paired well with Rothbart's defeat."

"The evil guy."

Her lip twitched up in amusement as a taxi stopped in front of them. This time, she waited for Jesse to open the door for her, and she slipped in, pulling the end of her dress up so it wouldn't brush against the dirty side of the car.

"I wondered what ending we'd get," she said as Jesse plopped down next to her, and the cab took off back toward her apartment.

His eyes widened. "There's more than one ending?"

"Tons! They die, they go to the afterlife, they marry, Odette turns human, Siegfried is left alone on the shore. So many!"

"Huh." He elbowed her gently. "I guess I have to see it again then."

Ana smiled. "It appears so."

In what felt like only a few minutes, the cab driver was telling them they had arrived, and she whirled around to see, indeed, they were at her apartment complex. She'd been so enraptured in their discussion she hadn't noticed.

Ana thanked the driver, and again, waited for Jesse to open the door for her, though it was mainly because he'd asked.

Ana smiled when he opened it with a flourish, extending his hand for her to take, and he pulled her out, telling the driver he'd be back in just a minute. Her hand found its way to the crook of his elbow, and he escorted her to the front entrance to her building. The light above the entrance was dim, likely due for a change in lightbulb, but the dull illumination was perfect for the end of a date — *evening*, she thought.

The soft glow touched Jesse's cheeks and traced his warm smile, outlining his entire face in dual shadows and light. Some wrinkles stood out prominently — the ones around his mouth, his forehead — but others smoothed into the dark, making him appear both older and younger. They looked good, though, like they were almost meant to be on his face, so she paid attention to the creases around the corners of his lips as they widened.

"I had a good time," Jesse said, his syllables in time with the crickets chirping in the bushes around them. He stepped one foot closer.

"Me too." Ana didn't back away.

"Maybe we can do this again." Another step.

"Maybe we can." Her head tilted up, Jesse a few centimeters away from her now.

"More than maybe?" he whispered.

Despite her heart racing in her chest, she still was able to pull her lips up into a teasing smile. "Maybe."

His laugh was breathy, as was hers, and he tilted his head just so. Ana didn't move as his lips once again touched hers, only sucked in sharply through her nose and filled her senses with his clean smell. She felt his hand cradle her elbow while the other touched her cheek, and her heart hummed as her eyes closed. As with the darkened theater, she was overly aware of every ounce of pressure and degree of touch; his dry, rough hands scratched her smooth cheek, and she felt herself leaning into it. His thumb brushed a rhythm against her skin, and her hand grasped on to his arm.

But the sensations departed as quickly as they'd started, and his lips left hers with such a delicate slowness that she was almost tempted to think they were still there. Her eyes crested back open, and he stepped back—one step, then two.

"Goodnight, Ana." Jesse's voice was quiet but sure. Before, at the museum, guilt creased his face after their kiss when she avoided his gaze, and she didn't have the heart to keep it on his face. Now, there was a surety to his movements, a precision to the press of lips as well as to his steps, even the ones away from her.

It wasn't until she'd whispered her goodbye did he turn, and she watched his retreating back, the way the shadows swallowed his dark pants until he stood near the headlights, his silhouette as defined as the performers on stage. The car door shut, the gear shifted from park, and the engine buzzed as he drove away.

Ana pressed her lips together. They still tingled from his touch, and the thought made something in her stomach heat. Though that, in and of itself, was an answer to the question Jesse had been asking, she...still had to think.

With one more glance at the empty road, Ana turned and entered her apartment.

Chapter Six

Two weeks.

Jesse had a flight back to America in two weeks. Normally, he'd be ecstatic. It had taken a few more weeks than anticipated to finish up work in Germany, so on any normal trip, he'd be dancing his way to the airport—especially because it was almost Thanksgiving, an ideal time to go back to his kids and grandkids.

He suspected two weeks would feel like two days—the thought sounded dramatic to his ears, but it didn't feel that way. The small planner in his back pocket weighed down his stride, remembering with every step the limited number of days he had left.

For the first time in a very long while…he didn't want to go home.

Ana. Ana, of course, was the reason. Lately, she was his reason for doing many things, including wearing a *tie*. He hadn't had to wear a tie since his daughter's wedding. And he'd worn one *again* since their trip to the theater a few days ago. Jesse was grateful he'd bothered to pack one.

Yesterday, they'd listened to a jazz orchestra. It was a cheap performance, an event for a charity where there were art vendors, food stalls, and games, so while he didn't *have* to wear a tie, he knew Ana was planning on dressing up and didn't want to show up in his usual grubby attire.

There was a chill in the air, but the stage was surrounded by heaters, so he barely needed his coat, instead giving it to Ana to drape across her legs. She had on black tights and a sweater dress, but snow was on the horizon, so the brisk wind was a little too chilly for thin tights.

Jesse, admittedly, wasn't the biggest fan of jazz, but he appreciated the organized chaos of a good performance, so he tapped his toe along with the rest of the audience, noting the way Ana swayed a little in sync with the beat of the song.

It was fun, and they bought gifts for family at the art vendors' stalls. Sarah, Monica, and Kelsey got matching mugs, and Jesse bought Jake a twenty-piece wooden puzzle with a dog on it. Ana, meanwhile, bought her parents a serving bowl swirled with delicate lines and a scalloped edge.

That evening was the first time Jesse had been to her apartment, helping Ana carry the bowl in while her hands were filled with their overindulgent number of snacks, which she plopped on her counter.

He flicked a couple more cinnamon-sugar nuts into his mouth before he left and gave her another goodbye kiss on the way out. They never lasted long, just a few moments, and while Ana didn't reciprocate, she never pulled away, like she was waiting in anticipation for it before he left. And that was one of the reasons he was sure—absolutely sure—she felt similarly to how he felt for her.

So, of course, the days he was making progress and maybe convincing her to kiss him back or kiss him first, he was leaving. Before those tickets, he thought he had all the time in the world to woo this amazing woman he'd met. But now, the days were counting down, and he wasn't sure what to do.

He wouldn't be seeing her today — or tomorrow.

Just last week, that wasn't too much of an issue. Sure, he'd be left with very little to do without his friend, but he had the next day or the day after to see her. With only two weeks left, those days were precious, and his stomach twisted just thinking of wasting it.

The end of her shift was two hours ago, and she said she wanted to work on her sewing for the next couple of days. She'd gotten behind, she said, and her mom gave her more than one to poke away at.

Jesse wanted to drop in and see her, but what would he even say? Hi, he missed her? He was leaving for America soon, so he wanted to spend all his time with her? His hotel room was just as lonely as ever?

"Hey, Ana, I want to take you on a date before it's too late and you forget all about me while I'm gone."

The confession hit a little too close to his heart, and he sighed. Jesse wanted to ask her out on a date because he had this terrible thought that as soon as he got back to America, whatever it was they had would scatter like sand in his palm, bleeding through his fingers to fly through the wind. And he couldn't deny that was a possibility; he and Ana didn't really talk to each other outside of the café or their walks, making further plans there rather than over the phone. He had her number, but he'd only used it a couple of times.

Once he returned to America, he feared neither one of them would dial their numbers, and when he was back, he'd... lose her.

The only solution he could think of was to ask her what he just confessed to the empty room — though without the self-deprecation.

Jesse could ask her on a date.

The thought was as nerve-wracking as when he'd asked Linda to move in with him, but...honestly, what was there to lose? He likely wouldn't have her as closely in his life if he didn't ask, and if he did ask and she said no, it would be the same result. But if she said yes...

Emboldened by the hope, he stood and quickly changed into fresh clothes before zipping downstairs to the street below. He jogged to the busy intersection, where he was likelier to get a cab at this time of evening, and he paused at a corner stand. A woman was packing up flowers, only a couple left still on display as she placed them in boxes.

"*Entschuldigung*," he said, catching her attention, and on a whim, he bought the last rose bouquet, a combination of pink and white, before she closed up shop. As Jesse jumped into a taxi, the vendor waved to him, and he called one last, "Thank you!" as he left. Within a few minutes, he was at Ana's apartment, and he paused outside as the taxi took off.

Taking a deep breath, Jesse climbed the couple of stairs and input the code for the building. Ana had given it to him yesterday, which was a great gesture, but he wasn't sure if he preferred surprising her at her door over the speaker to get inside.

The building was nice and well-maintained, and a decoration of square tiles lined the stairwell as well as the hallway, which gave the newer building some character. Yesterday, when he saw it for the first time, the pattern on the tile was quaint. Now, as he trudged up the last flight of steps to get to the fourth floor, the pattern seemed much more ominous. If Jesse was interested in Rorschach's ink test, he would wonder what kind of images he'd find in the tiles. Probably a skull.

Once he reached the hallway where her apartment was, Jesse made a point to avoid looking at the tiles. He instead had sights only for her door, which held a wooden welcome sign varnished in four different colors. The mat underneath his feet was simple, beige and black, and his shoes made a scratching sound as they slid over its surface.

He made it.

Jesse finally made it, and he was going to knock on the door.

A rose poked him in the eye when he lifted his arm, so he adjusted the bundle in his arms and sucked in one steadying breath before pushing a sure hand onto the door. He only had to wait a couple moments before it opened.

"Jesse?" Ana's tone was surprised; she must not have looked to see who it was through the peephole before opening the door. Either that, or the flowers covered her view.

"Hello," he greeted, a little awkward through the bundle of flowers in his hand.

"Hello." The response was slow, unsure, and Jesse's cheeks flushed.

"Sorry." He transferred the flowers to her arms with a quick, "These are for you."

"Oh." The paper wrapping crinkled as Ana shifted them in her arms. "Thank you."

"You're welcome." When she didn't move, her attention on the flowers, he cleared his throat. "Can I…?" He gestured behind her.

That seemed to startle Ana into action. She backed up, extending her arm in entry. "Yes, of course. Come in."

"I won't be long," he said as he shuffled in. Her shoes were sitting on the mat by the door, so he followed suit and removed his, wiggling his socked feet on the hardwood. "I know it's late."

"That's alright. I could do with a little break from sewing." With her free hand, Ana flexed her fingers. "Please, sit down."

"Uh, I think I'd prefer to stand, actually."

Ana raised an eyebrow at that, but shrugged, placing her bundle on the kitchen counter while Jesse followed her to the attached dining room. The apartment was open with the kitchen, dining area, and family room all one large space for Ana to organize as she pleased. She had a dark circular table with detailed beveling along the edge, kept on the outskirts of the kitchen area so she had enough room to maneuver. It was a convenient spot if she wanted a quick place to eat, and the accompanying chairs were cushioned, so the spot looked comfortable as well.

"Whatever you prefer," Ana said, her voice a tad strained as she reached for the vase on the top shelf of a cupboard. She was too fast in grabbing it for Jesse to help, and she placed the crème-colored pottery (decorated with delicate purple designs) beside her bouquet.

Unwrapping was louder than Jesse was expecting, so he waited for her to place the paper to the side before he spoke. "I have something I'd like to ask you."

"Feel free to ask me anything." Ana smiled—a light, happy thing—before she turned back around to grab scissors from her drawer. Strangely enough, Jesse had never really considered the extra steps needed for a bouquet, and equally as strange, he'd never seen his wife do it, either. He'd give her a bouquet, then the next he'd looked, it was already in that blue vase of hers on the kitchen table.

Shaking his head, he focused on the woman in front of him. As with all tasks, Ana was delicate and precise, holding the flowers by the tips of her fingers, and with one sure pinch, the scissors lobbed off the piece at the strict place she needed.

"Well…" Jesse shoved his hands in his pockets. "Well, I was wondering if…"

"If…?" His discomfort, though probably puzzling to her, seemed to be entertaining, and Jesse resisted the urge to grumble. Instead, he regained a little composure, while Ana snipped the excess length of stem off. It dropped to her counter.

"As you know, I have a question for you."

"So you've said."

"Right." Jesse took his hands out of his pockets this time. "I want to take you out somewhere."

She cut another two flowers and placed them in the vase. "Where do you have tickets to this time? Or is there a fair?" Ana perked up. "An art gallery?"

Jesse chuckled. "No, no art gallery. Well, I guess *maybe* an art gallery if you wanted."

Her brow furrowed. "What do you mean?"

Not wanting to extend the moment any longer, he blurted out again, "Do you want to go out on a date?"

Her hands froze, one with the scissors about to close around the stem, the other holding the flower crookedly in her hand. His eyes were locked onto it, waiting for movement. He couldn't see her face; it, and her, were turned back to her project.

Finally, the scissors sliced through the next stem, and Ana delicately inserted it next to a white rose.

"A date?" she asked.

"Yeah. A date."

"I see." A rose slowly spun in her hand, the de-thorned stem rolling between her fingers. Jesse didn't know why he was so sure, but the silence didn't seem to be one prepping for something terrible for his heart. Even from her back, he could tell it was a contemplative one, so he didn't rush her. His eyes darted back to her every time he noticed something new in her apartment, which was practically everything, but he still waited.

A red toaster. Ana. A snowman cookie jar he assumed was filled with someone else's baked goods. Ana. Some sort of fern in a glossy black vase. Ana. Always back to Ana, but he was alright with that.

"Where would you have taken me?"

The sudden question stopped him, and he turned to her fiddling with the flowers in the vase, the one between her fingers finding a home in the back.

"What do you mean?" he asked.

There was a pause, only disturbed by the heater whirring to life. If he listened hard enough, he could probably hear the click of the igniter lighting the furnace. Instead, he listened to Ana, who snipped the last stem. It skittered off the pile and rolled a few inches to the right, almost landing in her sink.

"When you asked me out for dinner when we met," she said, placing the last flower in the vase, right in the middle. "Where would you have taken me?"

"I'm not sure," he admitted. "Somewhere you could dress up, and I'd be forced into a tie again."

While she wasn't fully facing him, he caught the smile at his comment when she tilted her head, and that one upturn of her lips eased his mind enough for his shoulders to loosen.

"I'd pick you up like I did for the theater," he continued, "and then you'd humor me while I opened doors for you."

"I've already done that." Ana turned around, and her eyes twinkled.

"Humor me again?" His voice ladened with hope, and she smiled.

"I think I can do that," she said. "What else?"

Jesse stepped in front of her. "We'd sit at a candlelit table, and even if the food is overpriced, it wouldn't matter because—" He swallowed. "Well, we'd be together."

"What else?" she repeated, voice just a wisp of sound.

"Maybe we'd share a dessert, maybe not. Regardless, I'd pay, and I'd take you back to your apartment. And because it was our first date, I'd just..." Gently, he took her hand in his and brought her knuckles up to his lips. "Then the night would be over, and I'd think about you for the rest of it." He kissed her hand again. "How does that sound?"

Her cheeks, dusted with pink, pulled back to reveal her smile.

"Absolutely lovely."

Jesse grinned in response, and he shifted their hands so he was holding hers. He shrugged. "Well, too bad it didn't happen that way."

"Perhaps."

It was a short reply, but she squeezed his hand after.

"Ask me."

His eyes widened, and hers were serious.

"Ask me," Ana repeated, squeezing his hand again.

When Jesse had first asked her all those weeks ago—a couple of months now, even—he'd blurted out a way to keep her close, keep her talking just a few moments more. It was a silly thing to ask having only talked to Ana for two minutes, but it got her to stay. She'd raised her eyebrows in confusion, yes, but it was better than the retreating flare of her skirt.

Jesse could do better this time.

"Ana," he said.

She grinned. "Yes, Jesse? Is there something you want to ask me?"

"How did you know?" he joked, then drew his voice lower. "Would you like to go to dinner with me?"

Ana didn't make a show of thinking about it; there wasn't even a second at all before her answer.

"Yes, I would," she said. "Thursday at six? You pick the place."

The lightness in Jesse's heart couldn't be bothered to stress over having less than two days to find a candlelit dining experience, so he nodded with confidence.

"I'll be here to pick you up at six then." One speck of worry made it through, and he finished with, "Just don't expect a Michelin-rated place."

"Boo," she teased, then her eyes gentled. "Wherever we go is fine."

"Yeah?"

"Yes." Ana's eyes crinkled with joy. "After all, you said we'd be together, right?"

If he thought his chest felt great before, he didn't have words to describe the explosion of joy that radiated into his blood with every heartbeat. Jesse honestly couldn't fathom her saying yes to his date after so many times she'd made it clear she didn't want any of their outings to be a date.

Yet here they were, hands held loosely together, and both of them smiling like kids. Out of all the scenarios he'd thought of on the way here, this one was turning out to the be the best.

"I did say that," he agreed.

"So, it's a date!"

The way she emphasized the phrase, it was more than her qualifying what they were doing, and he chuckled at her cheeky humor.

"That's the phrase, right?" she asked. "Saying it's a date when you're making plans."

"Yes, that's definitely the phrase."

Her expression was pleased, and when she noticed the amusement on his own features, she winked. Unfortunately, after, she drew back and released his hand.

"Now that we have our plans, I need to get back to work." Her eyes flicked behind him, and they widened, no doubt finding the clock he'd noticed hanging there when he came in. "Actually, I have to go to bed soon."

Jesse saw the much-too-early time glaring out from her microwave, and he agreed. Time to go back to the hotel.

"I'll see you Thursday," Ana said, giving him a little wave as he tied his shoes.

"Thursday." With one hand on the doorknob, he used the other to wave back. Jesse kept his eyes on Ana for as long as he could as he shut the door behind him. The tiles looked a bit like flowers now.

Jesse shook his head with a smile. *Melodramatic old man.*

Chapter Seven

As Jesse tightened his black tie, he wondered how it was he'd gotten into three situations where he had to wear it in such a short time. But he shouldn't gripe. Each were worth it—though he may have to warn Ana he hit his formal-wear quota for the year. But, knowing her, she'd use it as an excuse to make him dress up for New Year's. He wondered what New Year's with her would be like...

Shaking his head, Jesse chastised his wandering mind. He was getting ahead of himself. All he was doing was going out to dinner with her. No need to have lofty delusions.

Swiping a hand down his clothes, Jesse sucked in a steadying breath, then nodded to his reflection in the bathroom mirror. Time to go. He left the hotel, his jacket slung over his arm, and directed the taxi toward the restaurant. Ana insisted they meet there; her apartment was in the opposite direction of the restaurant, so she didn't want him wasting cab fare picking her up. He tried arguing, but when Ana had something in her mind, there was no changing it.

Peering out of the window, Jesse was surprised to see they were almost there. He had thought the drive would slog along, his excited nerves chaining the wheels to going half their speed, but the opposite happened. The car ride took no time at all, and in just a couple of blinks, he was thanking the driver and exiting the vehicle.

Jesse was about to go inside when his eyes found a waving hand on the bench a few feet away from the door. His heart stuttered, fluttering like his jacket in the breeze. Ana's hand, painted with a dark nail polish, shifted through her bangs to keep them out of her face, which gave him a direct, glittering view of her eyes as they sparkled under the streetlamp.

"Ana," he said, approaching her. She stood, smoothing out her long, black dress with a soft smile on her face and cheeks flushed from the cold.

"Jesse," she said, and even with the hubbub of the cars rolling down the street and the passersby, he could still clearly hear the thicker pronunciation of the J in his name, something that didn't always peek out through her accent, but one which made an appearance tonight. There was more definition to the consonant, almost like a Z had slipped through in the front of his name. Only Ana pronounced his name like that, and every time she did, it sent a thrill through his spine.

"Ready to go in?" he asked, drifting his hand to the small of her back, fingers brushing against the waist of her jacket, and Ana seemed to lean against his hand before they walked forward into the small restaurant.

Situated on a corner, the restaurant had a small, modern-looking area out back covered by a light awning for a few outdoor tables. The couple took one of those, the waiter turning on the heated lamp in their corner as they sat. Hidden underneath the covering, the section was cozy and contained, and Jesse found the old-fashioned lanterns hanging from the exterior to be a nice touch.

Only one other table was occupied and, from the look of their plates, they wouldn't be there much longer—for more than one reason, Jesse suspected, seeing their legs intertwined beneath the table and their heads connected at the forehead.

Jesse and Ana, on the other hand, sat directly across from each other at their circular table, but he was completely happy with that. He rarely liked it when people sat next to him, especially in a booth. He liked his elbow room, and he didn't love knowing he couldn't stretch out.

Besides, he'd be able to see Ana's face, the way her eyes would crest in happiness, how she'd poke her tongue out just a little bit when she really got laughing. Unbeknownst to her, Jesse tried to see that every time they were together.

"Thank you for the last-minute reservations," she said, looking up from her menu. "It's wonderful to be outside like this."

His eyes drifted up to the clear skies. "It is, isn't it?"

"Almost like the person who chose Thursday knew it would be a nice temperature."

Jesse chuckled. "Doesn't that person check the weather multiple times a day?"

"You would too if you walked everywhere."

"I would less if I remembered to carry an umbrella."

Ana rolled her eyes, shaking her head as she turned back to her menu. He already knew what he was getting, though. As soon as he'd seen couscous on the menu, he'd decided. Jesse had no clue what it tasted like, but when Monica was about six, she'd watched some cartoon or something that mentioned it, and she cackled that it was the funniest name for a food. She thought it sounded like a bird noise and proceeded to "Couscous!" as she flapped her arms like a bird.

Because it was one of the stories parents embarrassed their kids with, Jesse knew Monica would still remember it, so Jesse figured he'd tell her next time he talked to her. Monica usually called him on the weekends, so he'd hear from her in the next couple of days. (Not that he wasn't heading back to America soon.)

At that thought, his eyes drifted up to Ana, who had already placed her menu to the end of the table. Ana really *was* fast at ordering. And if he wanted to, he could ask her about the paintings inside in the restaurant. He could order Ana another water because he knew she didn't drink. Jesse could check off everything he'd thought while out with Katerina because he was here, here with *Ana*.

"What's the smile for?" Ana asked, half of one tugging up her own lips.

"Just happy we can finally do this. Go out on a date like this."

"Honestly," she said, "it doesn't feel much different from our other not-dates."

"A little different." Jesse reached forward to lightly grab her hand, running his thumb over her knuckles. "I can do this now."

Her hand squeezed back. "So you can."

"And this," he whispered, drawing her hand up to his lips, where he brushed a kiss to the back of it. Her lips parted, but Ana didn't say anything at first, merely stared into his eyes, which he was happy for; Jesse could finally look into *her* eyes without feeling like he had to turn away.

The idea of being able to touch her in the open without fear of rejection was a thrilling one, and something Jesse planned to take full advantage of. He gently twisted their hands so he could lay a kiss against the inside of her wrist, and Jesse could feel her pulse skip against his lips. He released her hand with a wink.

After one more moment of charged silence, she cleared her throat and drew her hand back in front of her.

"There may be a few differences," she said, which made him chuckle.

It wasn't too much longer before the waiter returned, and they gave their orders. Jesse was always impressed with how smooth Ana's accent was—especially considering German was her third language—and his words always felt clunky in comparison. Ana never judged, though. If anything, she'd subtly use a word he struggled with in their conversation so Jesse could hear what it was supposed to sound like.

Evidently, he did fine—probably because couscous wasn't German—because she navigated the conversation to other topics. In that regard, their date *was* exactly like every other outing they'd had. Discussion and quips came easily, and they barely even noticed when their food arrived outside of the tantalizing smell.

Jesse hummed in approval at the first bite, perking up at the lemon squirted over the top of his dish, then he flicked his eyes up to see what Ana thought of her food. Even when eating, Ana was delicate and refined as always. Her napkin was laid out on her lap, her back was straight, and not one errant elbow rested on the table—unlike Jesse, who could be counted on to lean on one if not both of his arms as he ate (though he tried to make an effort not to while sitting across from Ana).

When Jesse wasn't worried about table etiquette or his meal, their conversation continued to flow, and Jesse found himself as enraptured in her speech as he always was. Ana's voice was beautiful—and not just because of the accent. It was smooth and soft, words sliding through the air like sleds over snow. Jesse wondered whether she had a good singing voice. He imagined she did.

Jesse didn't realize he had leaned forward until Ana mimicked the motion, laughter on her tongue, and placed both elbows on the table, resting her head in one hand. Her empty plate was stacked on top of his at the end of the table.

"Are you on the edge of your seat because of me?" she asked, evidently pleased at her correct use of the phrase.

Jesse rested his head on his palm as well. "No other way to be around you."

"Is that so?"

"I'm always waiting with bated breath for what you'll say." The cheesy grin coupled with his words made her laugh, her cheeks a warm glow of pink.

"What an old flirt you are," she said, grinning.

Jesse leaned forward as far as he could without looking foolish, and Ana did the same, interest in her gaze, so he laid a quick peck to her lips.

"I can be," he said.

Ana's smile morphed into a smirk, eyes just a little hooded, which made his heart skip.

"I am very aware," she whispered, reaching up to touch her thumb to his bottom lip, but she leaned back in her chair before his heart could completely explode. Jesse cleared his throat and readjusted his tie, which earned a giggle from Ana.

Before long, the waiter came back, but Jesse didn't want to leave yet. It felt like they had only been there for moments, not over an hour. He interjected before Ana could ask for the check.

"We'll have dessert." At Ana's lifted eyebrows, Jesse added, "That is, if you want some."

She shrugged. "I could have something."

He thought the situation didn't call for the kind of relief he felt at her answer, but he didn't care, concentrating instead on the fact they'd be together just a little longer.

They browsed through the couple of choices and settled on a unique one neither had heard of before: spaghetti ice cream. And once the waiter dropped it off at the table, Jesse understood why it was called such a thing: Ice cream poured out into such long strings that they resembled noodles, and the mashed strawberries and coconut flakes settled over them substituted the tomato sauce and parmesan.

"Clever," he said, poking at his side of the bowl before he slurped some up. "And good, too."

Ana's eyes were wide as she spooned some for herself.

"It *is*." She sighed, then enthusiastically dug in for another bite. "I love strawberries!"

He did too, and the similarity was just another reason for the warmth in his chest—that and the smile on her face as they tried to connect their ice cream noodle on their spoons. The melting vanilla fell apart before they could, so any *Lady and the Tramp* fantasies were gone too quickly, but still...Jesse had fun. It was a lighthearted novelty, and most importantly, it made her laugh.

They had moved to sit next to one another, being closer made it easier to share the dish, so it wasn't uncomfortable for Ana to press her shoulder to his after their last bites. Her hand rested on his knee, his hand over top of hers, and Jesse felt the contours of her grandma's ring on her forefinger, an opal she had passed down.

"Before you say anything," he said, "I'm paying."

"I wasn't going to say anything."

"Considering how stubborn you can be, I just wanted to address it now. Just in case."

Ana huffed, though there was no real annoyance in it. "I am not stubborn."

"If you insist."

In retaliation, she flicked him on the arm and separated from him as the waiter came to collect the bowl. They only had to wait another minute or so for him to return with the check, which Jesse took care of with cash. As soon as Ana finished her drink, they would be free to go.

Only a sip left before Jesse would need to walk back through the restaurant to the front door and then they'd...what? Part ways? The thought rallied against him, and he watched Ana's back as they walked out, contemplating whether he read the signs right, whether she was feeling the same as him.

Outside the restaurant and without the heating lamp, the night had cooled considerably, dipping down as the hours ticked by, but Jesse didn't feel the chill until the thought of Ana walking back to her apartment settled into his mind. Until the thought of sitting on his bed all alone burrowed deep into his being, leaving him almost breathless.

"Ana," he called before he lost his courage, though he didn't have to raise his voice; Ana was walking right by his side on the sidewalk.

She didn't respond verbally, only waiting with expectant features for him to continue.

"Would you...like to come back to the hotel? For drinks?"

Ana raised an eyebrow. "For *drinks*?"

"Well..." His face flushed. "Maybe not for drinks."

Jesse internally winced at how lame his offer sounded, and he waited, throat swelled up like he was sick, making it difficult to swallow.

He didn't have to wait long. Ana only took a few moments to respond, and when she did, his heart nearly exploded.

"I'd love to."

His steps faltered even as she continued down the sidewalk without a change in pace—like she hadn't just shaken him to the core by agreeing to go back to his hotel.

"Coming?" she called over her shoulder, eyebrow raised like it was silly of him not to be following her in the first place, and Jesse swallowed thickly. His walk fell evenly with hers.

"Are you sure?" he asked, hopeful about her answer but also not sure if he could handle it if she said no.

"If I wasn't, I wouldn't have said yes, Jesse." Ana caught his eyes, and the lightness sparked a smile from him.

A straightforward answer, but he appreciated it; the giddiness and fluttering made it feel like his steps were lighter than they were. Though presented in the disguise of coming back for a drink, there was no need for pretense—they were both very aware of what the invitation entailed, and warmth thrummed in his belly at the thought.

Jesse snuck a few chances of touch—an elbow against an elbow, a hand against a hip, fingers against fabric— and he didn't imagine the touches in response during their ride back to the hotel. Her shoulder pressed against his bicep, and her finger hooked in his beltloop for a moment before releasing.

By the time they made it to the building, Jesse had skittered his fingertips to rest on the small of her back while she retrieved the extra hotel key from her purse before he could (as Ana had given him the code for her building, he'd given her his spare hotel key). He politely ignored how she dropped the key back into her purse.

Jesse skated his thumb across skin bared by the low dip at the back of her dress, grinned, and immediately wanted to do it again. But he waited, trailing behind her through the hallway, heart pounding in anticipation so that he almost jumped when Ana turned around, leaned back against the door, and tilted her head to look up at him. Those heady, green eyes were mesmerizing as she blinked them, slow and telling—promising, really—and Jesse couldn't stop himself from leaning down to press a blazing kiss to her lips. Ana responded with fervor; Jesse pressed her against the door, and Ana let out the most tantalizing noise he'd heard from her. He planned to hear it many more times that night, but it reminded him—and her, it seemed—of where they were. They pulled apart, foreheads pressed together.

Jesse was reminded of the couple at the restaurant in the same position and what he assumed they'd be doing later, how they were pressed together like Jesse and Ana were over ice cream. He smiled in satisfaction at the thought of how his night was turning.

Though it wasn't directed at her, Ana smiled back at him, making his own stretch further. With one more lingering touch to her waist, Jesse stepped back so she could unlock the door, his eyes drawn to the unkempt strands of hair which had fallen from Ana's clip. They curled against her neck and shoulder, and Jesse had the urge to run his hand through her full locks, coiling those strands around his fingers.

The *ding!* and green light indicated the door was unlocked, and Jesse's attention shifted as Ana drifted through, Jesse not far behind her. He barely heard the door close behind him, attention solely on the woman in front of him.

They slipped off their shoes in silence, and Ana placed her purse on the side table. No words were spoken as Ana padded over to Jesse, her bare feet quiet against the carpeted floor. No words were needed, not after the prelude in the hallway. It wasn't until she lifted her hand to touch Jesse's face did he breathe out her name, ghosting it against the bridge of her nose as she leaned in closer.

Ana, in kind, whispered his name, and the syllables against his skin made him shiver.

Jesse had imagined a few times what it would be like for Ana to kiss him, something soft and light like the brush of a flower petal he dipped down to smell. Maybe, if his fantasies were a little heartier, the kiss would be more robust, but as usual, reality was much better.

The pressure was sure and steady, just like her decision to follow him home, and she slid the hand previously on his cheek to feed through his short hair, the other clutching at his lapel. His own hands drifted down to her hips and back, pulling her as close to him as he could; each curve against his body sent a thrill down to his toes.

Half of him couldn't believe this was happening, while the other half wholeheartedly enjoyed every moment, especially when Ana touched her tongue to his bottom lip over the same spot she'd brushed her thumb. Jesse didn't falter in following along, and when they broke for air, his mouth peppered kisses along her throat, behind her ear, paying more attention there when she whimpered.

His own breath hiccupped when Ana made quick work of his tie and skipped her fingers from one shirt button to the next. Within moments, she was urging the garment from Jesse's shoulders, the fabric fluttered to the floor. The tie came next, and the sound of the silk dropping to the ground was drowned out by the beating of his heart.

Then, Ana was kissing up his throat from his collarbone, stopping to breathe in his ear, "The bed."

She stepped away from him, but Jesse caught her hand before she could go too far. Ana tilted her head quizzically, but her question was answered when he saddled up to her, one arm touching the beading along her shoulder, the other reaching for the zipper on the back of her dress. Not taking his eyes off her, Jesse pulled it down—the noise magnified by their anticipation—and he watched her eyes darkened when his thumbs brushed her bare back. The zipper ended right at the small of it. Jesse's free hand tugged one shoulder of her dress down to her elbow. The other stayed put, and the fabric, tilted and uneven, held right at the top of her breast.

With a shrug, the second strap tumbled off her shoulder, and the top half of her dress bundled around her waist, exposing her strapless bra.

"There," he said, which made the corner of her lip tug up.

"Evening things up?"

"If I really wanted us even, I'd pull this off." Jesse ran a finger across the top of the lingerie. It was barely attached, but Ana wasn't concerned, standing before him with a straight back and all the confidence in the world with her rumpled dress pooled around her hips.

"Why don't you?"

"All in due time," he responded after a moment, distracted as he was with her smooth stomach and exquisitely defined waist. Jesse didn't know how he appeared to her, but he focused more on the way her hands drifted from his stomach to his chest, cataloguing every contour, muscle, and scar. She even dropped her head to press a kiss to the noticeable mark on his left side; a different kind of warmth, one soft and subtle like sun through a skylight, touched his heart.

The scar was one he'd gotten in a hunting accident when he was twenty-nine, still a stupid kid who thought he was invincible. Yet there Ana was, pressing such a delicate touch to something that reminded him of foolishness, probably thinking it was a wound from being heroic, perhaps from some rescue mission. Or—more likely—she didn't care what it was from, merely acknowledging the past hurt with a soft caress.

Jesse cradled her face in his palms. God, he cared *so much* for this woman. Her kindness, her wit, her absolute beauty. Slowly, he brought their faces together, and the kiss was the sweetest he could give her, saying everything he couldn't. After a few moments, he pulled back to gaze into her eyes, dark from the little lighting in the room, so they were little brushes of moss, soft and warm.

"Let me carry you," he said, and in response, Ana hooked her arms around his neck. She was as heavy as he was expecting, a sturdy figure with light limbs and lean muscle who was still shorter than Jesse even in heels. He placed her on his bed.

Though he could maybe claim their actions thus far leaned on the edge of urgency, the moment Ana's back hit the comforter of the hotel bed, everything slowed. Instead of a collision of forces, like that of a startling explosion, they came together like a cresting, hefty wave. Pressure rumbled underneath their skin through the beat of their hearts until it surged upward, bubbling and pressing out with every touch of skin. Each clutch of a hand, each slide of fingers across delicate places, created a steady build, tantalizing as Jesse hitched his breath in anticipation. And when the wave finally crashed, he could do nothing but let the current float him to shore like he was a shipwrecked sailor plastered against the sand.

Hips still aligned and heaving for breath, he let the last flecks of the beating wave filter through his body, breathing in Ana's shower gel, lotion, or soap; he didn't know what it was, only that it was tangy like citrus.

Afterward, when he'd rolled over to collect Ana in his arms as he did, they lay together, he on his back, her curled into his side, and on his chest, their hands rested with pinkies intertwined.

Jesse shifted a sheet up their skin to rest over their hips; it was like a tide slipping over their legs. The humming of cars, or maybe it was the heat through the vents, brushed against his ears like water against the shore, and his eyes drifted closed.

He'd never really loved water like some people do, but Jesse could appreciate the peace of floating on his back, ears submerged from the world. With the way the darkness of the room was only disturbed by the outside streetlamps stretching through gaps in the large, long window, he could imagine himself floating on his boat on a moonlit night, anchored to Ana.

They drifted. The only color he could see was the dark of his eyelids

His eyes snuck open when he felt Ana press a kiss to his collarbone. He caught her gaze through her lashes and returned the sentiment with a kiss to her hair. Ana hummed in contentment, and Jesse couldn't help the smile that overtook his face. There he was with a beautiful, amazing woman, naked in bed, in the room he'd only ever seen as solitary.

The light from the smoke detector didn't seem as red that night.

"I had a good time." Ana's voice was a whisper, though it was as loud to him as a shriek of joy.

"Me too," he said, nuzzling into her; Ana did the same, sidling up more, her bare chest against his was a comforting presence more than an amorous one.

"So…" he started, though trailed off, not wanting to disturb the peace with his next question. Unfortunately, Ana didn't let it go and poked him on the chest.

"So...?"

"*So*. Uh, where do you want to go next time?"

"Next time?" Ana hummed. "Would it be strange if we went back to the park?"

"Together, like this?" he asked—just to be sure.

"Yes, Jesse, together." Her voice sounded amused, but he didn't care. The happiness that bloomed in his chest was about as large as when she'd agreed to their first date.

He grinned. "I'd like that."

Jesse felt her smile pull against his chest. "Me too."

Chapter Eight

There was a coffee cup on the counter, the only simple one Ana owned. The rest she collected from art fairs or estate sales, but the one she hadn't bothered putting away was blue with the white logo of her school on it. Ana had forgotten about it until Jesse was already filling it with coffee.

"The others are too fancy," he said when she asked about it. "I feel like I'll break your others." He paused. "Though I promise not to break this one. It's your school, after all."

Ever since, her blue mug became Jesse's, and he used it every time he'd come over the past few days. And after he'd left this morning to pack for his trip back home to America, she'd washed it, and...let it sit.

Ana didn't know why she was being so sentimental about it. It was a cup. It wasn't as though Jesse wouldn't be back to drink from it. Perhaps that's why Ana kept it out on her counter—she was waiting for him to return and use it. Pretending he would.

Ana didn't know how long he'd be gone, and it turned out Jesse didn't, either.

"It could be a couple of weeks, or..."

"Longer?" she'd finished for him.

With that news, and knowing Jesse would be gone in a matter of days, it was no surprise Ana had taken him back to her apartment for a repeat of their dinner evening. She had found the mug the next morning—and there she was, days later, while Jesse packed up at his hotel.

He was leaving tomorrow.

Ana shook her head and pointedly shoved the mug back in the cupboard.

Jesse was leaving and he was coming back—eventually—so there was no need to sulk like a lovesick child.

Ana grabbed her bulky purse, then left. She needed to go for a walk.

The setting sun still held a smidge of warmth, but she was glad she'd worn her thick tights. The autumn breeze would've been a little too chilly for bare legs. As she walked, the air cooled further, and she snuggled into her coat. Then it became harder to see, and after even more steps, her shoes scraped against dirt.

Ana lifted her head.

Lebădă Pod.

Standing underneath the lamppost, exhaustion seeping into her limbs, Ana realized she had walked all the way to Swan Bridge. No swans were about now—only twittering sparrows and sleeping squirrels.

It was dark—late, Ana revised as she noticed the time on the clock, though she needed to squint to see it.

Ana had the urge to turn around right then. She didn't. Instead, she chose to walk further along the path, one step at a time with her arms hugging her sides.

Her boots crunched the leaves under her heel, a sharp sound which almost made her cringe. This time, she seemed to be the only one there, and the darkening shadows from the lamps against the wind-shaking branches were like hands shooing her away.

When Jesse was there, they seemed to beckon her closer. The colors were rich and warm in the afternoon sun, but in the evening, they were scurrying brown shadows skittering over her feet. She unconsciously slowed until she stopped, plopping down on a bench as the trees continued to groan against the wind.

The bench seemed so large without a body next to her.

Was that what Ana was going to do once Jesse left? Pine for his presence? She'd never done anything like it before, but when she stopped to mull over her feelings, she realized what the foundation of her unease was, and it was simple.

Uncertainty.

The coffee cup sat with a nebulous future—as did the chair next to the fridge Jesse liked to sit at, and the pillowcase she'd taken to using for him. The unfinished soda in her fridge she knew he liked. The key card for his hotel sitting in her purse.

Her bag was a big thing, almost a tote for how large it was. Ana adjusted so it was more firmly in her lap. Something jabbed into her leg from inside.

Dipping her hand in, it was...

Ana lifted the rectangle out. Jesse's gift. She'd planned to give it to him earlier, but after Jesse said he was leaving for America...there was the uncertainty again.

Her father told her a story once of when she was younger, probably six or seven years old. Ana didn't remember the event he spoke of, but she remembered the glitter of humor from her dad as he spoke.

When she was in school, a daycare-like setting, the kids would all play football (or soccer as an American like Jesse would call it). Every day, the kids would divide into teams, different every time, and Ana noticed a boy who always chose the opposite team from her. This same boy barely talked to her, and being as young a kid as she was, Ana was afraid he hated her. She agonized over it for days, even crying once to her dad about it.

Finally, she'd had enough and stomped over to the boy and asked him bluntly if he hated her. But, in fact, he had a crush and was too shy to talk to her.

Her father loved telling that story, chuckling at the end like it was a comedy, mainly because she was impatient enough to ask him outright.

Ana tightened her grip on the gift, then shoved it back into her purse. Her feet moved before she realized she was even standing, and she jogged to the main road.

No more uncertainty.

Surprisingly, even this late at night, Ana didn't have to wait long to hail a cab. Traffic was barely there; within only a few minutes, she was stepping out of the car and making her way through the doors of Jesse's hotel. A couple people milled about the lobby, two up at the desk, one sitting on a couch, but she didn't pay them much mind. Instead, she headed straight for the elevator and palmed the up arrow on the wall.

Ana was grateful everything had moved so quickly, because as soon as she stepped into the elevator, her nerves buzzed through her limbs, and she knew she was too late to turn back around now. Not that she wanted to, but in an enclosed space, Ana had nothing to do but *think*, and each scenario that played in her head made her stomach clench between her ribs.

The ding and settling cabin made her straighten her back, and Ana sucked in a deep breath. She merely had to exit, walk down the hall, knock on his door, and…

Well, there were a few things she wanted, most of them involving Jesse's arms around her, but Ana would settle for giving him her gift.

The elevator doors opened and—

"Jesse?"

There was Jesse, looking just as surprised as Ana. "What...?" Jesse blinked owlishly. "What are you... doing here?"

"Well, I—"

The elevator dinged, and Ana hopped out, almost running into Jesse. She fiddled with her purse, blushing.

"You're leaving," she said. "I wanted to..."

"Yeah," he said, smiling. "Me too."

Her shoulders loosened, and the tight knot in her stomach released. Ana was glad he felt the same. When Jesse turned back toward the hall, she trailed behind him, and they quickly made it back to his room, where she toed her shoes off, placing them neatly next to his tennis shoes, which she straightened.

Tilting her head up to him, Ana pursed her lips at the amusement in his face.

"You know I like things organized." With a teasing tug, she pulled his sweatshirt strings even, which made him laugh.

"That one's a losing battle," Jesse said, removing it altogether and tossing it on the chair near the window. Ana, on the other hand, made a point to hang her jacket in the small closet.

They stood on opposites sides of the room. Jesse, with his hands in his sweatpants' pockets, and Ana, her hands clasped in front of her. Jesse took a couple steps forward.

"So...do you...?" He made a jerky gesture with his arm that she didn't understand. At her puzzled silence, Jesse made a different motion she still didn't get, so she stepped toward him, grabbing his hand.

"How about you tell me instead of playing the charades game?"

Jesse's face flushed, and his smile was sheepish.

"Right," he said, then he lifted her hand to kiss her palm. His voice deepened as he asked, "Would you like to stay?"

In response, Ana drifted her hand to his neck and leaned forward. Their kiss was slow, a steady warmth which crackled all the way to her toes, and she smiled against his mouth, any remaining tension in her body melting away. He lay a light peck to her lips before they pulled back.

Every worry, every doubt, drifted away like blowing sand off a surface as she looked into his eyes. Without words—or maybe the words lit across their irises, sketched into the color—they moved to the bed. Each piece of clothing that slid off skin did so with tender slowness, and Ana's heart softened as Jesse folded her shirt with military precision, wrinkles smoothed across the surface. Ana did the same for his, though she hardly needed to worry about creasing the thick sweatpants; she doubted anything she could do would make those wrinkle.

Even the touch of his fingers to her skin was soft, and she peppered his shoulders and stomach and face with delicate kisses. Every brush of their skin was exact and determined, no motion wasted as they made love overtop of the comforter. With his head buried in her shoulder and her arms skimming over his back, she felt every shift in muscle and the tightening shake of the end. Ana barely noticed the chill against her naked skin until they were finished, and Jesse was attempting to maneuver the blankets around them.

Goosebumps erupted over her arms, her legs, her stomach, and she shivered as her sweat cooled from the temperature. Jesse always had his heat low when he went to sleep. As she discovered from sleeping with him a few times, he was a furnace at night, so when he moved away to reach for the blankets, the cold felt especially chilling.

Though…she thought it may be something else. Ana imagined the coffee cup, alone and desperate for use on her countertop. She thought of it collecting dust—for days, weeks—after Jesse's return, then eventually stumbling into him on the street.

"I've been back a while," he would say, and she imagined the coffee cup shattering on the floor, splintering into too many pieces for her to ever bind it back together.

Feeling exposed, Ana halted Jesse's hand as he pulled a corner of fabric over her. He tilted his head at her, but she didn't say anything, merely lifting herself off the mattress to grab her undergarments, which she shimmied back on. When she turned back to Jesse, he was sitting up against the headboard, comforter pulled over his waist and watching her with undiscernible eyes.

Ana didn't know what to say, but she sat on the bed in preparation to do so, curling her legs underneath her. Jesse still watched, and she swallowed thickly.

"You're leaving," she whispered finally, and everything she was feeling was stuffed into those words. For how quiet they left her mouth, they felt ballooned and bulbous on her tongue.

"I am," he said back, also quiet. The shifting sheets as he adjusted himself were louder than his response.

After a moment, he murmured, "I'll be coming back."

Ana didn't snap her head up like she thought she might, instead tilting slowly up, her hair curtained over one eye. The one with clear sight sought his own, and she looked to read what was so clearly in his irises earlier. It was blurry now, and she licked her dry lips.

"Will you?"

Immediately, Jesse reached his hand out to hers and grasped it in his own, threading his fingers between her own. The other hand brushed her hair out of her face, the side with her braid and bead, so when he pushed it behind her ear, it wanted to slip back out. It didn't, and Ana thought of that as some sort of sign, especially when he, with emphatic certainty, said, "Yes."

It was Ana whose movements bumped her braid out as she smiled, and it tickled over his wrist, his hand cupping her cheek.

"Wait here," Ana said, then shuffled over to her large purse, which she'd hooked on the coat hanger. Only a second of hesitation left her hand hovering over the entrance, but Ana shook her head and grabbed the gift from inside the bag. Her courage felt fleeting, wisping and turning in the wind, but Ana pushed one foot along the floor, then the next, until she was sitting on the bed once more. There was enough bravery left in her to make it, all transferred now to the gift.

Jesse's curious eyes tracked what was in her hands, and she bit her lip, tightening her grip on it. The corner dug into her palm, but after a moment, Ana turned it toward Jesse and transferred it to his hands.

His expression was blank at first, then his eyes widened—and softened.

It was probably the fifth time they'd gone to the park that she'd picked up her charcoal pencil. The last time she had was an entire year previous, but the lines on the page were exactly as she imagined in her head, her brain puppeteering her hand over the next weeks in order to transfer her picture to the page. Each swipe of the pencil was a relief in a way, more liberating than the sewing patterns she filled her days with, and the lines were freeing in their certainty of placements and purpose.

Lebădă Pod. Ana drew Swan Bridge—as detailed as she could make it—which the frame cradled behind its glass and was now in Jesse's hands. With a warm flutter,

Ana noted the way his thumb caressed the side, rhythmic and gentle.

"What does it say?" he asked, turning so he could point at the two words she'd penciled on the top. "I know bridge, but I don't know the other."

"*Lebădă nostru*. Our bridge."

His finger traced the letters. "Ours, huh?"

"*Al nostru*."

"*Al.. nostru?*"

Ana smiled, nodding. With more look at the drawing, he placed it next to him, then cradled her head in his hands.

"Thank you."

Jesse directed her head toward him, and their mouths met in the middle with a light-yet-lingering touch, and when they pulled back, Ana nuzzled her nose against his.

"How about we go later?" he asked, and Ana beamed.

"I'd like that very much."

"Good." Jesse kissed her again. "Very good." Then another.

With a laugh, she pulled back. "I need to leave."

"You don't *need* to."

"Yes, because you said you needed to get up at four in the morning for your flight, and it's already eleven. We both need to sleep."

Jesse sighed, but with the lightness in his gaze, she knew he wasn't too upset, and Ana stood to put on her clothes.

"Fine," he said, "then I'll see you when I get back."

Taking a moment to appreciate the orderly state of her clothing, Ana smiled. "See you when you get back."

It was relieving, she thought, and a little odd, how quickly the weight in the room dissipated with only a few words, and they chatted while they dressed, though Jesse left his sweatshirt on the chair. He was only walking her to the elevator, so he didn't bother putting much on besides his sweats and T-shirt.

Jesse helped her into her coat, and they walked to the call button, which he pressed while she adjusted her purse on her shoulder. Not knowing how much time they had before the elevator arrived, Jesse ducked down for a quick kiss.

"Goodbye."

"Take care of you," she said, then blinked as his eyebrows pushed together in confusion. She blushed. "Oh, I mean...take...care of me? No, just take care, I believe."

Jesse grinned, swooping in for another peck. "No, I think I like yours better this time."

"You do?"

"Yeah." He brushed a thumb over her cheek. "Take care of you, too."

The way he said it, that deep rumble and the warmth against her cheek made her heart skip, and it was her this time who caught his lips only to be interrupted by the ding of the elevator.

Backing away through the elevator doors didn't feel any different than any other time they'd parted, so already, Ana knew she was feeling better.

"What is it actually?" she asked. "The phrase, I mean."

The ding chirped in her ear, and the doors started closing. Through the closing gap, Jesse waved, then winked.

"I'll let you know when I get back."

They closed, and Ana bit the inside of her cheek to stop herself from grinning like a silly fool standing by herself.

I'll hold you to that, she thought, but Ana didn't expect she'd have to.

Chapter Nine

"**G**randpa!"

Jesse grinned, moving his suitcase out of the way for the toddler bursting out of the house. Jake grabbed on to his legs, but Jesse scooped him up into his arms, and a little giggle escaped the boy. From the corner of Jesse's eye, he saw Monica in the doorway, no doubt the one who opened the door for the little three-year-old to escape.

Sarah smiled at the two of them as she dropped her keys in her purse, then pressed a quick kiss to her son's head before she picked up Jesse's suitcase.

"You've got your hands full," she said before he could protest, pulling it behind her to the front porch. Jesse heard her thank Monica for looking after Jake while she picked Jesse up from the airport, and the two sisters went indoors.

Jake, on the other hand, hadn't stopped talking since Jesse had picked him up, and though he stumbled over his sentences, they were a lot clearer than the last time Jesse was home. Already, he was growing up fast—and Jesse meant that literally, too. Jake was taller, his arms able to wrap around his grandpa's shoulder a little more.

"And we made—we made big swords out of paper and took 'em home. I'm a knight now."

"Oh, are you?" Jesse said, adjusting the boy in his arms so he could go through the door. "And you made some newspaper swords?"

"Uh-huh!" Jake pointed down the hall to the room he always stayed in while visiting. "It's down there!"

"I'll have to see it after we eat then, huh? Maybe we can make one for Grandpa, too."

Jake nodded so vigorously he almost bonked his head on Jesse's, but—thankfully—Jesse was paying attention enough to lean back a little. The smell of a barbecue prompted the delay of sword show-and-tell, and he already heard Sarah and Monica clattering dishes in the kitchen.

Hotdogs, potato salad, chips, fruit, and beans sat out on the counter, and Jesse was practically salivating at the sight. After his flight, he was starving, so he set Jake down to grab himself a plate. He knew Sarah would get Jake something, so he piled up, kissed Monica and Sarah on the cheek, and went outside to see Kaylee cleaning up the grill.

"Hey, Dad! Good timing!" she said, then chuckled at his full plate. "I see you already found the food."

Jesse ruffled her hair, and she swatted his hand away. "Of course, I did. Thanks, sweetie."

"Oh, I had zero part in the preparation. I'm just on cleanup duty."

"I figured."

Like the youngest daughter she was, Kaylee stuck her tongue out and left to get her own plate. Kaylee was never known for great culinary skills, leaving that to Jesse or her sisters. Over the years, it had become an unspoken rule that she'd clean up afterward.

Jesse sat at the picnic table and dove right into his meal. It was a few degrees warmer than it had been the past few days in Germany, so he was happy to soak up the sun during what was likely the last nice day before winter truly struck.

His plate was half empty by the time the rest of his family had settled down to eat, so he was free to talk about some of the places he'd been while they finished, and while Sarah convinced Jake to eat everything on his plate.

Jesse didn't mention Ana.

He did tell Monica about the couscous again, and she laughed at Jesse's description of the food.

"Oh my god, I really can't believe you ordered it! Mr. Burger-and-Fries!"

"I've been enjoying sweet potato fries lately, actually."

Ana had ordered them, of course, the basket sitting between them in her apartment next to the rest of the to-go food. She'd already eaten ten by the time he had his first, and Jesse could see why she liked them so much.

"Fancy living there in Germany," Monica teased. "Mr. Schnitzel-and-Sweet-Potato-Fries then."

"That's me," he answered.

When his daughters finished, he got to hear what they were up to. Kaylee had a different boyfriend than the one before he'd left, Monica had a trip planned the next weekend with some friends from college, and Sarah gushed about Jake, barely mentioning her secretarial work at the law firm, but that was no surprise.

With each story, each laugh, something that couldn't be filled in Germany settled in his chest, and Jesse smiled at being surrounded by his kids and grandkid. *Being back is nice*, he thought.

Monica was the first to leave, her drive from his house the longest at an hour. Though Kaylee's was technically longer, she was staying with a friend in town, so she didn't leave until after they'd all finished their movie, a cartoon he'd never seen but one Jake seemed to enjoy.

Sarah picked up the empty cocoa mugs while Jake snuggled into Jesse's side.

"He missed you," she said.

Jesse rubbed his hand down his small back. "I did too. Missed all of you."

The mugs clicked against one another as she walked toward the kitchen. It was connected to the living room, so he still heard her when she asked, "How long are you here?"

"I'm not sure. No more than a month, I think. It depends on when the contract in Europe comes through."

"So not long."

The quiet disappointment wasn't difficult to hear.

"Not long."

Jesse pulled Jake into his side a little more. Jake stayed asleep, little whistling exhales unchanged. He'd had a busy day. They'd made newspaper swords for everyone, so Jake defended his room with Grandpa from the enemies. He dragged it along behind him on the floor for the rest of the night, and it sat leaned up against the couch while they watched their movie.

"I don't mean to sound upset." Sarah walked back in, sitting in the chair. "I just know how disappointed he'll be. He wanted you to come to his play."

"I might be able to."

"And you might not. Which is okay! It's not as though you traveling is new. Just, don't promise anything if you're not sure."

Jesse shook his head. "I won't."

"Okay, good. That's all." Sarah then pointed to her nose then pressed up a little with a laugh. "They're doing the *Three Little Pigs*."

"Yeah?" He chuckled. "And what part is Jake?"

"The wood vendor."

"There's a wood vendor?"

"They needed more characters." She shrugged. "It's a big class."

"So does that mean there's a straw and brick vendor?"

"Oh, yes. Very important parts. They each have three lines."

Jesse laughed. "Hey, I think I recall you having one whole line in your second-grade play."

Sarah groaned. "*Dad.*"

"And I think I remember you memorizing the completely wrong line. Your classmate was so confused when you said hers."

"That moment gave me stage fright for the rest of my *life*. Hopefully Jake takes after his dad. That man could speak nonsense in front of strangers. The confidence!"

"You have your own confidence," he reassured, then looked down at Jake. "I can see it in him, the way he says or does something like you did when you were little."

"Yeah? I mostly see his dad."

"I was the same way," Jesse said. "When you girls were growing up, I didn't see a lick of myself in you, not until your mom pointed it out. But Jake, he tilts his head the same way you did when you were trying to figure something out. Always the curious one."

Sarah didn't answer, and when Jesse looked over, her face was shifted in that particular way a parent did when seeing their kid. There was a simultaneous warmth and ache in his heart; his daughter was so grown up.

Jesse missed being able to see his children grow. He was still seeing it now, yes, but it wasn't like when they were younger, when he taught them how to ride a bike or how to roll up newspaper swords like Jake. His kids, now adults, learned more on their own, *taught* on their own, and they didn't need him in the same way.

It was something he never thought about when he was younger, only concerned about being independent from his parents, being grown up. Jesse never thought about how his parents felt, or if they were sad and proud to see him run past them.

He could see Jake grow, but it would be in a different capacity—in snippets and without as much of the mess as Sarah would experience. But, he supposed, there would be one more lesson he could teach Sarah: how to watch your kids sprout up and leave for their own adventures.

Jesse scooped up Jake, standing from the couch. That was a long way away, though.

Sarah gathered up his things, most notably Jake's newspaper sword and the stuffed bear Jesse had brought back from Germany for him, and Jesse followed her out to the car, where he strapped Jake into his seat.

"Good to have you back, Dad." Sarah patted his shoulder before ducking into her own seat.

"Good to be back."

He stayed in the driveway as she turned on the vehicle, the engine rumbling to life, and waved even through the shine of the headlights. Jesse didn't know if she was waving back, but he didn't really mind either way. He waved as she fully pulled out, and it wasn't until she made it past three neighbors' mailboxes that he put his hand down.

No other vehicle or passersby inhabited the road, and only the wind through the pine trees sounded in his ears. Even Jesse's steps were quiet as he padded back to the house. Inside, the kitchen light was on, casting the room in a reaching glow as it strained to fill as much of the house as it could. The rest of the house was dark. Quiet.

Always quiet when the kids were gone.

He almost felt like laughing to himself. It was astounding how easily one could destroy years of content solitude, but in only a few days, he'd already gotten used to having someone next to him at night. Craved it, really.

After so long without, a handful of days where Ana and Jesse spent the night together made him want to expect it as certainty.

Jesse wanted her here in his home, not just the hotel room that only had his water bottle on the table and suitcase in the corner as decoration. He wanted to laugh to someone about the mess and the dishes he told Kaylee not to worry about. He wanted unexpected lights on in the hallway because she was brushing her teeth or changing for bed.

On the couch, his phone perched on the armrest, its screen black.

Without thinking too much about it, Jesse swiped it up and poked through the contacts until he found her. They'd exchanged information the day before he left, but Jesse didn't actually expect to use it.

The phone screen was bright, illuminating his hands and face, and there was only a moment's hesitation where his thumbs hovered over the screen before he pressed on the letters of his phone.

Hey, Ana. How are you?

Chapter Ten

Growing up, if Ana was ever upset, she would go to her mother, Mary. Not because she would coddle, or comfort, or even give her meaningful advice; yes, she would do any number of those on occasion, but the main reason Ana went to her was so Ana could be *distracted*. Her mother always had some chore or errand for Ana to do. Pick up sticks, clean the bathroom, help make *papanași*.

It had been two weeks plus a day, eighteen hours, and twenty-two minutes since the elevator door had closed to carry her away from Jesse.

Ana needed a distraction.

The café had carried her through whatever shift she had, but the moment she had any free time, Ana found herself walking toward the park or to Jesse's hotel. She'd stop herself, of course, clucking her tongue at how silly she was being, but regardless...she always had the urge.

Ana hadn't really realized how much time they had spent together until he was thousands of miles away and only accessible through her phone. She hadn't realized how much she'd miss him. But she did—terribly.

Just the day before, a rather bizarre customer came into the coffee shop. After her shift, the moment she toed her shoes off in her apartment and settled into her chair, she was calling Jesse to tell him about it. She forgot, though, she was six hours ahead of him, and an eleven o'clock chat was a rude wake-up call. But that was her first instinct: to tell Jesse about her day, and the thought of that...

Well, she didn't particularly know *what* to think of that.

Thus, to fill some of the void she was feeling, she'd made her way to her parents'. Some of her parents' friends were having a potluck, and her mother had decided to bring a stew. A large pot sat on the counter, waiting for its broth and veggies, while Ana peeled potatoes and her mother peeled and chopped a stack of carrots.

Ana had always thought her mother looked quite at home in the kitchen. Her dad cooked, too, but there was something about the efficiency and speed her mother that made her an ideal cook. Ana could never recall a time where Mary ever had to stretch for an ingredient or spice. Everything was always in the correct place, and not one pot had ever boiled over. When Ana was a child, she imagined all the veggies and turmeric and garlic lined up like little soldiers, and her mother in her yellow apron was a drill sergeant, spewing commands in their faces. Even now as an adult, Ana wouldn't have been surprised if the onion hopped right into the pot itself. Her mother probably expected it of the onion.

Ana deposited her naked potato in the pile of to-be-cut later, and she picked up the next one, flicking off a spec of dirt that had clung to the outside despite the thorough washing.

As she dug into the first peel, her mother cleared her throat.

"Yes?" Ana asked.

She had to wait for her mother to chop the last bit of carrot before she spoke.

"Work has been taking up more of your time than usual."

If Ana hadn't been on autopilot, she probably would've cut herself. She barely stopped from inhaling sharply. Ana should've expected her mother to notice she hadn't been around as often. Of course, she would've.

Ana shifted her feet, trying to ignore the tinge of discomfort swirling right between her ribs.

"It has."

The tapping against the cutting board stopped for a moment, then it resumed as her mother said, "I thought you liked the hours you had."

"I do." Ana swallowed thickly, that feeling expanding in her stomach. "They've just, needed a little more help."

Her mother hummed, and when she left the conversation sit as it was, Ana breathed a little more deeply, blinking down at her completed potato in surprise. She switched it for the next.

With the silence, Ana could do nothing but turn back toward what she'd wanted to be distracted from in the first place. Why did her mother have to ask about her "long shifts" today? The first time Mary had asked what was making her daughter so busy, Ana had been truthful: a new friend. But the more Ana and Jesse were together, the less she could use that excuse unless she wanted her mother prying, which she certainly would. Even before Ana and Jesse's relationship became intimate, Mary had suspected her daughter's *friend* was what the emphasis implied.

For the sake of a little privacy, Ana had lied and said she had more shifts at the café. Being a café open more than just the mornings and weekday, Ana was able to do so, citing work whenever she was with Jesse.

"I have an idea for you, Annie," her mom said, pushing the carrots off the cutting board into the pot. Then, she piled Ana's peeled potatoes onto the board and retreated back to her section of the counter.

"And what's that?" Ana asked, a little wary.

"Ask for less hours at the—"

Ana groaned. "Mom, no."

"Hey, don't interrupt me before you know what I'm going to ask!"

"I know what you're going to ask, though."

Mary waved her hand. "Let me finish anyway. I know you like your job, but I would also appreciate the help. They can find another worker to pick up more hours."

Ana squeezed the handle of the knife a moment before sighing and cutting off the next strip with more aggression than was probably warranted.

"You can help me with the patterns more," Mary continued. "More than just one or two at a time."

"*Mom.*"

"What? I'm just saying it's an *option*, and one I think you should take."

"I know you think that—"

"And what's so bad, making pretty fabrics? You like art."

"Well, *yes*—"

"So, it should be a good transition for you. And you can still work at the coffee shop. Just less hours." Her mother set her knife on the counter. "I don't see what the problem is."

An age-old irritation simmered underneath her skin, and she clenched her teeth together. Ana didn't answer.

At only the sound of the knives, Ana heard her mother sigh, a full-bodied one that would've blown paper right off the surface.

"Honey, I don't mean to make you upset."

And just like that, her anger fizzled away, and she turned around to see her mother looking apologetic.

Ana breathed in, then out. "I know, Mom."

"I know you're grown, but I still try to find something that works best."

It was an uncharitable thought, but it popped up regardless, whispering in the back of her head.

Best for who?

Ana sliced it to bits like the carrots and nodded, the motion further shaking the pieces down and out of her mind. It wasn't her mother's fault that Ana hadn't mentioned her aspirations in years and repeated that she was happy at the coffee shop. It was Ana's, completely.

"I know," she repeated.

Her mother clapped her on the shoulder. "I'm glad. So, you'll think about it?"

Ana knew the only answer that would stop her mother from continuing. "Yes, I'll think about it."

A quick kiss on the cheek left Ana alone at her station again, and she continued with the last two potatoes while her mother finished chopping the carrots. The ingredients for the broth sat next to the pot, but they planned to drop them in after the more solid ingredients.

Her father used to make stews when her mom wasn't home. Usually, Mary would cook, but when Ana's dad did, he certainly liked his stews and soups. There was a bout of weeks where her father was the one to cook, and she *begged* him to make something other than soup.

"I'll even just eat bread!" her younger self had told him dramatically with her hands clasped together. Not surprisingly, he found it to be funny, so he relentlessly teased her about it for months afterward.

"Did you want bread instead?" he'd ask every time he'd serve her something, even if it was just a cereal bowl or cookie in the evening.

As if manifested by her thoughts, her dad ambled into the kitchen with one hand in his jeans' pocket, so his sweater bunched up underneath his arm. "Still working hard?"

"As always, Papa," Ana said over her shoulder. He came up to pat her on the shoulder and kiss her cheek.

"And what about you, Henric?" her mother chimed in. "Are you working hard on the shed door? I won't have our tools getting rusty."

"Don't worry, dear. All taken care of."

When her mother turned around to give her thanks, her face bright, Ana couldn't help but smile at her parents. She loved the way her dad's face softened, and her mother's eyes sparkled. That was always the way it was growing up. Their eyes sought each other's in the room, and there would be a moment, because a moment was usually all they had, where the world lessened to just the two of them.

As any child, Ana typically groaned at the display, but as she aged, she realized how special their love was. And she wondered...were she and Jesse like that? She thought they might be. Ana knew Jesse's eyes softened when he looked at her; she caught him staring at her through a mirror some weeks ago, and her heart stuttered just thinking about it. His eyebrows, tipped just slightly, framed his blue eyes, which had shimmered in the low light like a match through colored glass.

Ana wondered what she had looked like. Was her mouth quirked up at the corner as she read the logo on his sweatshirts? Or was she grinning like her mother, excited to be in the presence of someone she loved?

Turning back to her cutting board, Ana pursed her lips. There she went, thinking of Jesse again. She wasn't expecting it would be so hard to ignore the longing that pulsed in her chest at his absence, but even a trip to her parents was proving ineffective.

Thankfully, their attention turned back toward Ana, and she latched on to the words so they could scrub Jesse's smile from her mind's eye.

"How's your friend?" her dad asked.

Instead of wearing the image down, his question buffed it into clarity, and her heart throbbed.

"Uh…what friend?"

He chuckled. "Your new one, the one you met at the coffee shop."

Ana turned to grab the stalks of celery sitting near the refrigerator. "Oh, just fine."

"That's good."

Only a pause went by, Ana waiting to pull apart the stalks, before her mother clicked her tongue.

"That's it?" she asked loudly, directed at Ana's father, who shrugged in response. Then she addressed Ana. "You've been so secretive about this *friend*. Who is he?"

"A friend, Mother."

"So you say."

From her tone, it was like her mother was interrogating Ana in a police station, narrowed eyes and all. Ana rolled her eyes in response, breaking off the celery and cutting off the ends before she rinsed it. Ana hoped the knife against the board would drown out any further questions. She sent a pleading glance toward her dad, who just shrugged again—sympathetically this time.

Ana sighed.

"Are you dating?" her mother asked.

"Mom!"

"What?"

"No," Ana grumbled, "we are not dating." And that was the truth, but when she said the words aloud, they felt sharp; they sliced at her chest and nicked her heart on the way out.

Ana hadn't expected that statement to ache quite so much. She shook her head and swallowed before going back to her task.

Mary sighed. "Oh, alright. I'll leave it be. For now."

"Thank you." And if there was the barest hint of sarcasm sticking to those syllables, no one mentioned it.

They completed the rest of the stew, avoiding any of other sensitive topics, which Ana was grateful for. Instead, they steered conversation to family members, TV shows, weekly plans—really, everything Ana didn't mind bringing up.

By the end of the day, and by the time she made it back to her apartment after dinner, she'd almost forgotten what it was she needed a distraction from.

Then she saw his coffee cup in the cupboard when she reached for her own. She didn't stare at it, but she might as well have for how distinctly it branded itself into her thoughts as she made her evening cup of tea.

His name swirled in Ana's head, and her tea did nothing to distract her from thinking, and thinking, and *thinking* about him. Neither the movie she'd put on, her nightly routine, nor her bed when she finally slipped into her night clothes and burrowed under her sheets helped either.

Her mind didn't even have the courtesy of quieting after the lights were out, even though sleep was the highlight of her evening.

Ana stared at the ceiling. Despite the modern amenities inside, her ceilings suffered from a dated popcorn design, and she traced some of the shadowed lines with her eyes, hoping it would substitute for sheep jumping over fences.

After the third maze she'd created, Ana sighed, forcing her eyes shut. Like two similar ends of a magnet, her eyelids wanted to bounce away from each other, but she ignored the urge to open them and huddled further into her blankets.

A second, a minute, an *hour* went by. She still couldn't sleep. The world behind her eyelids seemed infinitely more fascinating to her brain than any amount of sleep, it seemed. She could feel her frustration rising...which made it even more difficult to sleep.

Groaning, she flopped onto her side. Then moved to her back. She rolled to her other side. Each move was punctuated by his name because the more she feigned disinterest in her thoughts, the more they rallied for attention.

Her phone buzzed on her nightstand. Ana sighed. Swiping her hand out grab it, she figured she wasn't getting to bed anytime soon anyway. A text message; she squinted at it. Then when she saw the name, her heart fluttered. Jesse.

Awake?

Ana chuckled. He certainly got right to his point when texting, and from the way she'd seen him poke at the screen with his finger, it was likely due to speed.

I'm awake.

After a few moments, her phone vibrated once more.

Call?

Ana didn't bother typing out a reply; instead, she called him as soon as she read the message, and after only two rings, he answered.

"Jesse," she breathed into the receiver.

"Hi," he said, and Ana could hear the smile in his voice. "Sorry for calling you late."

"That's alright." *It's more than alright*, she thought, considering it was thinking of him before the text that was keeping her awake. "What did you call about?"

There was silence, but she caught the sound of rustling from the other side followed shortly by an intake of breath.

"I miss you a lot more than I thought I would."

Her heart swelled at his words.

"I miss you, too," she whispered, and each syllable seemed to float in the air around her like little sprites, dusting her ears with their wings and making her smile.

Jesse breathed out, something like relief in the speaker.

"When will you be back?" she asked.

"On Tuesday morning."

"I'll make sure to have the day off."

A beat, then he asked, voice soft, "You will?"

"I will," she promised. "I'll be here."

"Good." They breathed together. "Good."

The darkness of her room held only silhouettes, her apartment far enough away from the road to avoid the direct shine of the streetlamps, so if she barely crested her eyes open, she could imagine the pillow next to her was Jesse. Her voice and his breath in her ear were soft; it was as if they were lying beside each other, whispering into her sheets.

Ana was surprised she enjoyed sliding up next to him so much. She wasn't a physically affectionate person, usually, and any partners she'd had in the past, she didn't enjoy cuddling with. Frankly, Ana liked her sleep, and she liked bundling up in her comforters, hands buried underneath her pillow. There typically wasn't room for a stray arm in that sleeping arrangement.

But Jesse, like many things, was different. His was a light touch, a hand on her arm or his forehead on her shoulder. The edge of the pillow tickled her elbow, a brush of his fingers against her skin, and she closed her eyes as she listened to Jesse describe his day with Kelsey.

She wondered if he was doing the same. Did Jesse imagine the pillow next to him could be her? Did he even *have* another pillow? Ana realized she didn't know what his house was like.

And, though she heard plenty about his daughters, it was so different to hear about them so presently. *That* day, he saw his grandkid—not a nebulous past day where he'd called Jesse "G'ampa" or a distant month ahead where he would see him. Ana had also never seen what his family looked like. Jesse wasn't well known for taking pictures or having many on his person, for that matter.

"I want to know more about you," she finally told him after he said what movie he and his daughter watched.

Jesse sputtered a moment, likely surprised she'd veered from his story, but he composed himself and replied softly, "Me too."

"I feel like I know you and don't at the same time."

Ana could tell he was confused by how he paused. "How so?"

"I can't picture where you are right now. I know your life here in Germany, but it's different in America. You feel so far away." She brushed her palm over the cool, empty pillow, her hand falling into the middle. "That's really what it is. Miles and miles away."

His voice came from a vacuous space as she talked to him, a singular form in a dark room. She could make up a scenery, but it wouldn't be the same, and Ana almost felt as though it was shameful to not know anything about his American home. Germany wasn't his home. America was, where his daughters were, so Ana should know *something* about his life there.

"I have a yellow mailbox outside." Jesse paused. "There's a start."

Ana's widening grin pulled against the pillow. "I wouldn't have expected that."

"Which color did you think?"

"Blue, to match your eyes."

He chuckled. "Flatterer. I actually don't remember why we chose yellow out of everything. I can't say it's my favorite color or anything. It's none of the girls' favorite color, either."

Closing her eyes, Ana let his voice fill her ears and the room while she snuggled into her comforters.

"Make something up," she requested.

Jesse hummed. "Let's see…"

"Something from the park?"

"The park?" She listened to the shifting fabric on the other end of the line, and she wondered what he was doing. "What about those flowers? The—what are they called—the daylilies. The ones at the east entrance."

"Oh, those!" Her smile was soft, half hidden in the pillow. She'd pointed those out to him during one of their first outings to the park. Despite their overabundance around businesses and homes due to their low maintenance (her mother, for one, complained about everyone choosing the same flower), Ana loved them. They reminded her of bright days and refreshing breezes; they even fluttered in the wind when she pointed them out to Jesse. There had still been a couple of weeks before the first frost at that point, so she typically drifted by them each time on their walk. Eventually Jesse noticed the direction they were headed, so he suggested ending their walks around the daylilies until they'd finally wilted.

"I like that," she whispered.

"Me too."

There was a dull sound in the background. Perhaps the television was on, or maybe he was outside. Ana didn't know what time it was in her area, so she wasn't positive about when he was talking to her over in America. She could only assume it was sometime during the day, in the morning or early afternoon. There could be breakfast in front of him—hashbrowns crispy and with pepper, just the way he liked them. Ana wished she was there with him.

"Jesse, when you get back, can we…talk?" she asked timidly.

"What do you mean?"

"I just mean that…" She sighed heavily. "I want to talk about *us*."

His voice was soft when he repeated it. "Us?"

"Yes." Ana couldn't see his face, but she imagined it might be knit in worry. "Us."

Her hand gripped Jesse's pillow, creasing it between her fingers.

"What about us?"

"Well," she said, "like you told me earlier…I miss you more than I thought I would. I want to talk about *that*." The conversation with her parents came to mind, how she said they weren't dating and how the lie had twisted her insides.

"I want to talk about it too." She heard a sharp inhale on the other line, then a light, jovial exhale. "Because I really care for you, Ana, and I want…well, I want *more* of this." He imagined her pressing her lips together, thinking about her next words.

"We talk nearly every day, whether you're here in Germany or there in America, and… and I want to continue that. Talking to you. Being next to you. I *miss* you," she repeated, feeling so much more gravity to that longing than she had before.

The pillow was lumpy under her hand, especially now that she'd clutched it to her chest. She wanted Jesse to be the one in her arms, instead. She wanted those lips on his coffee cup and on her own. She wanted to run her hand down his chest and smooth the wrinkles on his shirt before he left. She wanted walks in the woods and searing touches. She wanted exactly what they had already, but she also wanted *more* of it.

"I'd say we could talk about it now, but it feels too distant on the phone like this."

"I agree. I want to *see* you." Ana was only imagining his expressions. Even though she knew him well enough to remember the way his laugh lines stretched when he smiled, she still didn't know how his eyes would shine when he told her how deeply he cared for her. All she could picture was when he confessed how he felt after the museum, but the memory was tainted with her confusion at her own feelings, so she couldn't truly appreciate the image.

"Then we'll see each other Tuesday, though I wish I could see you now."

"I was thinking the same thing."

Jesse hummed. His next words were light and teasing: "What are you wearing? Since I can't see you."

Ana laughed. "I hardly think it's time for that."

"When I see you next, then."

Her chest felt like her pillow, someone holding it close to them so tightly it was about to burst. She grinned.

"When I see you next."

Chapter Eleven

When Jesse left the airport and took a taxi back to his usual room at the hotel, there was something almost surreal about the experience. After the novelty of the trips out of the country wore off, Jesse usually trudged his way to his hotel room, swiped the key with a sigh, plopped onto the bed, then counted down the days until he could go home.

But strangely, the hotel felt...warmer now, like something familiar and kind. Jesse knew it was because, with every step across the carpeted floor, the memory of Ana stepped behind him. On the chair, which had previously only ever held his sweatshirt, he imagined their clothes draped or Ana drinking from a steaming hotel paper cup with her legs curled up beneath her.

There were memories in this hotel room now, where before there were none beyond quiet nights by himself. Feeling something so opposite to what he'd come to associate the room and commute with was odd.

He didn't mind it, though.

In fact, Jesse was smiling as he dropped his luggage off, not bothering to sort through the clothes yet. He merely patted his jeans to make sure he still had his wallet, deposited the key card in the same pocket, and left. He bypassed the elevator and took the stairs, an excited energy buzzing through his veins.

Jesse was meeting Ana at what he'd started to consider their spot: the bridge in the park. In cartoons and movies, the happy characters would leap and flair their feet out in a little dance before trotting forward to their destination. Jesse could see how they'd want to as he walked there. He was tempted to skip up like that, all the extra, excited energy coursing through his legs like he had restless leg syndrome.

But he continued forward with decided, focused purpose—mostly because he preferred not to look like a loon as he got closer to the bridge. He didn't want Ana to regret her decision to meet with him. And to discuss *them*.

Thinking about their last conversation on the phone sent his heart racing. Her request to talk—though the question was one he'd heard from a breakup or two back in the day—had the same hope in its tone as was echoed in his every time he spoke to her.

When something was said enough times, Jesse realized it could lose its weight. In such a short time, he'd taken for granted that soft utterance every night between them, and *I miss you* became a mere substitute for *hello* or *goodbye*. But the repetition, the expansion of her words... it made his heart throb for Ana, and he wanted nothing more than to be beside her.

And with a similar confession from him, and a promise to meet each other, there Jesse was, walking up the pathway toward their meeting place. The wind brushed through his clothing to seep beneath the fabric, but he barely felt it as his eyes tracked the people in the park. A group of kids played duck-duck-goose (or whatever the German equivalent of it was), an elderly couple moseyed toward a bench next to the river where they gingerly sat, and a group of runners stomped by him, huffing and straining at the tail end of their run.

Ana wasn't there yet.

Jesse lifted his gaze up to the clock on the other end of the bridge, a tall pole which held the foot-long clock face. He was ten minutes early, it seemed, so he rested his elbows on the railing and cast his sights on the river.

With the wind, it appeared to be running faster as it sliced its way underneath his feet, but it could've been his imagination. Water was all the same to him, but he watched it anyway, counting the fallen leaves floating on top to distract himself.

Each minute went by excruciatingly slow, especially because Jesse kept pulling his head up to watch both ends of the bridge, though he knew Ana always came in the east entrance. And with each minute that passed, he ignored the fearful thought sneaking into his brain that said Ana wasn't coming.

Jesse shook his head.

Only three minutes had gone by. He was still seven minutes early, so he took a purposeful, steady breath and relaxed his tense shoulders. His stomach felt like a witch's cauldron, bubbling and brewing some kind of nauseating combination of nerves, excitement, and aching longing. He imagined it swirling with every swallow, and Jesse hoped it wouldn't boil over.

"Hello."

Jesse's head snapped up.

There she was.

The wind flipped her hair around her face, but he could see Ana's smile from underneath the locks she brushed out of her face with a gloved hand. A moment ago, his heart seemed to beat in rhythm with the untamed water lapping against the stones below, but her mere presence had soothed and slowed its cadence back to normal.

"Ana," he said, and he reached for her. The chill of her leather glove met his hand as they knit their fingers together, which he brought to rest on the railing. His thumb absentmindedly brushed against hers. Her pinky caressed in the same way. Using her free hand to brush hair behind her ear, that braid tapping against her cheek with another gust of wind, she smiled.

There was something about her smile, the way it tugged up a little more on the right than the left when she laughed, that flexed his against his ribs, expanding his chest to accommodate the regard he had for this woman. The care.

Jesse swallowed.

The *love*.

Being without her for those weeks, he knew he was well beyond the point of no return with her. There was no pulling back on his feelings, no way he could step away from her, especially not after he'd felt her against him. Not after she'd made coffee for him in the mornings and pinched the edge of his T-shirt at night to pull him closer to whisper goodnight to him.

"You're back," she said, leaning against his arm. It was warm against his.

"So I am."

Jesse breathed normally, all the urgency from earlier drifting away with the river. The anxiety was gone; each exhale ferried away his tension as her warm vanilla scent drifted into his nose with every inhale.

Jesse imagined her leaping into his arms like some play as the crescendo of music spiked to their loving kiss. He would spin her, and she would laugh, and they'd settle right in the middle of the bridge with a searing, breathtaking kiss. But the reality was softer; more gentle.

On this blustery day, scarf bundling at her neck and cheeks red, with their sides pressed together and hands linked, it was better.

The comfort of her standing next to him after so long apart was something he wouldn't trade for the dramatic telling of his dreams.

Her head came to rest on his shoulder, and he tilted his own to rest his cheek on her hair. How did he go so long without her? Those weeks left him wanting—her laugh, her wit, and her soft caresses. It had been a long while since he was so desperate for one person's attention, and though embarrassment swelled up a time or two thinking about it, the comfort of having someone in his life he wanted to spend so much time with rendered the feeling into nothingness.

"The swans haven't left yet." Ana used her free hand to point to the trees a few feet from the river's edge. And when he squinted, he could see the tail of one poking out from the tree trunk.

"I looked it up," she continued. "They're mute swans."

That caused him to look down at her in disbelief, remembering the way one hissed at him when he walked too close. "I wouldn't call them *mute*."

"They're quieter than other kinds." Her lips were turned up. "Anyway, I found out they are only partially migratory."

He smiled at the precise pronunciation, consonants a little too harsh to be natural saying the uncommon word, but he didn't interrupt her, only listened as she explained further.

"They only leave when the lakes freeze."

Jesse turned his attention back to the swan, which had waddled unobstructed into his view to nibble underneath its wing. The white of its wings was a stark contrast to the dark tree trunks and browning leaves in the face of December's cold. It shuddered after it was done, righting its feathers to their correct places, and it took small steps to the water's edge, where it settled atop a large rock. There it stayed, gazing out over the water.

"They leave sometimes," Ana said, and her voice quieted, a ripple of sound over the trickling water beneath them. "But they come back."

His eyes were drawn to hers. The green was light in the sun, and they glittered meaning into her observation.

"They do," he agreed

"I wonder why."

There was a moment where he considered continuing their veiled conversation, perhaps saying the swan came back for another or enjoyed the bridge. In all likeliness, he would've done so before his trip. But Jesse had gone days without Ana's company, had imagined her in everything he's seen and done while he was gone, so he knew he couldn't lie.

His hand left hers to drift up her arm. He cradled her neck, while his other hand settled on her waist. In return, she clutched at the material of his jacket; it crinkled under her fingers.

Jesse caressed her cool skin with his thumb.

"Because I love you."

It was why he returned. He didn't follow the confession with a kiss, another fantasy he'd quashed in favor of reality, he simply drew her closer to his chest and watched for a reaction. She blinked as she let his words settle, then smiled so brightly it lit her whole face. Jesse couldn't help but join her.

Both of her gloved palms cupped his cheeks, and she leaned up on her tiptoes to lay a kiss on his lips. Both grinning like fools made it a juvenile motion with teeth and awkward landings, but neither of them cared.

Ana pressed her forehead to Jesse's and whispered, "I love you, too."

He kissed the tip of her nose, and she giggled, stepping back as she wrinkled it.

"I want to be with you," Jesse continued with no fear of rejection, not after her reply that hummed through his chest like she'd played a beautiful score across his ribs.

"I'd like that as well."

Again, they smiled at one another.

"Now what?" he asked.

"Now," Ana said, stepping closer to him so their chests almost touched, "I believe it is customary for a girl's date to escort her back to her apartment."

His voice lowered. "Is it also customary for him to follow her inside?"

"Certainly."

Ana kept one hand looped around his as she turned to walk, so he trailed behind her. He glanced at the river, and his smile was soft as he viewed the bank.

The swan was still there.

Chapter Twelve

The afternoon was a nice one despite the shortening days. There wasn't much wind, and the sun against Ana's black jacket warmed her skin nicely as she waited outside her apartment for Jesse. He'd insisted on picking her up for their first "official" date, as he said. While she could appreciate the traditional approach, Ana didn't care where they met so long as they could be together.

She admitted to feeling a little giddy at the thought of him taking the relationship seriously, of him wanting their date to be something special. Ana thought it was quite sweet, and she pushed down the incoming smile, so she didn't look silly grinning all by herself.

Ana wondered where they were going to go. Before dating, they'd already gone to so many different places. Would they go to the movies, the theater, or the museum? Or was she completely off base, and planned to surprise her with something new for both of them? Had he been ziplining before, or rock climbing? Those didn't sound particularly pleasant for her, especially in her white blouse, but Ana thought she'd be willing to try if he was really enthused.

After all, Ana found herself doing more than she thought she would before Jesse. She was *dating* him, for one. When she'd first met him, Ana certainly hadn't expected that outcome (looking back, she wasn't positive what it was she was thinking, outside of curiosity).

Ana was glad Jesse hadn't walked away after that first poor attempt at a date. She chuckled to herself. She could still remember the cute flush on his cheeks after he'd blurted out his invitation to dinner.

She was happy with herself, too—for saying yes to the walks and the outings. And for giving him a chance. Without her realizing, not until he'd kissed her, she'd been falling for this genuine, sincere man from day one.

A car approached, stopping in front of her, and she waved to Jesse as he got out to pay the driver. He waved back, and something light fluttered in her stomach at the clear excitement on his face.

He wasn't dressed to the nines, but Ana could tell he'd made an effort. A V-neck gray T-shirt substituted his baggier ones, and the collared, zip-up sweatshirt overtop resembled something closer to a sweater; it didn't have a hood and was a fetching maroon color.

So likely not the theater, she thought, not unless he changed later.

Jesse ducked down for a quick peck before he greeted her. "Hello."

"Hello." She returned the kiss, and she felt him smile against her lips.

When they parted, he offered his arm. "Shall we go?"

Ana hooked her arm into his and gestured forward. "Lead on."

They left the complex, and Jesse led her on a quick bus ride—only two stops—before taking meandering steps toward their destination. They passed a boutique, a soap shop, an insurance agency, and Ana furrowed her brow, wondering where he could be taking them. Then he stopped, and she blinked up at the sign.

Ana laughed.

"A coffee shop?" she asked, eyebrow raised.

His grin was a little cheeky, which made her own smile widen.

"It's where we met, after all," he said. "And I figured you wouldn't want to have a date at work."

"You are correct."

"So, what do you think?" He pointed his thumb to the door. "Ready to go in?"

"Like I said—lead on."

Like the gentleman he was, he opened the door for her, which didn't have a bell overtop like she was used to, so no eyes darted up when they entered. Only the waitress saw, and she directed them to the empty table near a bookshelf.

The chairs and tables had a garden aesthetic, metal with twining vine patterns and cushions tied by strings to the back rungs of the chairs. She noted each cushion stitched with flowers, which only added to the theme.

Jesse settled into his chair after pulling hers out, an action which made her heart hum with pleasure, and picked up their two-page menu. One page for drinks, the other for desserts and baked goods. There were teas and coffees, cookies and cakes and bagels.

"How about I order us dessert?"

Ana tilted her head. "You have something in mind, I take it?"

"I do," he said as the waitress approached. Ana ordered a tea, feeling oddly like she would be betraying dear Elaine by trying anything other than her fanciful coffee creations.

Jesse, on the other hand, got a hazelnut coffee, then pointed to the dessert on the menu for the waitress. The woman scribbled it down on her notebook and headed back to the kitchen.

"A surprise then?" Ana said.

"I think it'll be a good one."

Jesse's lips tugged up in a smirk, and Ana attempted reading what the dessert would be from his expression, but his eyes only glittered in amusement at her guesses.

She huffed. "Fine. I'll wait."

His smile only widened, but he soothed the teasing with a gentle hand hold, slipping it under Ana's palm, which rested on the table. He squeezed.

"Now it'll be my turn to think of the next date," she said, squeezing back.

"Oh, yeah? Where would you take us?"

She raised an eyebrow. "I see you don't want any surprises in return."

He chuckled. "Okay, keep your secrets."

"I can perhaps give you a hint."

"And what would that be?"

Ana's free hand came up to tug on his shirt. She thought a shopping trip for a nice, maybe navy, long-fitted shirt to replace his usual collection of hoodies would be a fun date. Of course, plucking at his hem was a terrible hint, and at his puzzled frown, she elaborated slightly. "Your sweatshirt."

"What about it?" He glanced down at the garment in question. "Well, now you have me curious."

"Only now?"

"Obviously not," he answered, lifting her hand so he could kiss her knuckles. "You captivated me the moment I saw you."

Ana giggled. "Charmer."

They released hands as the waitress came over with their drinks, placing them down with a friendly smile before she turned back to the front counter to grab a green serving platter. Ana moved her tea back to give the woman room.

The plate clicked down in front of her, and something soft and gentle nestled into her chest at the sight. Small round cookies with red jam in the middle crowded the dish.

She smiled. "The cookies I gave you."

"And the coffee you made me," he added, snatching a cookie for himself, but he waited until she grabbed one too before eating it. They were small enough that she could pop the whole dessert in her mouth like Jesse had, but she bit into half, savoring it. A couple crumbs landed on the table, and Jesse plucked up another cookie, his coffee in the other hand.

The whole affair was a simple one—going for coffee and cookies—but sitting there together felt like so much more. Because they were *together*. They weren't pretending or denying; they were conscious of what their confession meant.

It was nice, she thought, being in a committed relationship with him. The second half of her cookie went into her mouth, and the almond of the dough as well as the raspberry of the jam dissolved in a pleasant bundle of sugar. It was so sweet of him to remember. Ana didn't imagine many others would've. She didn't imagine *she* would've. But that was Jesse—sincere, considerate, and a bit of a romantic as she'd come to discover.

Most of all, though, whether he was taking her on dates or merely talking with her on a bench, he made her happy.

A sip of her tea hid her smile, but Jesse caught it anyway.

"Having fun?"

She reached over to again grab his hand on the table; she noted with amusement there were a couple crumbs clinging to his fingers.

"Very much."

He grinned. "Good."

Not that she honestly anticipated it happening, but with every shift in their relationship, there was a moment or two of weary anticipation that their easy camaraderie would spoil, but just like the first time they ventured out after the physical change in their partnership, not even an official dating title could dampen the enthusiasm of their conversation.

Their words sprinkled the air like glitter, and even the silence settled into something beautiful. Without her notice, her tea was gone when she went to take a sip; Jesse's second coffee held only a sip or two more, and their dessert was just a scattering of crumbs. Their bill sat upside down on the end of the table, which Ana furrowed a puzzled brow at. She didn't remember the waitress dropping it off.

Jesse grabbed the check before she could, and she pursed her lips.

Noticing the expression, he chuckled. "You can get it next time. Besides, this is reminding me of all the coffees I bought so I could see you more."

"Oh, is that why you always stop by the café? Elaine will be so disappointed." She leaned forward over the table and kissed him. "But I would say you were reimbursed quite nicely for your troubles."

"I wholeheartedly agree."

Ana went to take another sip of her tea, but it was still empty. She frowned, placing it back down in disappointed, which she covered by grabbing her coat from the back of the chair.

"I can make you some tea," he said.

Her eyes drifted up as Jesse jiggled her empty cup in his hand.

"I hope not with the hotel-provided packets."

Jesse laughed and stood to grab her coat from her hands, helping her into it. She obviously didn't need the assistance, but the gesture was sweet, and it made her smile.

"I rather hoped I could make it for you at your place."

"Very smooth."

Jesse merely winked in response as he put on his own jacket, and they left for one more stop, picking up dinner from a pizza place before hopping into a taxi to take them back to her apartment. She handed Jesse the pizza, while she opened doors for them. Once inside, he plopped the box on the counter and grabbed plates. Ana stopped to watch him, marveling at the domesticity. He knew where her plates were and was comfortable enough in her apartment that he didn't hesitate to set the table for them.

She wasn't upset by that either; they weren't going too fast for her tastes, and she didn't think he was making himself at home. No, in fact, it felt very natural, like their relationship could only go in one direction, and this was where they currently were with Jesse bundling up two cloth napkins from her drawer to set next to her cream-colored plates.

As Ana put her coat away, she noted Jesse had hung his own in her closet. The gray complemented her black pea coat, and Ana took a moment to admire them hung next to each other. As a flighty whim, she hooked the hollow arms around one another so they touched. Laughing to herself, she closed the door and settled next to Jesse at the table.

"Dessert before dinner?" she asked, snatching a slice of pizza from the box.

"Eh," he said, shrugging. "Food is food."

"My mother would be appalled."

He let out an inquisitive hum, mouth full.

"She had a very strict timetable when it came to meals. We had dinner at the same time every day when I was growing up, and I couldn't have dessert until at least thirty minutes later."

"Definitely not like my house. It was a bit of a free-for-all. If we had dinner planned, great, if not, we made sandwiches or something."

"Was that what…what you and Linda did for the girls?"

His next bite hovered near his mouth after her words, then he set his pizza down on his plate. For a moment—only a moment—her nerves escaped through her fingers, and she tapped them on the table…but there was nothing to be concerned with. Not really. It wasn't the first time she had mentioned his late wife, and she made a point to do so when it was relevant. Ana didn't want someone so significant in his life to be a taboo subject.

An old boyfriend of hers would get angry if she talked about some of her old friends, and conversations became increasingly more delicate and rickety, like traversing an old, rope bridge. With each word, she only prayed the rope wouldn't fray beneath her feet.

Until, finally, it did.

Ana never wanted Jesse to feel the same.

His voice was gentle, as were his eyes, and he locked onto hers with gratitude, which made Ana's nerves flutter away into nothing.

"Nah," he answered, "but it was a family affair. Everyone chipped in where they could. Probably because those girls were a right menace when they were hungry, so all hands on deck meant food earlier."

"Sounds very warm."

He seemed to consider that a moment, then smiled. "You know, I think warm is a good way to describe it."

Between them, her apartment felt warm, too, accentuated by the golden glow of her lamps. Ana basked in all of it. There was such an even continuity to the feeling that she thought nothing could disturb it, not even when they drifted from the kitchen to her bedroom. If anything, their actions only added to the illuminating certainty that everything was right, and she couldn't help but smile into Jesse's bare chest. His finger fed through her hair, and she sighed in contentment.

***

Ana woke the next morning to the smell of coffee and wrinkled sheets beside her. After a cat-like stretch, she shuffled into some clothes and padded out to the kitchen. Jesse was pouring coffee into his mug, and the image settled a satisfied hum through her veins as she reached from behind to wrap her arms around his torso just as he finished.

With one hand, he grasped her forearm and squeezed. From the light bubbling noise, she assumed Jesse was sipping his coffee—as evidenced from his usual sigh at the first taste.

"I have an idea," she said into his back. "What do you think about staying here for the weekend?"

"I like that idea a lot." From the lightness in his voice, she could tell he was smiling.

"Good, because now that you're back, I'd rather not let you go." To illustrate, she tightened her arms around him playfully.

It wasn't really a novel plan, Jesse staying the weekend. It wasn't the first he had stayed before he had left America, but this would be the first since he returned, and there was a selfish desire in her to claim his time for her own after having been denied it for weeks.

He happily complied, only leaving after breakfast to grab some clothes from his hotel; and, as Ana noted with a quick sniff, Jesse apparently decided to take a shower while he was there.

His hair wasn't wet anymore—with how short it was, she assumed it dried quickly—but she ran a hand through it anyway, asking, "Didn't want my volumizing shampoo?"

Jesse chuckled. "I can't say it would benefit my hair much."

"It could. You could have flowing locks if you grew it out."

"Doubtful."

Just like the previous night, Jesse confidently navigated her apartment, placing his duffel on the chest in her room beside rarely used puzzles. Ana could almost feel the glow on her skin again, and she stepped forward to bring his head down to hers. His lips tasted like coffee; he must have gotten more at the hotel, but Ana's train of thought quickly left her as he pushed her against the wall.

The pressure from his body was tantalizing, and she hooked a leg around his hip. When they needed to part for air, she grinned at the flush on his face, but it went beyond her sight when she closed her eyes to his next kiss.

Ana didn't realize how much she missed the physical side of their relationship, more concerned about the loss of companionship until Jesse was back. She selfishly wanted to take her fill now that she had him, which she fully intended to do.

Her back hit the bed, and the rest of the weekend consisted of various repeats of that thrilling action—sometimes not as quickly as she wanted it to, but she was patient—and Jesse had multiple ways to interact.

The weekend wardrobe for both of them was of comfort and ease. Jesse had his sweatpants and T-shirts while Ana puttered around the apartment in the baggy cotton dress she reserved for staying at home. The apartment became a blessed haven, where they could shut out the rest of the world; they didn't even need to order food and disturb their peace with errant knocking because Ana had thought ahead and bought supplies to cook.

During one such meal, Ana strapped on her lemon-patterned apron, got out the ingredients for bread and a roll recipe from her great-grandmother, and directed Jesse on the steps he was helping her with. It seemed only fitting to make when her father had given her some of his soup to take home, which she and Jesse planned to share that night.

As Ana looked at Jesse's clothes, she wondered if it would've been better for him to wear the apron. Little puffs of flour clung to his elbow, chest, and wrists, but she found it commendable he decided to help at all — though, she was using a bread machine, so the process was much easier than hand-kneading it.

It was her mother's old machine, but it still worked, and she planned to keep it for as long as she could. A simple machine, Ana only had to explain to Jesse how to add yeast to the mixture, tunneling a hole for it in the middle. He figured out the buttons fine on his own, so she hoisted herself up on the counter and watched him finish.

It was endearing, the way he double-checked every measurement and completed each task with military precision.

"This is your family recipe," he said. "I don't want to mess it up!"

It was just like the coffee mug. He was so considerate of everything she consisted of: her job, her family, her friends, even her taste in cookies. Ana couldn't help but smile as he clicked the last button on the bread cycle with a decisive beep.

Turning around to her, Jesse grinned, and she waved him over so she could brush the smears of flour off of his clothing. He settled between Ana's legs and leaned one arm on the counter.

"How does it feel to be a baker?" she asked. "I'll have to show you how to knead it by hand next time."

Jesse shrugged. "Sure. Maybe a long weekend when we have more time."

That startled a laugh out of Ana. "More time? What else do we have planned that's so time consuming?"

He wiggled his eyebrows in a corny fashion that made her laugh even more, and a calm warmth settled over her. Ana was reminded of a cartoon she watched as a child, where the background would shift to golden bubbles, almost like a dull lens flare, when the characters would have a heartwarming moment. The music would sing a sweet tune, the characters would smile softly, and the background swelled with an incandescent glow.

Ana was so confident those animated orbs would appear in her periphery that she was half-waiting for the music to kick in. She could do nothing but lift her lips as she straightened Jesse's sweatshirt string, ignoring his remark about the task being a losing battle. For the tenth or twentieth time since Jesse had come back, there was a certainty to how he belonged there with her, and she accepted it wholeheartedly.

"I don't think I said…"

He lifted a questioning brow.

Ana cupped his face in her hands.

"Welcome back."

The soft look in his eyes made her chest expand to overwhelm her with love, and she was glad it was his turn to say something instead of her.

Jesse pressed his forehead to hers, and his voice rumbled down her skin.

"Glad to be back."

Chapter Thirteen

The cool river splashed against the side of the boat, and the mist it spritzed onto Jesse's skin made him shiver. The temperature inside the boat had been a little hot for his taste, so he'd stepped outside for the moment. His reddened cheeks were already cooling, and he didn't imagine he'd stay on deck for very long; their tour boat, which ferried passengers to the city of Heidelberg, wasn't quite hot enough to make him prefer the freezing outdoors.

Ana, during another one of their days together, had turned to him in bed, pushed herself up to her elbow, and declared she wanted to go on a trip.

"We've gone to so many theaters and galleries when we weren't dating, so I want our next date to be special. Something we wouldn't have done before."

He didn't need much convincing, and they eventually decided on Heidelberg, the "City of Love," as many in Germany called it. *An appropriate destination*, he thought, a little giddy.

Because of the approaching holiday, there were a couple of boat rides on the Rhine River left before it closed for the winter. Jesse imagined Heidelberg would have lights and Christmas decorations galore, but he was excited to see the castle, which was perched on the hill overlooking the town.

The sun spattering through the mist rising from the river gave the area a mystical, glittering effect, and Jesse wondered if he'd be able to see it from the bluff where the castle rested. What would it look like as the sun set as the lights turned on? He'd heard it was beautiful, and he was looking forward to it—as was Ana.

Inside the boat, she was poring over brochures and a booklet she'd plucked from their luggage. She had an itinerary planned that would begin as soon as they checked into the hotel. At the very least, she had a selection of activities she wanted to check off, including the world's largest wine barrel.

"I know I don't drink," Ana had said, pointing to the listing in the brochure, "but how fascinating! I wonder if there's any branding on it, or if it's a different structure."

Though he'd never been interested in wine barrels, Jesse could certainly find some interest in old wine, so that was something else he was eager to see.

Regardless of what they explored, Jesse was just happy to be there with Ana. Not including travel for work, he hadn't gone on a vacation since the girls were still in grade school. To visit an area not because he was there for work, but because he *wanted* to was a novel experience; one he planned to enjoy thoroughly.

A gust of wind shuffled his coat around; he quickly fastened a button on his jacket, so he didn't accidentally whip a passerby with fabric. More mist prickled over his skin, and he wiped it with an equally wet hand. They were approaching the Neckar River, a branch from the Rhine which slithered along against the banks Heidelberg. Jesse wasn't particularly fond of water, or water-related activities, so the sooner they left the boat, the better.

A hand on his lower back turned his attention to his newfound company, and he smiled.

Ana slid next to him, and Jesse moved his arm around her shoulders so she could huddle for warmth.

"I thought you'd be cold by now," she said.

"Not yet." Jesse rubbed his hand down her arm. "But now I won't be."

"Though I will," she said, shivering.

"That's because you came out without your jacket."

"I wanted to see the view from out here. Besides, I figured you'd keep me warm."

He nuzzled the top of her head at her words—from her, a statement of fact instead of some sweet nothing. In fact, Ana didn't even look at him when she said it, merely settling against him to gaze out at the river. The boat chugged along smoothly, and outside of the few stray breezes, the air was still.

Jesse could certainly enjoy the water if he had Ana against his side, warming his heart and the fabric of his clothes. They stayed like that, enjoying one another's company, all the way until they were urged by the captain to retrieve their belongings.

Docking was quick process with each crewmember efficiently securing the boat before laying the plank to allow guests to disembark. Within a few minutes, Jesse and Ana were shuffling off to their lodgings, which was a five-minute walk from their landing point.

The hotel was quaint; it was only four floors, and their room was cozier than a typical hotel with a few knick-knacks and coordinating pictures to match their fluffy bedding. The wooden floors were covered by a dark, patterned rug, something he imagined was easy to clean and hid any stray coffee spills from clumsy guests.

He waited for Ana to hang her blouses in the closet, then they were off. Though their hotel wasn't the more luxurious and popular option of the historical *Hotel zum Ritter*, one of the few Renaissance buildings left alone by the French in the 1600s, theirs was still in Old Town, so they weren't far from many of the attractions of the city.

And there are certainly plenty, Jesse thought, taking in the many Christmas decorations. Heidelberg celebrated the season with an outdoor market, and he could smell and hear it in the air. Bells chimed various carols through the streets, and cinnamon wafted to his nose on the breeze from every direction.

After her foray onto the deck without a coat, Ana's first order of business was to get a warm drink, and they grabbed *kinderpunsch,* a Christmas drink with hibiscus tea, cider, orange juice, and star anise. They enjoyed the drink next to two flute players who piped out a handful of Christmas numbers.

Ana hunched over the tea as if she could hold in the warmth with her shoulders. Jesse settled an arm around her shoulders, and she sent him a grateful look even as she shivered again. With both of them huddled together with their drinks, it didn't take long for Ana to warm up; it was only a few minutes before they ducked into an eccentric-looking shop with baubles and art he couldn't place, though he imagined most of it was pop-culture related. From what he'd seen Elaine wear, he wasn't surprised when Ana found a small souvenir for her there.

Jesse kept an eye out for anything for the kids and grandkid, but he hadn't found anything. Besides, he didn't know if they would care which area in Germany a present came from, just that it was from Germany. He still browsed, of course, but he wasn't straining to search for anything, merely tagging along behind Ana through both the indoor stores and outside stalls.

There were a few different Christmas markets—one in each of the squares—so they wandered down

Haupstrasse, which was the street that connected the markets to the next square. They came upon Christmas music being played through a speaker rather than live performers, and the main entertainment was a merry-go-round with two rows of horses. Already, there were scores of children giggling atop their saddles.

"Where to next?" Ana asked, which turned Jesse's attention back to her. "We could..." Ana trailed off, peering around Jesse's shoulder with wide eyes.

"John?" she said, and Jesse turned around to see a man—blond, around thirty, and admittedly handsome—stop in place. Once the blond saw who it was, his puzzled expression quickly transformed to one of joy, and his white teeth seemed to sparkle like the fake snowflakes around them. Something about it made Jesse shift uncomfortably on his feet.

"Ana?" The man grinned further when she nodded. "How amazing! It's so good to see you!"

"John!" she repeated, walking forward to embrace him. "I can't believe it!"

And the moment her arms went around John's shoulders, Jesse's throat seemed to tighten; though the hug lasted all of a couple of seconds, it freeze-framed in Jesse's mind, etching the image onto his eyes.

He blinked it away.

Ana's smile was wide when she pulled apart from John.

Jesse blinked again.

"How long has it been?" John asked.

"Years! I can't believe you're here!"

Jesse stood to the side. He didn't know whether he should introduce himself or not. Their chatter of where they lived and what they did now was in rapid-fire German, but even if it was as slow as an English toddler's cartoon, Jesse wasn't sure if he'd be able to focus anyway. At least—not on anything outside of the way Ana's long scarf was brushing against the guy's leg when the wind blew. Did they have to stand that close?

Jesse shook his head. There was no need to be rude, he thought. Stepping forward, he stood next to Ana.

His movement brought Ana's attention to him, and the way her lips tugged up eased the niggling feeling in his brain.

"Oh, yes," Ana said. "This is Jesse. And Jesse, this is John, a childhood friend."

He hoped his mouth didn't look as strained as it felt when he stuck out his hand to shake. He and John exchanged pleasantries, then Ana spoke again.

"We're spending the weekend together. We thought it would be nice to have a little vacation before work."

If Jesse wasn't watching him, he may have missed the way John's eyes widened slightly as he darted them between Ana and Jesse. It made that niggling in the back of his mind spread.

"O-Oh," John said then cleared his throat. "Well, sounds like a good time! I hope you're having fun. You're always working hard, Ana, so you deserve a break."

Her voice was soft as she said, "Thank you, John."

Though Jesse was dimly aware of joining for a sentence or two, the rest of the conversation, hummed the way the distant marketplace from the hotel window, leaving him standing aside from it, unsure of where the sound was coming from.

Jesse only came fully back to the conversation as John was saying his goodbye, and hugged Ana once more. Jesse could've sworn the second one lasted longer than the first. His handshake felt stiff, but Jesse blamed it on the cold and smiled to the man.

Then he left, and Jesse stood dumbly next to Ana who still had a bright smile on her face.

"Oh, it was so lovely to see him! I'm glad we ran into him!" She turned her grin to Jesse, but it felt odd to see such a glowing smile on her face that he hadn't caused.

"R-Right."

"Come on!" she said, grabbing his hand. "Let's go to that stall!"

Without a word about what just happened, Jesse was dragged to a stand selling hand-crafted nutcrackers. He glanced at Ana, who had snatched up one of the crimson-and gold-painted soldiers up to get a closer look. She didn't turn to him. He wanted her to, but she didn't.

Jesse shoved his now-free hands into his pockets.

Ana didn't say anything about John at the next stall, either, or the one after that, and the longer they went on without a word, the more Jesse started to feel like he shouldn't be concerned.

But he *was*.

And that thought lingered with them at the next market, too. In fact, it tumbled about his thoughts so loudly, he barely remembered buying them dinner and sitting to eat next to a heat lamp outside. When Jesse came back to himself, all that was left were their French fries—his regular and hers sweet potato. Pride flared in him as he watched her munch on them. Jesse knew to order those for her because they were her favorite, and a small thought, just the size of a mosquito, buzzed to the forefront of his mind: Would *John* know to order Ana sweet potato fries?

Probably, his mind provided too quickly for him to ignore it. They were childhood friends, knew each other for years. He probably knew a lot about Ana.

Jesse swallowed and gave his head a rattle. He and Ana were soon tossing the remnants of their meal away, then continued their way through the fair.

Despite the many distractions, Jesse couldn't seem shake off how incredibly insecure Ana's interaction with John had made him feel. The though seemed to dim and strengthen depending on the second. It was frustrating. Maddening. Jesse didn't want to be bogged down by the image of what Ana and John looked like together as they hugged. He also didn't want to linger on what *Jesse* and Ana looked like to strangers. He especially didn't want the ugly feeling of wishing John had never been in Heidelberg in the first place.

He needed to sort his head and was desperate to swat away anything negative—and he was successful, for a time.

Jesse managed to shake it off for most of their day, and he enjoyed Ana's absolute awe at the sprawling grounds of the Heidelberg University campus. Plaques and dedications dotted the property, and Ana practically skipped to each one, taking time to appreciate the architecture of the buildings.

When that was finished, they headed back to Old Town, intent on going to one more place the evening crawled in.

Their hotel told them *Alte Brüke*, Old Bridge, led to their next destination, a trail on the north side of the bridge called *Philosophenweg*, the "Philosopher's Walk." It was named for the scholars of old who took these contemplative paths, and reinforced by the many poets, artists, and composers who lauded Heidelberg for its beauty.

As they traversed the path at sunset with all the glittering lights from the town below twinkling like stars. The path took them up, up around the other side of the river. From there, they could overlook the town from above and were close to being an even height with Heidelberg Castle in the distance.

Mark Twain, apparently, called the lights of Old Town "a fallen galaxy." He couldn't see it, but he imagined the hoary river mist clinging to the cobblestone streets and the dim opacity against the lights really would make it look like a fallen galaxy, especially with all those colorful Christmas strands.

As the sun drifted behind the skyline, their shadows stretched over the path to join their brethren down below. Or, at least, Jesse's was. Ana's shadow touched his boots as they climbed, and he felt more like he was chasing it rather than watching it ascend with his together. His hand drifted up, and he traced her shadow's shoulder.

He blinked in surprise when she reached her hand back to grasp his. Over her shoulder, with a teasing glint to her eye, she asked, "Tired?"

"No, not yet."

"Good." She pulled his arm, so he took a larger step to stand next to her. "We're almost to the viewing platform."

And they were. Only three more minutes of walking, and they arrived at a circular, flat area with a couple of plaques and benches. Up by the railing, they could gaze down onto Old Town and see the lit-up castle. If the town was the stars, the castle would be the sun, everything and everyone converging around it.

The warmth of it seemed so far away, like there was more than just a river's distance between them.

"Beautiful," Ana breathed, and she removed her hat so she could brush errant hairs out of her face.

Standing back from her, Jesse could imagine her as a painting. The colors could even be a dim Christmas presentation; the trees not yet dead, but a deep green next to the faded, red-bricked homes below, straining to be seen against the fiery glow of the sky. It could be a sepia-toned picture, too, with Ana's silhouette a form of beauty comparable to the scenery.

Jesse wondered what he would look like next to her—another silhouette—but the figure he imagined appeared more blond than Jesse's encroaching gray.

Shaking his head, he dispersed the phantom clinging to the image and strode through it to stand next to her.

"It's gorgeous," he agreed.

Ana leaned against him, and his arm drifted around her shoulders.

"I'm glad we came here," she mumbled into his coat.

Ana's smile when she pulled back from John zapped into Jesse's mind, and he clenched his jaw in an attempt to banish it.

"Me, too." He held her tighter, fully wrapping her in his arms.

"Oh, are you cold?"

Jesse pressed his face into her hair, smelling her shampoo mixed with the rich, wooded air. "Yeah. Cold."

Ana's arms around him did nothing to abate the chill.

If he could have held her any tighter, he would have.

But he couldn't.

Chapter Fourteen

Something was wrong with Jesse.

Ana couldn't pinpoint precisely what, or even when he started acting strangely, but he was, and she didn't know what to do.

She first noticed it last evening, before their walk on *Philosophenweg,* but she'd assumed his distant attitude was due to fatigue or disinterest. When they were shopping, he was quiet, and she noticed he hadn't bought anything other than food, so she assumed he must have been a little bored. Ana had tried to engage him a number of times while they were out, and in the moment, it seemed to work, but as soon as Jesse was left inside his head, Ana could tell he was thinking deeply about something.

Then, about an hour before the market closed on their way back from the trail, they ran into John once more. The carousel spun happily in the middle of the cobblestone square, but there were less children than earlier—less people, in general, than earlier. Only about a third of the carousel was occupied, but there was John on a white horse next to a young girl who couldn't' have been older than six.

Ana had stopped to wave, and after the third cycle around, John finally noticed her and waved back just as enthusiastically. Once the ride slowed and passengers hopped off, Ana approached John—as well as the dark-skinned woman and two kids who crowded around him.

"I can't believe I didn't ask who you were with," Ana said in greeting, and John laughed, putting one arm around his wife while using the other to keep the youngest from toddling away.

"Eh, we had a bunch of other stuff to catch up on."

Introductions came next, and Ana found she quite liked John's wife, who she could already tell already was quick-witted and kind. She seemed like a good match for her friend, and their children were precious. Ana's heart almost melted when she saw Ben, the youngest, yawn and rub his eye with his little fist, accidentally knocking his earmuffs crooked. John easily righted them before hoisting his son into his arms, and the boy very quickly snuggled against his chest, disturbing the earmuffs again, which made John roll his eyes with affection.

"Guess we should head back," he said, and they all waved to each other.

It wasn't until she and Jesse had gotten back to their hotel that Ana realized he had barely spoken.

Today, Ana's plan was to cheer him up—distract him from what plagued him—and what better way to do so than the main attraction of the city? They didn't have enough time to take an indoor tour of the castle, but they could explore the grounds and the giant wine barrel.

She was pleased to see he was already excited, and for most of their journey to the old castle, Ana almost thought she had been imagining his change in attitude. But—she noted it cropped up a few more times. At one point, they suddenly stopped holding hands, Jesse abruptly releasing his grip and shoving it into his pocket. At the time, Ana thought it was because they were going through a crowded area, so being linked was a tad awkward.

The other instance was when Jesse pulled her to stand opposite him, away from a particularly tenacious salesperson, which she found odd. The man, probably a couple years older than her, didn't seem to be rude or annoying.

Ana shook her head and vowed to make the day enjoyable, odd behavior notwithstanding.

The first stop was the wine barrel held in a separate building from the castle. When Ana entered, she was tempted to open her mouth like a gaping fish. The barrel was roughly five times the height of her, a hulking figure of dark wood. When she'd heard it was one of, if not the, biggest wine barrel in the world, she expected it to be large, but not nearly as gargantuan as what was in front of her. Furthermore, she certainly didn't expect to see stairs that led to a wooden platform, similar to a deck, which one could use to stand atop the barrel.

Back home, Ana knew a woman who had been here many times, and she felt compelled to repeat the woman's saying: "It's a dance floor."

"Really?" Jesse squinted his eyes up at it. "Huh. Guess the castle-goers knew how to party."

She laughed. "Evidently so. I've never been much of a dancer myself."

"Me either. Boots don't allow much grace." He gestured to said boots. "I didn't know how much walking we'd do, and these are pretty comfortable."

"I find your practicality very endearing."

"I can't say I've ever gotten that compliment before."

His smile was playful; though she wanted to flush from his teasing, Ana ignored the minimal embarrassment in favor of enjoying the normality of the moment. It reminded her of all the times he'd correct her turn of phrases, that glint of humor in his eyes, and she sighed in relief.

With nothing in the moment to worry about, Ana was free to study the crest poking outward from the top-middle of the barrel. The sign was probably as tall as she was, but because it was so high up, Ana had to crane her neck to see the thick golden threads carved to nestle the unclear sign. A red crown perched on top, and she wondered if it was the actual size of the crown.

Ana assumed most people were interested in the fact that it was a monstrously large supply of alcohol, but that was of less intriguing to her. She didn't drink. She'd tried some when she was young, of course, but she never solidified a taste or appreciation for the flavor, only regretted the headache that came from too much—or in wine's case, very little.

Jesse was one of the few people who never pressured her to get anything at restaurants or get-togethers. She had told him she didn't drink, and he merely said, "Okay." And that was the end of the conversation. Jesse would occasionally order something for himself, but it wasn't often, and even if it was, Ana knew he didn't care about drinking alone.

It was nice, she thought.

Jesse pointed to the dance-floor balcony, then gestured with his head to the stairs on the right, which curved around to the higher platform. "Think you'll have better luck seeing up there?"

"Probably," she said, then followed a couple heading up as well, but when she didn't hear footsteps behind her, she paused, frowning.

"You're not coming?"

"Nah." Jesse waved his hand. "It's a bit crowded up there, so I'll just wait."

She hesitated. "If you're sure..."

Instead of a verbal response, he gave a thumbs up. She waited a few seconds more to see if he might change his mind. *Another oddity*, she thought, then shook her head. Jesse was already turned away, gazing at the face of the barrel and not looking at Ana, so she took the steps two at a time to make it up. The stairway curved and wasn't steep like many old staircases were, so the climb wasn't very strenuous, but Ana did have to wait in line before it was her turn to enjoy the landing.

When they'd first arrived, she'd marveled at the high ceilings necessary to shelter the landmark. But now, from where she stood, the stone ceiling was a mere hat's throw away from the top of her head. Then she looked down, and the floor seemed so far away, like she was peering down from the top of a Ferris wheel.

Jesse stood to the side with his hands in his pockets. Ana bit her lip. What was upsetting him?

Two more tourists ascended the stairs behind her, so she was quick to glance down at the crown, which did, indeed, appear to be lifelike in size. Instinctively, Ana turned to her left to talk about it, but only a stranger stood there, and she sighed. She'd seen enough.

When Jesse greeted her with an enthusiastic smile. Ana transferred her observations from the top floor to the bottom, and they traveled to another building, which held a kind of pharmaceutical museum. They didn't stay long as the building a bit too crowded—and besides, they were keener to explore the grounds and see the castle.

The castle wasn't just one material, or one degree of decay—it was starting to fall apart. As old as it was, there were various denizens who built or rebuilt or saved portions, so it was a fun architectural hodgepodge.

Actually, it was quite somber to behold how some towers or walls were no more than piles of stone in unrecognizable lumps. That was one reason Ana loved museums so much; they were the preservation of people's work from long ago. Ana wondered what the builders of the castle would think seeing some parts in decay but an equally great many areas still intact. Were their ghosts circling what remained?

The chilly December wind seeping into her jacket made her think they were here, pushing her to and from their hard work. The whistling breeze through the rocks and trees only accentuated Jesse's silence, casting a foreboding anxiety to him.

He was gazing up toward a window opening, and Ana saw his eyebrows lift like he noticed something...but instead of sharing, his attention drifted to the next area.

"You've been quiet today." Ana turned her head just enough to see him cast his sight down.

"Have I?"

"You were quiet yesterday, too."

Her observation seemed to surprise him.

"O-Oh." He cleared his throat. "Right."

Ana waited, but nothing more came from him.

"Is that all?"

He looked over, and there was something hooded about his eyes, but he attempted a nonchalant shrug to cover it.

"I'm just a little tired."

Ana narrowed her eyes, waiting once more for further explanation—but again, silence. She sighed. "Alright." She tugged his hand so they could get a closer look at the clock tower with a lookout's nest poking out from the top. She would love to go in there, but remembering how high the barrel seemed, she imagined she would be clinging to the railing if she actually managed to make it up there.

Ana pointed up to the one-man lookout with its indigo-colored roof and railings—admittedly hard to see against the overcast clouds and browning trees—but she thought it looked a little like a small gazebo, scrunched to fit just one person.

"I think you would've made a good gazer." Ana had chosen the malapropism on purpose.

At the wording, Jesse furrowed his brow at before he pulled his head up, then his smile was small as he said, "Yeah, maybe."

His attention left shortly after, without any mention of her phrasing, and Ana's ire started to rise.

"This way," she said, directing him with sure steps toward a secluded bench. She perched herself on the edge and patted the space next to her, but he didn't sit.

"You don't seem to be having much fun," she said finally.

Something unhappy twisted his mouth, and her confusion grew.

"I am having fun, Ana."

"Then why have you been so—so silent?" She frowned. "Would you like to leave?"

"What? No!" The answer was quick, so relief came to Ana fast as well.

"Then what?"

Jesse shook his head. "It's just—I've had some things on my mind."

"Clearly."

He pursed his lips at that. "Yeah, I'm sure you'd rather have someone else accompany you around the castle."

She sent him a small smile to indicate that wasn't true. She only wanted to know what was wrong. "Well, this is not quite what I had planned for our date today."

"Well, maybe you can take someone *young* and *blond* next time, if I'm that bad of a date."

Ana startled a little at the harsh tone but tried to keep the conversation going, unsure of its meaning. "Is that another American movie reference? You put a lot of emphasis on young and blond, so I assume so." She paused. "Are you trying to get me to watch that Harrison Ford movie again? Because, *surprisingly*, I have yet to see it since last weekend."

When he didn't respond with a laugh or quip, she turned to him to see his clenched jaw and narrowed eyes.

"You're serious," Ana said, unbelieving. *Young* and *blond*, he'd said. Young and blond the day after she'd run into *John*, the moment he started acting strange. That was when the anger billowed, surging up like someone had thrown pine needles into a fire. "I cannot believe you would think such a thing! And about John and I, no less!"

As her voice rose, his expression seemed remorseful—just the smallest bit—but that hardly mattered to her now. He accused her of trading him out for the newest, prettiest model, like she was a bored, rich housewife hoping to spruce up her kitchen with a nice dishwasher. And he accused her of doing so with her childhood friend who was *married*, not to mention the fact that he thought so low of her to assume she'd be so vain in the first place.

"Well, you were awfully friendly." He crossed his arms like *she* was the one who was being unreasonable.

"That is because he is an old friend! *Friend!*" Ana copied and crossed her arms as well, frowning at him. "I cannot believe a single hug has caused you to act so childishly."

He sputtered. "*Childish?*"

"Yes!"

"It's not childish to see what everybody else sees!"

"And what does *that* mean?"

"Exactly what I said! I mean, did you *see* him?" He waved his hand to the side as if John was standing there.

"See...?" Ana let out a noise of frustration. "Yes, he's handsome and blond. You've lingered on that *plenty*."

Jesse shook his head. "No, did you see his *reaction*?"

"What?"

Here, Jesse paused, face partially turned downward and away as he said his next words without looking at her.

"His reaction," he said. "When you told him we were there together. Did you *see* it?"

"I—" Ana closed her mouth. She *did* see it.

She pretended she hadn't.

When John's eyes widened and his lips parted in surprise, she ignored it. She set it aside in favor of how John and Jesse's hands shook in greeting. With that gesture, she was officially bringing Jesse into her world. Going out on actual dates and on vacation, leaving the confines of their walks, it made Ana realize how secluded their relationship felt before that, how separate it had been. Yes, they had gone to theaters and galleries, but there wasn't a complete merging of lives yet, not until people drifted closer.

That was what she concentrated on. Not the disbelief.

Ana let out a breath and stepped closer to him, though her eyes were still narrowed. "Jesse, that does not *matter*."

His expression contorted into one of disbelief, and he scoffed. "Of *course*, it does."

"No, it doesn't. Why should it?"

"Why...?" Jesse stared at her, then ran a hand down his weary face. The sun through the gaps in the stones cast angled silhouettes over the grass, and the glow dripped over his face in a contrast of light and shadow. "Well, I'm not exactly..."

"Young and blond?" she finished for him. Each word slowly lowered the volume, until it became just a little easier to relax her shoulders and crook up the corner of her lip. This seemed to be the case for Jesse; he huffed out a small laugh. It certainly sounded hollower than usual, but it was better than their yelling before.

"Yeah," he muttered, taking a step to the side so he could pretend to look for wandering tourists, but Ana didn't let him drift away from the conversation. She stood from the bench and stepped directly in front of him.

"I didn't know you felt that way."

"I didn't either," he whispered. "But then..."

"John."

Ana didn't need a verbal confirmation. The shame in his eyes was enough of an answer for her.

"Silly man," she said, then brought her hand to his face. She traced her forefinger along the creases on his forehead before moving to his crow's feet, then drifted down to touch the laugh lines around his mouth. She cupped his cheek.

"It doesn't matter. Because I love you."

His breath shuddered. Ana leaned in to caress his lips with a kiss. It was sweet and soft—sincere in her devotion—and she heard Jesse sigh happily when they released.

"I love you, too," he whispered, and from the heat of his breath, Ana felt as though the words were misted onto her cheek like a foggy window, drawn in his handwriting with a solid press of a finger.

His arms wound around her back, and he held Ana tightly to his chest, her own arms hooking around his body. She added to the comforting, weighty pressure with open palms against him for extra support.

"I'm sorry," he said into her ear, which traveled down her spine, so she felt his apology completely. "I was being..." Jesse seemed to consider a moment, then his laugh brushed a strand of hair away from her face. "Childish. I was childish and...jealous. I'm sorry."

Ana didn't think she could tighten her grip further without it being uncomfortable for either one of them, so she elected to lean away from the hold completely.

Besides, she wanted to look him in the eyes when she spoke.

"I forgive you."

The way he cupped her face was probably the softest she'd ever experienced, and the hold was reverent. "You're too good to me."

"I already said I forgave you," she teased.

"Maybe I'm collecting a few extras in case I need them."

"If only that worked, my dear."

A quick peck touched her lips. "Worth a shot."

"I suppose." She smiled. "I'm glad this is over. I thought you were turning into a Max."

A deep chuckle escaped him, bursting out like a popped bubble.

"Yes, yes," he said, "don't be a Max."

When he was in America, they had read a book together, a story appropriately about romance and longing. But there was a character who became easily jealous, and they joked how they promised to never be like him, especially after her past relationship. Thus: "Don't be a Max."

An audible noise of relief came from Jesse, who stepped back to plop down on the bench.

"Well, now that we're alright, what were you saying about being a spotter?"

His grin was a crooked thing, and she rolled her eyes, already reaching to grab his hand to pull him up.

"Oh, come on," she said. Ana didn't release his hand; in fact, Jesse swung it between them as they continued their exploration.

It felt nice.

Chapter Fifteen

Ana tutted, swiping Jesse's feet off of the coffee table as she replaced them with a steaming cup of chamomile tea. Ana didn't particularly like the floral teas, so hers was citrus with cinnamon. She sat next to Jesse, curled her legs up underneath her, and hugged the mug to herself. She heard Jesse blow on his before taking a sip.

They were back in her apartment for the evening, electing to lounge in comfortable clothes with tea instead of braving the snow outside.

"I wonder if they've given up your room," she said, poking Jesse on the arm.

"As long as no one steals my suitcase, it's fine by me. The sweatshirt from my favorite diner is in there."

"What a travesty that would be. Do you want to get it now? We can remind the workers you stay there."

His arm came up to wrap around her shoulders, and she snuggled into his side. "I think I like it here."

"There's certainly more room than your little hotel suite."

"I should hope. If your apartment was as small as my hotel room, I say we should go there instead. At least there's room service."

His fingers trailed along her arm from shoulder to elbow. It tickled a little, which would've made her shiver if she wasn't so warm against his side.

"What would you get if you ordered room service?" she asked. "I've never done it."

"I hadn't either before I started traveling so much." He considered, cup against his bottom lip as he thought. "You know, I think I'd get a tuna melt."

She pulled back to raise an eyebrow at him. "A what?"

"A sandwich with tuna and cheese."

Ana wrinkled her nose. "Fish and cheese. I'm not sure I would like that."

"I can always make it for you next time."

She leaned into him with a grin. "So, I *do* get room service."

Jesse laughed. "I guess you do." He ducked his head down to kiss her neck. "What kind of room service do I get?"

"I can think of a few things." Her voice was breathy.

"So can I."

His voice rumbled against her skin like rolling gravel, and that did make her shiver.

But after a short kiss, she leaned back with faux disapproval.

"Hey, we're supposed to be watching a movie tonight."

"True." Jesse settled back against the cushions. "I can always order room service for dessert."

Ana rolled her eyes, but she couldn't hold back the giggle that escaped her.

Christmas and New Years had passed, but Ana didn't want the cheeriness of the holiday to end—as evidenced by their Christmas movie playing and the snowman decorations dotting her apartment. If she had any peppermint hot chocolate left, they would have been having that, but tea was a good substitute.

Besides, the two of them agreed to exchange gifts that night, so Ana couldn't very well have a Christmas-free apartment before that. Her miniature Christmas tree sat atop an end table, so her gift for Jesse was leaning up against the legs. Jesse's gift for her was in a tiny box she had barely noticed when he placed it under the tree itself.

Shaking her head, Ana returned to the movie, smiling at the charm of the black-and-white film. Her parents weren't particularly interested in television, now or when she was growing up, but Christmas was the exception. Ana imagined many families being the same with household members off from work and blood relations and friends gathering together.

Coming from Romania as they did, their Christmas was always more intimate, with just Ana and her parents. They didn't have family in Germany, so it was rare for her to celebrate Christmas outside of her parents. Occasionally, during school, she'd participate in a white elephant party if there were gift exchanges, and merely a merry get together if there weren't.

Exchanging a useful, thoughtful gift with Jesse was something foreign to her but equally as enticing. She wondered if he'd like what she'd gotten him and what that small box he'd gotten for her was.

The movie finished after another half hour, and Ana hummed in contentment, stretching her sluggish limbs. She didn't anticipate they were going to have a late night, both having just finished challenging, long days at work. Ana, amused, noted the bottle of p.m. pain killers Jesse already had waiting for him on the coffee table next to his water. She certainly wouldn't begrudge him their use; she was tempted to take some, too. Her feet ached from her ill-fitting boots, which always reminded her she wasn't so young anymore. Unlike her twenty-year-old self, who strutted the streets in cheap heels, Ana couldn't afford to wear uncomfortable shoes anymore.

Perhaps she shouldn't have chastised Jesse for putting his feet on the table. The cool metal frame of the glass coffee table would probably feel splendid on her feet.

Jesse lay a quick kiss on her cheek, then stood, startling her out of her thoughts. She watched in anticipation as he walked to the Christmas tree and pointed to the gifts.

"Ready?" he asked, picking up his tiny box.

"Yes!" Ana's chirp of enthusiasm was probably more excitable than the situation warranted, but she didn't mind. She sprung up and grabbed the bundle from the floor, then they settled on the couch once more.

Ana could tell he was trying to study the bulbous, unidentifiable shape in her arms, just as she was attempting to discern any details from his small box, so with laughs from each of them, they exchanged.

Jesse pressed on the squishy package, crinkling it under his fingers. The satin bow tied around it helped give it a vaguely rectangular shape, but he didn't take long before he was untying the ribbon then tearing into the package.

At Jesse's grin, Ana breathed in relief. He held up a maroon-colored sweatshirt with a silhouette of Heidelberg's castle in the middle, a script font of the name stenciled underneath it.

"Do you remember when we went to the coffee shop?" At the unsure pull of his mouth, she amended, "I mean when we had the thumbprint cookies."

"Yeah, I do." He examined the sweatshirt again.

"Then you might remember me telling you our second date was supposed to be related to your sweatshirt. Well, it's not at all what I had planned, and it's not our second date, but still…" Ana gestured to the gift.

He grabbed her hand before she could rest it at her side again.

"I love it," he said then brushed his lips on her knuckles. "Thank you."

Ana squeezed his hand then released. "You are very welcome."

Her heart warmed when he pulled the new garment over his head, and Ana let herself wander an appreciative eye down him; maroon was a very good color on Jesse.

"Your turn," he said, nodding to the box in her left palm.

It was smaller than a ring box and made of simple, textured, white cardboard. Rather than wrap it like Ana had, Jesse placed a small, stickable bow on top to act as decoration. Ana used it as a handle to pull the lid off.

What lay gently atop cotton bedding was a small charm. Picking it up, she realized it was a building with columns carved into the metal.

"The Museum of Natural History," Jesse said. "I know it's not exactly where you're thinking of going to work, but I thought it might be a nice reminder of your future anyway. I wasn't sure what you would want it on, either, so I figured I'd just give you charm and not a chain or bracelet."

His explanation registered, though it may have taken a few extra moments to comprehend as she stared at the silver charm. He'd gotten her a museum. Ana hadn't talked about her career plans with him for a long time, yet he seemed to intuitively know it had been something she'd been thinking about for the past week or so.

Ana held it to her heart. "I've…actually been thinking of looking for another job soon."

"Really?" Jesse beamed at her. "I wondered when it would be time."

When it would be time, Ana noticed, like he had all the faith in the world for her. The overwhelming amount of *feeling* that overcame her made her reach for his sleeve, and he seemed to know exactly what she wanted; he moved the last pieces of the wrapping paper and scooted next to her, wrapping his arm around her. The charm between them, still clasped in her hand. Ana could feel the imprint of the edges, but she didn't mind, even tightening her hand so she wouldn't lose it.

"Do you have an idea of which one?" Jesse asked. "Are there any that are hiring?"

"One right now, but a friend of mine told me a small art gallery will be looking for someone within the next couple of weeks."

Though Heidelberg was close in her memory, she didn't feel worried about mentioning her friend. Perhaps it was because they'd wrapped up the issue of Jesse's jealously, or maybe it was because he'd vowed to tell her if he was ever feeling similarly. Either way, Ana only waited a moment or two in case he needed to tell her before continuing, "They're setting up a meeting with the curator for me when they're close to hiring."

"That's amazing, Ana!" Jesse squeezed her in excitement. "I didn't realize you were so well-connected," he joked.

"I didn't think I was either!"

Ana had been understandably surprised when she'd gotten the call out of the blue, though she shouldn't have been. They last time she had seen her friend, Jonas, he told her he'd keep an eye out for anything she may be interested in.

"Actually," Ana said, "you would be familiar with the person who is setting up the meeting."

"Oh?" Jesse tilted his head, loosening his grip so he could see her. "Besides Elaine and...well, John, I haven't met any of your friends." There was a flicker of sheepishness as he said her old friend's name, but Ana didn't comment.

Ana said, "The gallery we went to before dating, the one with the Nolde painting. The Expressionist one with the two boats."

The last sentence seemed to spark a memory, and Ana smiled.

"Yes, that one," she said. "Well, the artist we went there for, his name is Jonas."

"Oh, the hanging glass piece upstairs."

Ana brightened. "Yes! That one!"

"Where we had our first kiss," Jesse said, leaning in for another, and she accepted happily. It was a soft touch, even the hand that brushed against her cheek, and she tasted the chamomile tea on his lips.

When they pulled back, their faces were still close, so she only had to whisper.

"Also, where you utterly confused me."

He laughed. "Because I kissed you?"

"*Yes*, and you know you did."

His shrug was small but cheeky. "Guilty."

Jesse tilted down for another kiss, this one with a little more pressure, and Ana's free hand slid across the outline of the castle on his sweatshirt. She traced it with her fingers while his caught in her braid, snagging.

She pulled back with a slight wince as he apologized.

"That's alright. It was a bit loose anyway."

Using a hair tie wrapped around her wrist, she pulled back all of her hair with the exception of the braid. After a moment of hesitation, she finally set her charm down on the table so she could have both hands free to remove the bead. Ana set it on the table, too, then fed a finger through the braid to release it fully.

Just as she was about to divide the strands for the new braid, Jesse clasped his hand over hers. Ana furrowed her brow.

"Do you mind if I...?" He nodded to her hair.

"You...know how to braid?" she asked. No one but her or her mother had ever touched that strand before, let alone the bead itself. Ana wasn't necessarily opposed to the idea, but the decision felt more intimate than she expected. Ana had honestly never thought anyone would ask, so she never had to consider what it would mean to her. A barrier sat before her that she didn't even know existed, and she bit her lip.

His face was patient as his hand gently crested over hers; his callused thumb brushing against the crease in her palm where she'd clutched the charm, and it soothed the ache there

"I was a single dad with three girls," Jesse said. "I definitely know how to braid."

Ana wondered if his offer meant as much to him as it did to her. For her, it encroached on tradition—though saying it in her head felt a little dramatic, and she noted the way the voice in her head sounded so much like her mother's. For him, she wondered if it was something special he did with Sarah, Monica, and Kaylee. Would they have sat on their mother's old vanity chair, or stand in the bathroom with a selection of hair ties scattered around the countertop?

Or did it mean nothing?

But from the way Jesse waited, staring at her with those storm-cloud blue eyes, he knew what he was asking, and Ana didn't imagine he would be upset if she said no. He'd merely release her hand and let her do it.

Ana made her decision and grasped his hand gently in return.

"Yes."

She directed his hand to her hair, and her heart fluttered as he hooked it around his forefinger with care, bringing it to his lips.

With the touch of his kiss, she breathed out, and each moment was weighted with significance like she'd given him the right to perform a sacred ritual.

When she was a girl, she read all about braids, having been fascinated by them when she pointed a stubby finger at a statue and announced they matched, wiggling her own braid at her parents.

Braids could be traced back to 3500 BCE. Paintings on a Stone Age rock found in the Sahara depicted a woman with cornrows. The Egyptians wore them as a sign of royalty and divinity, while the Greeks used intricate braids woven with flowers and metal and fruit to indicate their luxurious wealth and status. At one point in their history, the Chinese used them to indicate social rank, and rice farmers braided them down their backs.

Never mind their importance in religion, culture, or as art symbols—braids made Ana feel as though hers held just as much weight; she remembered promising to never lose the bead or go a day without its steady presence near her temple.

The bead—*her* bead—had first been worn by her grandmother, who eventually passed it on to her mother before it was finally given to Ana. She vowed to carry on the tradition.

It meant family, she realized, and sitting before Jesse with his fingers weaving through her hair connected him to her more intimately, more *solidly*, than anything else ever had. Her allowance implied something, whether he understood it or not didn't matter, and the idea of it both thrilled and terrified her.

His deft movements stopped, and Jesse pulled back.

"All done," he said with softness in his voice. Ana wondered why he'd only offered now and not earlier.

Then she looked down.

Her braid, with the polished blue bead attached as usual, cascaded down her chest to rest in the middle, where she noticed a new addition: the charm. Jesse had braided the charm near the bead, so it hung at the end of her braid.

Ana reached down to feel the smoothness of the familiar against cool ridges of the unfamiliar; they were side-by-side and it felt like they were meant to be that way. With the charm in her hair, Ana couldn't imagine any other place she could possibly put it.

"Do you..." Jesse shifted in his seat. "Do you like it? Is that okay? I can take it out if you don't want it there."

"No," she immediately protested. "No, I love it."

"Yeah?" he asked, hopeful.

Ana didn't answer verbally, instead, she lean forward to touch a searing kiss to his lips. When he pulled her toward him, palms on her back, she hopped up to straddle his legs. When she pulled her body to his, she could feel the charm and bead pressed between them. It wasn't until later, as they settled against her bare skin, that she realized the charm felt even better there than it had in her palm.

Like how a single braid's meaning had evolved over the years from a statement into a tradition, Ana knew the charm was a turning point; then and there, she vowed to keep this new tradition alive.

Chapter Sixteen

It was strange how differently Jesse took the news he was going back to America than he had a half a year ago. Before, he'd practically jump with joy immediately call one of his girls to share the good news with them.

But with Ana in his life, it was bittersweet. Disappointment hit him in equal measures to relief as he thought both of how much he'd miss Ana and how much he wanted to see his family. Thankfully, the trip home was a short one, only a week, so it wouldn't be long before he was back with her.

Ana didn't seem too disappointed and teased him about all the things she could do while he was gone.

"I can look for a new dress," she had said as she stood in front of her collection.

"I could help you choose."

She'd merely gestured to his clothing before staunchly telling him no.

Thinking of that refusal, he straightened the strings of the hoodie underneath his jacket. He figured he'd save Ana the trouble of doing it herself.

He was headed to the park, probably for one of the last times of the season. It had gotten a little too chilly for their taste. Winter had officially arrived in the city and brought with it blustery winds and a shock to the lungs when stepping out of the house.

Ana had finished her shift, so they were meeting in their usual spot on the bridge. It was only slightly overcast; a stray streak of sun peeked out during Jesse's walk, which he in his too-thin jacket appreciated wholeheartedly.

Jesse had known he was going back to America this month, so he thought he wouldn't bring his thicker jacket until then, but he couldn't have predicted the cold snap two days before he was leaving.

He didn't mind a little chill, though, if it made Ana happy. She said she wanted to experience their walks in all seasons, a sweet comment said while making dinner that further cemented the fact they were together, dating. They would still need to explore the park in the spring and summer. Leaving the two best seasons for last felt fitting, Jesse thought. Finally together—and conquering their first fight in Heidelberg—their future looked bright.

When he arrived at the park, it was to a calm stillness. The wind was contained to the trees, occasionally disturbing them with its light sigh of breath. Perhaps it was because evening was near, or maybe because it was winter, but Jesse didn't see anyone in the park, save for the few animals not yet gone or slumbering.

One may call it eerie, but Jesse found peace in the faded hues and whispered sounds of the season, so he didn't mind waiting for Ana to arrive. Surprisingly, he even found the trickling of the river soothing. There was a delicate glassiness to the current unlike anything he'd seen on the water before. Perhaps it was a lack of leaves tumbling through that gave it more clarity than usual, or maybe it was him being figurative and flowery; he was waiting to see Ana, after all.

She could probably come up with something better. For English being her third language, she was astoundingly adept at it, and her few and far between poor remembrances reminded him how impressive she was.

Sarah understood Spanish, and Jesse knew she found etymology fascinating in both languages, but it was likely due to her work in the legal office that dealt only in precise language. Jesse thought she and Ana could probably have great discussions about what they'd learned, and Jesse wouldn't be surprised if the conversation inspired Ana to learn Spanish, too. She'd mentioned recently she wanted to study another language.

"It's quiet here today."

Jesse turned. Ana stood at the end of the bridge, bundled in her black peacoat with a long purple scarf wrapped twice around her neck. Her hands were covered by bulky mittens; one waved at him.

"Very quiet," he said. "Maybe this is the time when we should come instead."

"We certainly wouldn't have to worry about anyone taking our favorite bench."

He huffed a laugh at the memory. "I can't believe those kids didn't wake up. I almost thought they were dead!"

"It was very alarming." Her voice came out both bewildered and annoyed. "You looked so concerned. I thought you might try reviving them yourselves if not for the little one twitching in his sleep."

Shaking his head, he laughed as he recalled the three children huddled together on the couple's usual bench. It was the middle of the afternoon on a Saturday in the busy park, and the kids slept through it all; he'd never met anyone as heavy a sleeper as those kids were.

"Jake definitely isn't like that," Jesse said, shaking his head. "He wakes up at the drop of a hat. I remember

Sarah having the hardest time with his daytime naps because he was always waking up from some noise or another."

"Then maybe he takes after his grandfather. Unless Sarah is also a...uh..."

"Light sleeper," he provided.

"Thank you. Light sleeper."

"Nah, Sarah was an anomaly among babies. She slept through the night, didn't wake up really early or stay up late. We had no idea what everyone was talking about when they said they couldn't sleep because of their kids."

"Even I know that is very lucky."

He laughed. "Yeah, everyone was definitely envious when we told them, but once Monica came around, we finally got it. Oh, she was a right terror. Colicky, never wanted to go to bed. I don't think I moved from bed the first time my parents took the girls for a night."

"I can only imagine." She chuckled softly, then asked, "What about Kaylee?"

Jesse shrugged. "Very inconsistent, actually. One week she'd sleep every night just fine, then the next, she'd be rattling the bars of her crib."

"Sounds like you had your hands full with them."

"Yeah, but it was worth it." Jesse knew his smile probably looked a little dopey, but it made an appearance most every time he talked about his daughters. "And they're all grown up and helping me out when they can, so those sleepless nights have all been paid in kind."

"From how you talk of them, they sound like truly lovely people."

Jesse nudged her side with a light touch. "You'd get along with all of them, I'm sure."

"You think?" Her pleased smile was shyly hidden behind her scarf.

"Especially Monica, I think. Likes all that D.I.Y stuff, so I usually get some beautiful things for Christmas from her."

"Like what?"

"Well, she's been really interested in ceramics lately, so she gave me a really nice serving bowl."

Ana brightened. "Oh, I'd love to talk about that. I've only worked with clay a little, so I'm sure she's got wonderful recommendations for techniques."

"You should call her sometime!"

Ana paused at that, biting her lip.

"Oh," he said, realizing what he said. They didn't know each other. "Right."

Jesse imagined what it would be like for Ana to be able to pick up the phone to talk to his daughter, and his heart warmed like the two of them together held it in their hands. He imagined Ana making Sarah coffee in the morning, telling her what concoction she'd used to flavor it and probably credit Elaine for the idea. Ana and Kaylee would be admiring photographers on his youngest's phone, and Ana could teach her about angles, saturations levels, and whatever else there was to know about photographs.

The idea wouldn't leave him, though it wasn't the first time he had thought of Ana in the midst of his family. Each time it appeared, the renditions collected in his brain like photographs, and he wasn't too proud to admit he hoarded them, slipped them into an album in his mind, and shelved them carefully until the next was spewed out like a Polaroid fluttering into his hands.

A gloved mitten around his hand turned his attention back to Ana.

"Should we…tell them?" Ana asked.

He could hear hesitation clearly in her voice, but underneath, he could also sense there was excitement.

"I—I don't know."

Now that the possibility was open, he hesitated, though the reason wasn't clear.

"I don't know either."

Hearing the same from her made his shoulders, which he hadn't realized he'd tensed, relax, and he squeezed her hand.

"I think about it sometimes," Jesse said. "I'll be on the phone with them and think, hey, wouldn't it be nice to tell them truthfully when they ask how I'm doing. How I'm *actually* doing."

He'd considered it many times, but the thought never lingered in his mind long enough to form, and the moment to share seems to pass. Jesse couldn't explain why the thought of sharing with his daughter's seemed to flit away, but they did, so he stayed silent on the subject every time.

"I've thought about it too," Ana admitted. "When I'm with my parents or even working with Elaine…"

Jesse chuckled. "Like she doesn't know."

"True." She nodded. "But it's never…in the open. Always implied or entirely avoided."

He bit his lip then asked, "So… what now?"

The once-in-the-hour wind shuffled by them, and it pulled a few strands of hair out from Ana's scarf; they tickled against Jesse's cheek. Ana used her free hand to tuck them back in as well as she could with the mittens on.

She left her fingers to rest on her cheek, like she didn't know what to do with her hand now that its task was complete, then answered, "Maybe…Maybe we should."

Jesse inhaled through his mouth, the icy air felt like frost in his throat. "You think?"

Determination seemed to bolster through her, and she straightened her back.

"Yes," she said. "Why not? We are happy, in a relationship, and it has been months. Why keep it a secret?"

Some of that confidence drifted to him, and he nodded.

"You know what, you're right."

Seeing her inspiring grin, he wondered what his reservations were in the first place, especially when he couldn't distinctly name them. Why *didn't* they tell anyone? As Ana said, they were in a happily committed relationship, something they had thought through and persevered to end up where they were.

Those pictures in his mind could become reality. They could be transferred from his imagination and morphed into memories, and that alone made him want to call his daughters at that second. But he knew he should wait.

"We can tell them when I go to America. You tell your parents, and I tell my daughters."

"I like that idea." She sucked her teeth a moment. "Divide and conquer? That's it, right?"

"Divide and conquer," he repeated, nodding.

Ana beamed, then skipped a little next to him, bouncing their bound hands.

"I cannot wait for you to meet my family. They can help you with your Romanian," she teased, elbowing him.

"I think I might need some more practice."

Ana waved a hand, dismissing the thought. "You are fine. I think you would get along with my father, though. My mother, too, but she's a little...abrasive."

Jesse chuckled. "From your stories of her, I can imagine that."

They stood in silence, just enjoying each other's company. The park seemed brighter all the sudden, though Jesse suspected it was all in his imagination.

He wondered if there were any swans around. The nights were getting colder, but he wasn't sure if the water temperature had fallen enough to warrant their departure. No clues of the birds could be seen, but he imagined them beyond the tree line, puttering around with their families or by their lonesome.

Come to think of it...

"Hey, Ana," he said, "Have you ever seen a family of swans here? There always seems to be a swan by itself."

She blinked at his odd question but answered after a contemplative moment. "I cannot remember for sure. They must be around, though."

"Maybe we'll see some babies waddling around in the spring."

"As long as we avoid the mother, that will be quite lovely."

Jesse tilted his head. "The mother?"

"Yes, they tend to get aggressive when someone wanders too near their nest." Ana paused to point at her ankle. "One nipped at me once."

His eyes widened. "I'm surprised you want to frequent a park we've dubbed Swan Bridge then."

Ana shrugged, laughing. "It's just I was near their babies, and as a curious child, I didn't know to back away."

"Then I'll keep that in mind this spring. Be careful, or Mama will bite back."

She wiggled their hands between them. "I'm sure you understand, Papa Bear."

Jesse laughed. "I suppose I do."

They quieted in favor of watching the dead leaves drift by in the river. A snatch of sunlight illuminated the water, and it sparkled in glee until the clouds caged it away again.

"I'm looking forward to meeting your daughters," Ana whispered, leaning her head on his shoulder.

He rested his on top of hers and said, just as quietly, "I'm looking forward to meeting your parents."

Their whispered words claimed the still air around them, and Jesse wondered how long they would linger before the wind blew them into the night. As of that moment, everything seemed to hold, and he hoped their excitement, anticipation, and *love* lingered.

It felt like it would last forever.

Chapter Seventeen

The table was set, the dinner was almost ready, and his daughters were chatting at the dining table. No grandson that night, but Jesse figured that was for the best. He was going to tell his daughters about Ana, and a rambunctious toddler probably wasn't ideal company in a serious conversation.

The timer on the oven beeped. Jesse swiped up the heat pad and removed the casserole from within. It was nothing fancy because he didn't want to fill the kitchen with ingredients he'd need to pitch before he left for Germany again, so he picked something easy. Besides, it was a favorite in the household, something he used to make a lot when the girls were younger.

"Smells great, Dad!" Sarah said as he walked into the dining room. She had already put down a couple heating pads on the table; he placed the dish right on top of them.

"Thanks, sweetie." He ruffled her hair, and she playfully swatted his hand.

Monica was talking about some work event that Kaylee seemed particularly interested in, but they managed a quick thanks before each dug into their portions. It reminded Jesse of when they were younger, Kaylee just starting high school and Monica fully entrenched in her junior year, talking about an extracurricular teacher he'd never heard of. Whatever social media thing they were discussing went over his head, but he enjoyed the back-and-forth anyway. It was just nice to be back home.

Upon his return, he'd talked to a few of his coworkers, and hearing about spontaneous lunches or surprise visits made him, admittedly, a little envious. It wasn't as though he disliked the traveling part of his job—he loved it, in fact—but being away from home made him appreciate everyone's company all the more when he returned.

He didn't bring up his relationship with Ana.

It wasn't the right time. Whether he thought so because he didn't want to surprise them over dinner or because he was putting off the conversation, he didn't know.

Being in his old home, even if it had been solely his for almost twenty years, brought thoughts of Linda, and Jesse admitted to being unsure of how his family would react.

They had all been close to their mother, obviously, and the memory of her was a hard one to define when compared to his own loss. For his daughters, losing Linda when they were still girls, they cherished the memories so tightly that they'd calcified to a state that didn't leave much room for evolution. He found that was what happened when you were a child; many things—memories, routines, comforts—became stark and rigid, especially when they were tied to something very personal.

Kaylee, for instance—whenever she didn't understand something, it was "stupid." If she didn't know how to use a new math equation, then it was stupid. It wasn't that she was upset about learning something new or needing to ask for help...it was simply stupid because it was unknown.

It was the same when it came to Linda. They had forgotten some things about her and remembered others, and that was unlikely to change, but he worried this unknown person would automatically be considered something stupid. His girls knew Linda as mother, partner to their dad. He didn't know how they would react to someone encroaching on that spot. Yes, he had dated in the past, but no one for long enough to meet them.

Sarah, in particular, had wanted him to start dating more proactively, so he hoped she would have at least a lukewarm reaction.

Dinner wrapped up, and Monica was quick to gather the dishes, but he knew it was because she was expecting dessert shortly after. He decided to not make her wait and threw the dirty dishes in the sink in favor of retrieving the apple pie from the fridge. It was Monica's favorite and Sarah's second favorite, only falling behind the chocolate cupcakes he used to make around Halloween.

The pie was from the store, but it was a local place that made them from scratch. The store owner's wife baked them every couple of days, and the apple pie was a fresh one Jesse immediately snatched up. From personal experience, he knew they went fast, but it was understandable; they were absolutely delicious. So delicious, in fact, that the grocery store was added to his sweatshirt collection in royal blue.

Within a few minutes, they'd made a sizable dent in the dessert with their plates practically licked clean, but Jesse didn't quite enjoy it as much as he usually did. He was preoccupied by the perfect moment to bring up Ana. Once again deciding the moment wasn't right, he ended up pushing Kaylee away from her usual dish-washing duties to do it himself.

He ran the water, let it get warm, and added soap.

His daughters sat behind him at the peninsula on barstools so old he couldn't remember when it was he'd bought them.

Them to his back and him turned away, Jesse thought this might be closest to a perfect moment he would get. The deep breath he sucked in smelled of soap.

"Hey, girls?" he asked, wetting the washcloth now that the water was hot. "I have something to tell you."

Their chatter quieted.

"Yeah, what's up?" Kaylee asked for them.

Jesse cleared his throat. "I know toward the end of my last trip, you girls were guessing about who I was texting so much."

Monica leaned forward, the barstool squeaking, and he could hear the poorly contained excitement in her voice as she said, "*Yes?*"

"Well, you were all right."

Kaylee clapped her hands together as he turned to look at her sisters. "I *knew* it! So, are you dating? Are you just talking so far?"

Jesse smiled at her questions. "Dating."

"It's really nice you've found someone, Dad," Sarah said over Monica and Kaylee's squeals of excitement.

"It is," he said. "Which is why…well, we decided to tell everyone. And I'd like for you all to meet her at some point."

"Oh." Monica's eyes were wide. "It's that serious?"

"I guess it has been a while since you've been back," Kaylee added. "So, who is she? What's she like?"

"Her name is Ana." Even without an outside view, he knew his voice softened and the corners of his mouth had curled into a smile. Even just telling them so little was a relieving balm to the anxiety that writhed in this stomach.

"That's a pretty name—at least, in Europe. *Anna* always sounds so nasally here when we say it."

Jesse laughed, turning back to the dishes. "Yeah, I suppose it does."

"Where was your first date?" Monica asked.

"A coffee shop. That's where we met."

"How cute, Dad!"

His cheeks flushed. He was glad he was turned away, scrubbing the plate.

"I hope you took her somewhere nicer afterwards," Kaylee piped in.

"*Yes.*" Jesse almost rolled his eyes. Out of all of them, Kaylee had the most refined taste when it came to dates, but that was probably because she wanted to avoid another incident like the boy who took her to McDonald's for their first—and only—date. Jesse remembered many instances where she bemoaned the location before even going, and he was always quick to tell her to have an open mind. Just because one guy took her for fast food, which they ate while sitting in his smelly car in the parking lot, didn't mean they all would.

"I've taken her to art galleries, art fairs, and museums, thank you very much."

Sarah's lips pulled up in amusement. "Sounds like she likes art."

"Yeah, she's planning on becoming the curator of a museum."

"Oh, does she work at a museum now?"

"No, not yet." He rinsed the plate and stuck it in the rack. "Even though it's been a few years since she graduated, she's worked other jobs because of family stuff, so she wasn't able to pursue other career options."

Silence. The atmosphere of the room shifted, and he glanced back, wiping his hands on the towel.

"Dad, did you say...?" Monica ran a hand through her hair, pinning one side behind her ear. "A few years since she graduated?"

His brow furrowed. "Yes. Why?"

"Was she…Did she go to school late?"

"Yes. When she came to Germany." His answers were slow as he turned a puzzled gaze between them.

"Wait, she's not from Germany?" Kaylee asked.

"No, she's—"

"I think," Monica cut in, louder, "what Kaylee means to ask is…Ana, how old is she?"

Oh. That was what the pointed questions were leading to. This time, Ana's name did nothing to soothe the roiling mace-like spikes in his stomach. Their attention was solely on him.

"Thirty-two," he answered.

"Thirty-two." The repetition from Monica was deadpan.

"But we can all have dinner together, and I'm sure you'd all get along with Ana."

"You're—" A hiccupped laugh tumbled from Kaylee's lips. "You can't be serious, Dad."

"*Thirty-two.*" Monica's voice was a little bit higher pitched that time.

"I *am* serious." He stood before them all, arms crossed. "Ana and I are together. Yes, there's an age gap—"

Monica's laugh was derisive.

"But that doesn't mean we don't care for each other."

"*Dad*," Kaylee stressed as if that alone could change his mind or make him see reason.

All of them sat in silence before him, each one of them avoiding his eyes. Monica even had her hand covering her face. Jesse swallowed the lump in his throat, then leaned back against the counter, and focused on the pressure of its edge digging into his back.

His eyes drifted to his eldest, who had been quiet up until now, but she steadfastly looked downward.

"Sarah?" he said in a small voice.

From across the counter, he could see her clench her hands together.

"I-I don't—" She snapped her mouth closed and took a deep breath. "I don't know, Dad."

"Just '*I don't know*?'" Kaylee asked. "That's really all you're going to say about it?"

"Of course not!" Sarah snapped before her gaze flicked over to Jesse, then back. She licked her lips. "I just don't know how I *should* feel about it."

"Yeah, well, I'm sorry, Dad, but I'm *not* feeling okay with it." Kaylee glared at her sister. "And neither should you."

"Kaylee—"

"You could straight-up be her dad."

"That's uncalled for."

"No, it's not!" Kaylee surged to her feet, facing away from him.

Sarah's chair squeaked as she shifted uncomfortably, her face back to staring down toward the granite countertops.

"She's four years older than me," Sarah said, and the whole room quieted as she spoke; otherwise, they likely would've missed it. What he didn't miss was the way Monica's lip curled in disgust behind Sarah.

Throughout the conversation, their words pierced like a thrusting lance, and no wound had time to heal before another judgement opened them further. The cuts wept, pooling in and clogging up his innards. He'd never seen his daughters look at him like that.

Kaylee's next words hit him like he'd been slammed into a wall. "What about *Mom*?" she asked. She sounded just like she had as a young girl when she asked what happened to Linda.

Each beat of Jesse's heart broke it further, and the pain of it made him wince.

"Yeah, Dad, what would Mom think of all of this?" Monica piped in.

"I—I don't..."

"I can only guess, but I bet she'd be disappointed."

With that, his heart shattered completely, and all that remained was heat, flaring up. He thought he heard Sarah snap at Monica, but he wasn't completely listening.

"*Don't*." His voice was stern. "Do *not* bring your mother into this. If she were here, we wouldn't even be having this conversation. But she's *not*."

And maybe it was cruel to be so harsh but using Linda's image to cast their own hurt feelings about the situation was not something he could stand by. He knew the subject would be brought up. He figured it would take precedence over the age gap, but he didn't expect the sneers that accompanied their mother's name.

Behind Monica, he saw Kaylee's lip tremble, and the indignation left him as quickly as it had come. Now he just felt exhausted.

"Look," he said, pinching the bridge of his nose. "This obviously...This obviously isn't going as any of us planned, so maybe we should just...talk later."

There was silence as everyone seemed to absorb the conversation, the atmosphere, and their own feelings. Kaylee stood, nodding, and she pretty much scurried out of the kitchen. In only a few moments, the front door was opened then shut.

"I don't know if I want to." Monica's arms were wrapped around herself, but she didn't let him respond because she whirled around and left too.

Only Sarah was left.

She'd barely spoken, and she'd barely moved. Finally, like she'd been put on pause and someone hit the play button, she stood with slow and steady movements.

"Sarah?" he called when she still didn't speak.

Her sigh carried through the entire kitchen, and the tension in the air was tangible.

"I need time to think, Dad."

And with that, she left as well. Sarah closed to front door gently, but to him, she might as well have slammed it.

A sudden emptiness replaced the roiling in his stomach. It snaked its way from his core to his limbs and became heavier by the moment. As it threatened to pull him to the floor, he chose to ignore it in favor of motion: he pushed the stools in, placed the half-drunk mugs of tea and coffee in the sink, and finished washing the dishes.

There were two pieces remaining of the apple pie. What had brought such delicious joy half an hour ago now turned his stomach just to look at it.

He snatched it off the counter and dropped it in the trash.

Chapter Eighteen

A key shifted the deadbolt on Ana's door, but she didn't turn to see who it was. She knew it was Jesse. Not only did he have an extra key to her apartment, but he'd told her he was coming from his hotel for a visit.

She scrubbed the pan in her sink while she listened to Jesse clatter his shoes off at the door and plop his duffel bag down. Before long, he sat at the table, groaning about his old bones.

Her hand stopped.

She listened to his mindless chatter for another moment, then refocused on her task of scrubbing the pan with the bubbly cloth in her hand.

Jesse sounded like he normally did. He didn't seem like *Ana*, who was staring blankly ahead, lifeless, and tired. Why was that? He'd told her how his daughters reacted over the phone, his voice thick with emotion, before he came back to Germany. Yet here he was babbling out a story about some humorous mishap at work. He hadn't trudged into her apartment with a long, sullen face; instead, he walked in as usual.

Ana doubled her efforts and scrubbed hard against the pan. The caked-on food had released after two swipes, but she hadn't noticed, and continued to drag the washcloth against its surface. It wasn't until an ache swelled in her fingers that she stopped.

"Ana."

She breathed, and she smelled soap.

"Yes?"

Jesse probably wondered why she didn't turn around; there were a few moments of silence, and she wasn't sure what he was thinking.

Finally, he asked, "Are you okay?"

Her mouth stretched into a smile, bright and wide, and without conscious thought, she looked at him over her shoulder. "Of course!"

"It's just...you've been very quiet."

Ana rinsed the pan then grabbed for her towel to dry it. "Have I?"

"Yes, you have. You...haven't said anything since I got here." He tried for a smile. "Not even a welcome home kiss."

Blinking, she realized, no, she hadn't greeted him even a dim hello. Guilt curled her lip, and she moved forward to apologize with a quick kiss to his lips. He didn't try to elongate it, which she was grateful for, but the contact did make her feel a little better.

"Welcome back," she said.

"Glad to be back." Jesse caressed her face with the backs of his fingers, and she closed her eyes to the sensation. His touch drifted from her cheek, then one finger crested underneath her eye, pressing on the softness there.

"You look tired," he whispered, and she snapped her eyes open. There was an inky smudge underneath his eyes as well.

"As do you."

His lips twitched. "Well, to be expected, what with the flight and...my daughters."

The gnawing ache in Ana's stomach that had been lingering since she spoke to her parents only worsened, and she pressed her lips together.

"Have you…spoken to them again?" she asked, but she knew the answer in the way he held himself. Perhaps he acted normally when he came in to pretend everything was fine. If she'd bothered to look at him, she would've noticed the longer hair, the exhaustion in his eyes, and the slope to his shoulders.

Jesse sighed. "No." And that one word alone croaked out of his mouth like it was forced through broken glass. Ana's throat felt tight and swollen as if she was allergic to the day.

"And what about…?"

His trailed-off inquiry made her bite her cheek.

She didn't answer him, so Jesse reformed the question in a soft voice. "How did it go with your parents?"

"Fine." Ana counted it lucky she could get the word out. Maybe because it was lie.

He seemed skeptical, though cautious. "Really? Just…fine?"

"*Yes.*"

Jesse didn't speak for a few moments, electing to stare at her instead, which made her squirm—and bristle.

After revealing who she was dating to her parents, Ana didn't particularly want any more scrutiny centered on her.

She relaxed when he said, "Okay."

They stepped back from each other, and she went back to the sink while Jesse deposited himself on the couch. Only a stray spoon was left in the basin, and Ana stared at it. What was so fascinating about it, she didn't know, but she shook her head and grabbed for the cloth again so she could wash it.

It didn't take nearly as long as she wanted, and she even pretended it was covered in food when it wasn't. She slowly dried it, then she put away the pan, taking her time to remove the other stackable pans on the shelf to place the clean one in it. Ana hefted the other pans back onto the shelf then grabbed the clean spoon and walked to open the silverware drawer.

When the drawer closed, she was left with nothing else to do. The only other option she had was to sit next to Jesse and risk him asking about her parents again. Ana was tempted to make a second option, but they all ended the same. At least she would be on a comfortable couch if he decided to go with the first option.

She took small steps, then settled tensely onto the cushion next to him. He had some cooking program on, and they sat in silence, though she relaxed when Jesse reached over to pat her leg before returning his attention to the show.

His hand had been warm through her leggings, and she craved more of the touch. Instead, she leaned back and tuned in as well as she could to how the show presenters prepared a recipe with chicken and apples.

As it had since it happened, the conversation with her parents looped in her brain, and she was unable to ignore the playback of their words and expressions. How she hadn't talked to or seen them since. Before her visit to tell them about Jesse, they had already agreed to meet yesterday for more pattern sewing.

Ana didn't show up, and her mother didn't ask where she was.

She breathed in deeply, which loosened her swollen throat enough to slip out, "She told me to leave." The words were whispered, and she both hoped and didn't hope Jesse heard her.

He did.

At first, he didn't say anything; he squeezed the fingers that grasped his so desperately and brought it to his lips. Jesse didn't let go as he settled their entwined hands on the couch between them with such gentleness it made her chest tighten.

Then he said, "I'm sorry."

Ana inhaled sharply. She was grateful he didn't say anything further, for if he had, there was no guarantee she would be able to hold in her tears. They already burned on the bottom of her eyelids. She refused to blink, and her vision blurred.

Despite her best efforts, one trickled down her cheek anyway. She felt it slide down until it stopped near her mouth—not even having the decency to complete its route—and lingered there like it had found its permanent place. Ana was hyper aware of its presence, and she willed it to fall from her chin to her clothes so she could forget it had ever existed, but it didn't. It remained rooted in place, and she clenched her jaw in frustration.

His thumb brushed the stubborn tear off. She moved her eyes to Jesse, who was already wiping his thumb on his sleeve.

"That must have been difficult, I know." Despite his close presence, his eyes were hooded with pain, just as hers were. He *did* know. Ana could only imagine what his daughters had said to him, and when she thought of her mother's words, she knew exactly how he was suffering.

Ana's emotions swelled, and she couldn't stop them from pouring out over her edges.

"Oh, god," she said, overwhelmed. "I've never seen her so *disappointed*." The tears that had gathered on her bottom lids finally streaked down her cheeks, and she cursed their descent and the way they lingered. One after another they fell, and before she knew it, Ana was crying.

She couldn't remember the last time she had cried like this—whimpers and sobs of despair that could only be quelled by someone she loved squeezing her tightly.

Her mother had said such cruel things about both Ana and Jesse and had made Ana feel like an unruly *child* who'd brought shame upon their family.

The word her mother had said was, "*Shameful.*" Ana dating Jesse was *shameful*, but when Ana had tried to explain, her mother wouldn't hear it. She chose, instead, to block her daughter's explanation with more hurtful words.

Then her father. He'd looked at her from behind her mother, his usual place, with such *sadness*, like she was someone who needed to be pitied.

Between both of them, they had portrayed every kind of reaction one could have outside of acceptance. They were angry, they wanted her to choose someone else, they were sad, and they were disappointed.

Her mother didn't want to see her.

More tears streamed down Ana's face, and Jesse, a solid presence, never let her go. He held her and waited until her breathing evened and she was left only with a flush on her cheeks and a sniffling nose.

Pulling back, she grabbed for a tissue and got up to relieve the pressure, though it did nothing to help her eyes, which were swollen and squeezed dry of all moisture.

She'd *hated* crying ever since she was a girl and realized she could hold it in if she tried hard enough. Tears always felt intrusive, pushing forth from the depths of her soul to reveal her mood and leak out of her eyes. Beyond that, it exposed her vulnerabilities; Ana didn't like people knowing what it was that could upset her. She didn't want anyone to have the satisfaction of adding another piece to the puzzle that was her.

Ana used another tissue to wipe her eyes, grateful she hadn't bothered to wear makeup that day. It was her day off; she had fully intended to not go out at all. Wallowing alone and then with Jesse seemed like the most she could handle emotionally, so with her hair up and a baggy T-shirt on, she probably looked disastrous.

Arms wrapping around her almost made her startle, but at the familiar scent of the hotel shampoo, she snaked her own arms around him and relaxed into Jesse.

"Thank you," she whispered into his chest.

"You don't need to thank me."

"Maybe not, but I will anyway." She tightened her grip on the fabric of his shirt. "Take me to bed."

That craving from earlier, that comfort in his hand on her thigh rose up in her, and she eagerly followed him as he pulled her toward her room. They shut the door behind them and left the lights off.

They blocked the world out, and Ana thought that was for the best.

Chapter Nineteen

When Jesse woke up the next morning, one image in particular stood out in his mind. When he went to work, it lingered, and every second for the rest of the day was filled with one thing: the sight of Ana crying.

The day before was an emotionally heavy day before he'd even arrived at Ana's. Having never seen her so upset, Jesse had been surprised when Ana had merely teared up. So, when the heaving sobs arrived, a sound he'd never heard from her before, he couldn't fathom how to make things better. Each stuttering breath smashed into him like a wave against a rock cliff, every keening whine eroding pieces off, and they shivered down the cliff face like the tears down her cheek.

Holding Ana in his arms as her sniffles dampened his shirt made him realize how truly close she was to her family. Not that he wasn't aware of it for how often she mentioned them and visited, but the utter devastation on her face as she talked about how disappointed her mother was…it was difficult to watch.

It was hard to erase the memory, and every time he tried, his brain spotlighted it and made it impossible to ignore the line of tears down Ana's face like rain droplets on a window.

The next day, and the one after that, Ana continued on as normal, though Jesse knew how much the fight with her parents weighed on her. Ana would roll her bead around in her fingers, a forlorn downturn to her eyebrows, but as soon as she noticed him, her grin would stretch into a facsimile of her usual dazzling smile. With the strain, it dimmed, and Jesse could only do so much to brighten it. He found he was having a harder time brightening it as the hours went by.

Trailing behind the image of her tears was another thought, one Jesse knew would shatter him. It nagged at him like a woodpecker jabbing away at a tree, poking and poking until he wanted to tear his brain out.

Jesse couldn't tell if it was louder when they were together or not, but he knew there wasn't a moment where it wasn't rattling around in his head. Though, he could admit it didn't help that he still hadn't talked to his daughters since he'd arrived in Germany. It only made the mess in his head echo and echo.

The next day, though, brought clarity. They met in the park after Ana's shift at work, and all was exactly the same as usual until he noticed her face. There were bags under her eyes. She didn't have much makeup on. Her braid was uneven.

She looked so *tired*.

More than that, their conversation was pitted as they avoided the very glaring topic of their families, which encompassed half of what they usually talked about. There were stutters and pauses, and both knew exactly what caused them.

Neither had talked to their families. The hole in Jesse's life was ever-present and raw.

He hadn't even been able to see Jake before he left.

And for the fourth during their walk, Ana's breath hitched when she was about to say something about her childhood; the woodpecker's beak pecked into his gray matter again to replay every action and every word of their interaction.

They went to their respective homes, and it continued to berate him as he sat on his hotel bed. Ana was preparing to leave for the meeting with the gallery curator her friend had set up. Thankfully, she was excited about it, but even with that opportunity on the horizon, Jesse knew the situation with her family was forefront in her thoughts. Ana's enthusiasm for the meeting had been dimmed when she'd discussed it during their walk.

The thought he had was one he knew would break him. But the more he mulled in about in his head, the more it became his only option—for both of them, but mainly for Ana's happiness.

"I can't be with her."

He said it to the room and let it settle in the air and the carpet. He let his heart and body feel it as it bounced from the walls back to his ears.

Each second the thought floated around him it consumed more of him. It chewed away at his head, his heart, and his very soul before it seeped down into his lungs; he felt like he couldn't take a deep breath.

"I can't be with her."

He said it again, hoping it would help quell the all-consuming ache in his soul.

Jesse kept saying it until he felt numb to the words, like holding ice for so long it turned his fingers unfeeling.

"I can't be with her."

At the final declaration, he nodded and pulled on his shoes and coat. If he didn't hurry, he'd miss her, and he wanted to get this over with before she left.

The taxi ride there and ascension up the steps were over in a blink of an eye as he repeated the thought, numbing himself further. He rapped a quick knock on her door, then greeted her surprised face when it swung open.

Jesse sat on her couch and watched Ana bustle around the apartment as she changed from her work clothes into a nice blouse and pencil skirt. If Jesse hadn't witnessed it this morning, he would've never have guessed she was feeling so weary. Her makeup was pristine, her braid redone, and her straight-ironed hair shining down her back.

She was beautiful—not that she wasn't earlier.

He repeated the phrase—*I can't be with her*—then his heart started to ache.

Jesse watched as she stacked her luggage by the door. She was spending the night at a hotel; he wondered if it looked like his.

Ana said something to him, but it was muffled in his ears. Repeating the mantra in his head wasn't working anymore, not when he turned his head to see those green eyes looking toward him. So, just as he'd practice so many times in the last hour, he said it out loud.

"We shouldn't be together anymore."

Keys dropped to the floor, and he winced at the sound. "*What?*"

"I think it would be best if we broke up."

A myriad of emotions fluctuated on her face—confusion, despair, surprise, anger—but she finally settled on the first. Jesse was glad it was that and not any of the others. It made it easier to continue.

"I don't understand."

"It's for the best, Ana."

She stared at him, which made the nerves in his stomach scurry over his heart.

"The *best*," she repeated.

He didn't respond, only waited to see how she would process. It was a nerve-racking wait.

"Why—why would it be for the best? We—we're happy, right? I don't understand." Her voice wobbled, and he watched her pause to visibly swallow. A terrible ache settled into his very soul at the sight. "I—well, I know we've had some troubles lately, with our—"

She stopped. She sucked in a breath. The next seconds slogged through magma-like air, churning and creeping with searing heat.

"The *best*, you said." Ana whirled a glare around to him. "Because of our families, you think it is for *the best* that we part?"

Jesse had seen many adversities in his life, but he quailed like a little duckling at the ferocity in her gaze. Swallowing, he held strong.

"I do think that."

Ana shook her head, more violent than usual; her hair thrashed out to whip the air.

"I cannot believe you," she said. "I cannot *believe* you!"

"Hey, I—"

"*No*. You do not get to *speak*." Her well-practiced accent slipped, and harsher consonants and foreign vowels cut into her sentence. "Did you stop to consider when making a decision about *us*, a unit of *two*, that I might want to be consulted?" She scoffed, and the sound slammed into his heart. "No, apparently only you know what is best for *us*. And apparently, it is such an easy thing for you to say."

"This isn't *easy*."

"Isn't it? The way you are speaking so casually, I would assume so."

She leaned down to snatch up the keys she'd dropped.

"Look," he said, standing up, "maybe…maybe I approached this wrong, but I don't think I'm wrong."

"*Really*."

"I *don't*," he snapped, but breathed in deeply so he could soften his words. "Ana." Her green eyes were as sharp as shards of glass. "Our families are important to us. My girls…when I told them, I've never seen them like that before. And you…"

She breathed. "What about me?"

"You cried." He brought a hand up to her cheek, but he couldn't make out her expression. "After your mother—"

"Don't." Ana turned her face to rid herself of his touch. "You weren't there."

"No, but I was there afterwards."

"And that's reason enough to *break up*? I *cried*! That is all!"

"Because of your mother!"

"You think I do not know that? There's no reason that should mean we give up!"

"I'm not giving up."

"Yes, you are!" she shouted, and they were both in each other's faces.

"Being together is tearing your family apart, so I'm just doing what needs to be done!"

Ana sucked in air, ready to shout once more, but she stopped. It was so abrupt it made Jesse blink in surprise, but alarm shot through him when her face twisted in rage.

"Jesse." The delicate purr of her accent on his name shifted into something harsher, like glass scraping against gravel. She paused only long enough to make the next word hit harder, and it did.

"Leave," she said, and his insides dropped.

"W-What?" he croaked.

"Leave," she repeated. "I want nothing to do with your selfish self-sacrifice or whatever you want to call it."

"My…?"

Ana crossed her arms. "You said *your* family. Not *our* families. You're right. Maybe you do know best. You knew that *us* really meant you and I separately. Because if you really considered this problem as *ours*, you would not hide this break up behind only *my* family." The sharp press of her fingertips against his chest could've been a shove for how weak he felt.

"You *gave up*, and you blamed *me* for it." This time, it *was* a shove, and he stumbled back a step. "Now *leave*. I honestly cannot bear to talk to you right now."

A whimpering, mewling part of his heart came alive, and unable to stop himself, he asked, "Ever?"

Her eyebrows shot up and her mouth turned down. Her expression was an even mix between her lingering anger and...sadness. She seemed to consider him before turning away, and his next breath was an inhale of hurt, which he knew was terrible of him to feel when the entire situation was his doing.

He'd achieved what he'd wanted when he came in. Jesse had broken up with Ana, but there was no satisfaction there, not when she'd scraped her insight across his mind, which now throbbed with an aching rawness he could only describe as shame and regret.

Her back to him was one of the worst outcomes, but did he really expect anything different? Did he really expect her to sigh and go along nicely with his plan? Jesse never should've thought of it as an option, let alone the ideal—yet there he was, wallowing in a hurt he had no right to feel.

Jesse thought his steps toward the door would be slow, but in a flash of panic, he rushed to the mat where he'd deposited his shoes. He slipped one on and tied the lace. Ana still hadn't moved. If his fingers trembled or his entire arm, Jesse didn't know, but even then, his second shoe went too quickly as well.

He wanted to say something. To apologize, maybe, or to say goodbye.

Jesse didn't know what felt right anymore.

In what seemed like a single blink, his hand was on the doorknob. He turned it.

"Jesse."

He never stopped an action so quickly, and he whipped around. Ana's back was still to him.

"Yes?" His voice quivered with hope and devastating acceptance, both warring for a majority.

"Only perhaps, but..." Her shoulders lifted and fell with her large sigh. "Perhaps we can talk when I'm back from my trip."

He didn't know what to say. He just mumbled, "Okay."

Jesse left, blindly descending the stairs one step at a time. Once outside, he stopped to stare up at the cloudy sky painted in an assortment of grays. He was glad there was no sun; not as he walked home, cold from rushing over to Ana's without a hat or gloves, and not as he entered his too-dark room. And not as he collapsed into bed, wishing the day hadn't happened at all.

He didn't sleep.

Chapter Twenty

Jesse had never experienced déjà vu quite so heavily as he did then. His menu was face down on the table, while his date puttered between decisions. Thinking too much, *too much*, about Ana. It was the day after Ana was supposed to get back from her trip, and he hadn't heard from her. Not once. Not even when he'd pitifully texted her in the middle of the night to ask her if she'd gotten back yet.

There was only silence.

Sitting here in the restaurant, Jesse wasn't sure if he could accurately track how it was he'd gotten there. All he knew was, one day, he'd practically begged himself to stop thinking about her. He'd wished he could rewind time to the moment he first had a date with Katherina. Jesse had cycled Ana's age through his head, so he could be more attentive to the woman, maybe be more interested in her stories, and stop comparing everything she did to Ana.

Jesse couldn't quite remember the steps he took to get to this point, but he'd somehow ended up with Katerina, yet again, across from him in a restaurant.

He was surprised when she accepted his invitation, and equally surprised at himself for being desperate enough to go on a date so soon after Ana's steadfast silence.

The thought of it made his chest clench.

Katerina set the menu down.

"So," she said, lip tilting up a little, "still someone else?"

Jesse sputtered, and she laughed, shrugging.

"It's obvious."

"Yeah," he said, internally wincing. "We've done this before, haven't we?"

"Yes, we have."

He tapped his fingers on the table. "Can I ask why you accepted?"

"Can I ask why you asked?" An important question, but one she didn't wait for a reply to, instead continuing with, "Honestly, I was curious. And from your message, I didn't get the feeling you were interested in me. You were nice to talk to, though, so I figured…why not?"

He couldn't help but smile. "What a good attitude."

Her answering grin was a little crooked, one side pulled up more than the other, and he was again reminded of how Ana's laugh would pull the right side of her lip up. Before any other memories could come forward, he shook his head and asked, "Have you had any luck yourself?"

"A little, actually." Her cheeks reddened, expression softening. He recognized that look, and there went the ache in his chest once more.

"I'm glad."

"Do you want me to ask you, too? Or do you want to talk about anything else?"

"I think…" He cleared his throat. "I think I'd rather talk about anything else, if you don't mind."

"Not at all. I'm sure you've gotten what it is you want out of this."

Surprisingly, he had.

Jesse realized something, sitting across from Katerina in just the same way as months ago: he was in the same exact spot. He'd distanced himself from Ana the first time because of her age. While he may not have thought of all the repercussions concerning what it truly meant to date someone much younger, there was still an ever-present gravity to the decision, of how he knew if they moved forward, things would change irrevocably.

Yet he decided to pursue her anyway, even when it seemed she wasn't interested, and especially after he realized she was.

Though it was under the guise of their family difficulties, the core reason for all the arguments was, again, because of Ana's age versus his. But he didn't continue this time. No, as Ana said…he'd given up. And he made *her* give up, too.

No wonder she wouldn't speak to him.

If he was really so committed to the idea of being with her after his first date with Katerina, what was different about now? Nothing, besides the outward disappointments from his daughters. Realistically…he knew it would happen. He really did.

Frankly, Jesse felt rather cowardly, tucking his tail when the situation became difficult. He deserved Ana's anger and coldness.

He would make it right, though.

***

She wasn't answering. Since his date, he'd tried texting her (with no reply) and calling her (also with no reply). Jesse didn't want to overwhelm her with notifications, but he had to fight the urge to bombard her phone with his calls.

But if she didn't want to talk, she didn't want to talk.

He could work with that.

Maybe.

First, he tried sending her flowers. Jesse found someone in the area with daylilies, though it took him a few phone calls to find them. He was thankful there was somebody who would fill the request. He didn't know if it was an odd one, because he didn't know anything about flowers, but he was still appreciative regardless.

Jesse got a call the next day saying no one was able to take the delivery, so they left them outside the door. Although a little disappointed Ana wouldn't get them immediately, he figured she was at work, so she would find them later.

He never got a call, even a full day after. Disappointment drooped his shoulders, and he was left feeling like he didn't particularly know what to do next. Briefly, he considered the other standard apologies: chocolates, cards, and flowers—the last one being a bust.

What else could he do to show her how sorry he was and how much he wanted to talk to her again? He groaned in frustration when he couldn't think of anything, and he plopped down on his hotel bed.

He stared at the light of the fire alarm.

Within a few seconds, he was digging out his phone.

"Hi, Dad," Sarah answered after a few rings, and he grinned, relieved.

"Hey there, squirt." He paused. "I wasn't sure if you'd answer."

"You know, this isn't the first time I've answered since—since then."

"Still," he said. "Thank you."

Sarah sighed. "You don't have to thank me for answering the phone. You're my dad. I'm going to answer."

"Your sisters don't feel the same."

"Dad." His title came out pained, and he felt a twinge of guilt.

"Sorry, sweetie. Don't worry about it."

He directed the conversation elsewhere, which ended up being conversations about Jake, something he didn't mind one bit.

"I just bought him a new coat, and it's *adorable*," she gushed. "It's red with a couple dinosaurs on the front. You'd love it."

"I'm sure I would. Maybe I'll see it soon."

"When are you coming back?"

"W-When? Uh…"

When *would* he be back in America? It would be too soon if he couldn't contact Ana. But perhaps that would be a sign of some sort—didn't really matter from where it came, only that the sign was telling him it wasn't mean to be between himself and Ana.

What if he went back without seeing her—with so many things said and unsaid? Jesse didn't know if he could handle that lack of closure. His throat tightened.

"Hey, Dad?" He shook his head, noting the soft tone of his daughter's voice.

"Yeah, what's up?"

There was a pause. "Are you…okay?"

"You don't…" His lips screwed up a moment. "You don't want to hear about that."

"Well, maybe…Maybe I do."

There was conviction in her voice. He'd heard it enough times from her when she was growing up that he definitely recognized it.

His reply was hesitant. "Sarah…"

"Tell me," she said. "I want to know, to understand. Tell me."

Jesse didn't know if she would change her mind halfway through, but he decided to take the opportunity, so he told her. They were the shortened notes, of course, and he left out specifics of their argument, but she hummed in response to much of what he said and remained silent for the rest.

"Is there something special, between you? Like a food or something?" she finally suggested. Jesse hadn't expected guidance on how to win her back, especially not from his family, but again, he would take it.

"I mean, I already tried to give her the daylilies. I guess I could try coffee, but the one I'd want to give her, I'd need to ask the barista working at the same place as Ana."

"Right, that wouldn't do." Sarah took a moment, and he could picture her running her thumb over her bottom lip, the thoughtful mannerism she'd had ever since she was a girl.

"What about a place? You get all the business's sweatshirts, so maybe you could get one for her from somewhere you guys like."

"Hey, that's an idea." He perked up. "There are art galleries, yeah! And there are a few museums we've gone to, but...Hmm. I guess I don't know if there's any one in particular she likes more or would remind her of us."

"Nothing else?"

One place came to mind, of course. He knew it was the place they'd spent the most time together, even beyond the coffee shop or the time they'd spent in her apartment.

"Well, there is a park we go to a lot."

"Great! Is there anything you could buy, like merchandise?"

He laughed. "It's not Yellowstone."

"I *know*, but sometimes parks have little stickers or keychains or something for the big ones."

"Not for this one."

"So, there's *nothing* you could get that would remind her of the park. A plant, or a mushroom, maybe…"

"Not really." Jesse frowned. "It's just a normal park with a bridge. And that's really the defining feature. I guess I could maybe—"

Wait. His eyes widened, and he rolled off the bed to riffle through his suitcase. When he grasped on to what he was looking for, he inwardly cheered, then addressed Sarah.

"I have to go, sweetie."

"I take it you thought of something?" Her tone was amused.

"Sure did."

"Good."

After telling her he loved her, Jesse tossed the phone to the side and fully pulled the item from his luggage.

It was the drawing Ana made for him, tucked away in its secure frame. He carried it with him when he traveled. In America, he set it on his nightstand, and here, he placed it on the TV stand. He didn't really watch much TV when in hotels, so instead of glancing at a cooking show, he'd look to the sketched drawing of their bridge.

With Ana still upset with him, he couldn't bear to keep it out, so he'd left it in his suitcase.

Now, Jesse wrapped it up and mailed it, though he did take the time to add a little something to the frame. He made sure to be extremely careful with the packaging, ensuring it wouldn't break on the way.

And, as with the daylilies, he waited with tapping fingers and jiggling legs. Anxiety and anticipation were a nauseating mixture, but he endured it because he deserved it for screwing up so much.

And he waited.

He'd almost completely lost hope for contact with her again—but then, he got a text one late afternoon. Jesse didn't think anything of it. Could've been someone from work, Sarah, or even Jake, when he got a hold of his mom's phone on occasion.

Instead, his heart leapt when he saw the name.

Ana.

But his heart plummeted when he read on.

I'm in the hospital. Please call me.

Chapter Twenty-One

Ana felt a little guilty for how short she'd been with the driver when she entered the cab, but she was still seething about—about the *breakup*. She preferred to feel the anger instead of the drowning sadness, so she let it linger as he drove her to her hotel.

She clenched her fists, digging the nails in until it *hurt*.

How could he *do* that? How could he come to her apartment to say he wanted to break apart like what they had was nothing? How *could* he?

The more questions she asked, the more furious she became until she wished she was out of the car so she could pace her frustrations out onto the sideway. But she was locked in the moving vehicle; she merely bounced her leg in aggravation.

The anger roiled under her skin, but it didn't know where to go, where to direct itself, so it merely simmered, centered on Jesse, then her parents, then herself, then cycled back to Jesse until she was nothing left but a boiling pot of nauseating *rage*.

Ana didn't typically stay angry for this long. She was someone who blazed searingly hot for a few moments before fizzling out. She wasn't someone whose veins pulsed magma, but there she was, not able to let go of how furious she was.

How *upset* she was.

And perhaps that was the reason for the turmoil. She wasn't *just* feeling anger, was she? Ana was hurt, so very *hurt* by Jesse's decisions. And she was devastated by her parents' attitude toward her choices.

Most importantly, though, Ana was ashamed. Because for a moment—a single, fleeting moment—Ana was relieved when Jesse wanted to break up.

Her senses came back to her right after, thankfully, but the undiluted reaction lingered in her memory, and she wondered if she would've come to the same conclusion as Jesse if she'd had more time to think about the future.

She would've liked to think she'd have made a better choice, but who knew? As Jesse pointed out, she was exhausted, tired from fighting and avoiding her feelings. Would she really have chosen differently? "*It's better this way.*" She shook her head at the recollection of those words. Perhaps not if she went day after day without mending her relationship to her parents.

Shifting in her seat, Ana rested her head against the window. It didn't really matter, did it? And besides, she had other things to think about, like how she was on her way to talk to a curator! Finally, after so many years, she was making steps to achieve her dreams.

Of course, Ana didn't want to get her hopes up too far; she would be happy if the woman was just kind enough to answer her questions. Now that she had started envisioning her future amidst art pieces and history, Ana didn't think she could go back to being content at the coffee shop, not really. Of course, she would miss Elaine, but Ana had to leave eventually.

Feeling lightened by the upcoming introduction, Ana wondered why it took her so long to really *try*, but...

Ana pressed against the crescent moon indents in her palm, still sore from when she'd clenched her fists.

Jesse was the reason she had decided to follow her dream.

He was also the reason she started drawing again.

Her eyes burned from unshed tears, and Ana blinked them away. *Why* did he have to leave her? *Why*? And, she growled, *why* was she crying so much lately?

Ana huffed. She would think about it later. She—

The driver cursed, his eyes wide with fear as he bodily pushed down on the horn, and Ana turned her attention to where he was looking. Headlights.

There was a moment just before the car hit, a second's blink of disbelief, like she was watching a movie. The vehicle wasn't going to hit *her*; it was a trick, or a dream, or something else altogether.

But the moment ended, and the front end of the oncoming car careened into the passenger's side of her cab.

After that, nothing, only darkness.

*   *   *

There was a lake near Ana's house in Romania when she was younger. Most days, depending on the season, she was over there to swim or to ice skate. She remembered how she used try talking underwater; she found it funny how, when she submerged herself in the water, her own voice as well as those on the surface were incomprehensible, just a dull whoosh of sound.

Now, Ana heard those same noises, which didn't make sense; she knew she was no longer a child, and she hadn't been swimming in ages. Some of the sounds were familiar, but not enough that she could place them, and any time she got close, darkness encroached on her consciousness.

It seemed to be a bit of a pattern. She'd wake enough to have some sort of vague connection to what was outside of her own head, then she'd sleep.

Ana felt like she slept for too long.

When her body finally committed to waking, Ana winced as her eyes opened, the light a shot of discomfort into her cornea. Trying again, she noticed voices, but she didn't understand them at first. Ana imagined her brain fastening together like a quilt, patch by patch, until each seemingly unrelated thought was sewn into her consciousness.

The voices, she realized, were her parents.

"M-Mama?"

There was a cry of relief. "Yes, baby! I'm here."

Her mother took her hand. Ana couldn't see her do it, but she felt it, just as she felt another gentle pat on her forearm. Her father.

"Where…?"

"You're in the hospital. You were in a car accident. Do you remember?"

Surprisingly, Ana did. She couldn't recall much about the aftermath, which Ana didn't mind at all; how she got to the hospital was a blur, but she definitely remembered the moment of the crash.

Her parents proceeded to tell her a car had run a red light and smashed into the side of her cab, which folded in half, narrowly avoiding folding Ana, too. The driver, thankfully, made it out with only a broken arm and bruised ribs and had been released days before Ana.

According to her parents (and the doctor, who visited after being informed Ana was awake), Ana had a punctured lung from a set of cracked ribs and had needed extensive surgery, not to mention the fractures and bruises and cuts scattered throughout her body.

Even if the beeping machines and surgery bandages hadn't given it away, Ana's sore chest would have confirmed the diagnosis. The doctor advised her she'd need at least another week of observation before she could be released. Only one week, and it would be boring—terribly, horribly boring—but she could endure it. Being bored was infinitely better than being dead.

It was a sobering thought. She almost *died*. She very well could've. Sometimes, half asleep and half awake, the light of the room glared like the headlights. It made her gasp and flinch like a small child afraid of monsters in the dark. It was frustrating, but the doctors told her it was a normal reaction to a trauma like hers.

Ana wasn't particularly used to the word *trauma* in association with her. Trauma felt too severe a word to use for a simple car accident, but she didn't know what else she could call her nighttime frights.

The doctors also mentioned she may not be able to climb in a car easily, and if she couldn't, to contact a therapist.

"It'll be alright, sweetheart," her dad said earlier, patting her arm in that gentle way of his. "You'll heal just fine."

For some reason, her father's confidence always seemed more significant than her mother's—likely because her mother did most of the talking, and her father only occasionally piped up.

Ana couldn't say enough how nice it was to see her father again. His presence was a comfort, one that reminded her of childhood and a hand that rubbed her back when she was frightened.

He used to sit next to her at night when there were boogeymen under the bed and ghouls sprouting from the trees. The touch of his gentle hands was nestled in the special part of her brain reserved for the most precious of childhood memories, the ones that felt magical by how clear they were or warm they made her feel when she thought of them.

Getting jostled around by a car shook up a few old memories, and she wondered what other sentimental scene would take her by surprise next. Perhaps something about her mother, or a time when she toddled around the kitchen as a baby.

Either way, her difficulties with her parents seemed so silly after the accident, especially knowing how much they had been around during Ana's recovery and surgery. How could she not think they could overcome that fight?

Unfortunately, though, they couldn't be there every hour of the day, which made Ana's thoughts linger on other subjects. She hadn't realized until now how much the argument with her parents had overwhelmed her brain until she didn't have to worry about it anymore.

Ana had other problems to mull over during the long minutes and hours alone in her room. Jesse, mainly. The fight with Jesse and the memories they shared to be more specific.

Ana was reminded of their dates and touches and sweet words, which overshadowed the hurtful ones.

If anything, she was grateful her stay in the hospital provided her with time to reflect. That was practically all she could do trapped there, but there was much to think about, she knew, and this time, she wouldn't have frustration punctuating each line.

With blank walls and nothing else to do, she yearned, as always, to talk to Jesse. Even though the thought of him also sparked her irritation with him, she couldn't get him out of her head. One moment she'd wax to angry, and the next it would wane to sadness. So, she thought of him some more. She remembered their dates and touches and kind words, which overshadowed the hurtful ones. She thought of him again and again—she knew she missed him.

Ana missed him.

She closed her eyes. Yes; there was plenty to the think about in this empty room.

***

The doctor had come in a number of times already that day, so Ana furrowed her brow when he lingered after his last check on her breathing. The man clasped his hands together in front of him. Ana became a little impatient by the pleasantries...until he finally revealed his real reason for being there.

"You're pregnant."

Ana stared at him. The syllables registered in her ears, but their meaning—they felt like just words, something out of context she'd read in the middle of a book.

You. Pronoun, used in this case to address whoever the speaker is talking to.

Are. Verb of "to be," one of the first she memorized when learning English. A slippery little thing that changed forms often.

Pregnant. And it was around this point that her brain categorized the sounds of the word so distantly that it completely lost its meaning. There were vowel sounds, a G in there, and it ended on a solid T.

She *felt* the word more than she understood it, and her hand drifted to her stomach as her eyes widened.

"Pregnant?"

The doctor nodded. "We discovered you are with child before the surgery, and don't worry, the baby is fine.

A nurse will be in here soon to give you some information and to answer any questions you have."

Ana nodded, though it felt awkward—like knowing how to nod had gotten scrambled in her brain from the accident. The doctor continued by talking about prenatal care and obstetricians, but it was hard to concentrate when she was stuck still on *pregnant*.

Pregnant, pregnant, pregnant.

Pregnant—with Jesse's child.

Chapter Twenty-Two

For the past hour, Ana had done nothing but lay in her bed with hands resting over her stomach. For the past hour, Ana had done nothing but think about what the doctor had told her.

She was pregnant.

She was pregnant with Jesse's child, and he hadn't been to the hospital to see her. Her mother said she contacted him, but he still hadn't been there. Ana loathed the look of pity on her mom's face when she wondered aloud where he was.

Why hadn't he been there? Was their parting really so permanent that he wouldn't even want to visit her in the hospital? Even before they were dating, they were close friends; he was someone she could connect with and rely on. From the way he had asked if he could see her again after their argument, Ana assumed he would want to at least *talk* to her.

Obviously, Ana assumed wrong, which made her insides twist. It was a sensation she never questioned before, but it felt new now that she had another being growing within her.

Surreal, it was. Ana knew people she had gone to school with who had kids, people she talked to while they were pregnant, so she'd heard all the stories, but Ana didn't think there was anything that could truly prepare anyone for the realization that they were pregnant.

For Ana, it was like her body didn't belong to her anymore. There was something foreign there—but she felt an odd protectiveness toward it, too. It was a puzzling sensation. She wondered if those who received transplants felt the same, like their body was not fully their own.

Perhaps that's why it was difficult to accept. Thinking back, she'd missed her period, but since they were usually so inconsistent, she hadn't concerned herself. Evidently, she should have.

Because she was *pregnant*.

Shaking her head, Ana knew she needed to wrap her mind around it. The doctor told her she was pregnant, she had a list of prenatal care supplements she needed to take when she left the hospital, and she already decided abortion wasn't an option for her.

The last thought made her squirm uncomfortably in her bed. Knowing the baby was *hers* made her want to wrap her arms around herself as another barrier of protection, and knowing the child was *Jesse's*...

There was a cold shiver of panic and a disheartening amount of sadness weighing her down, but underneath both was a happy flutter in her chest that was only growing, regardless of the negativity that clung to Ana's bones.

Over the next few days, as the oxygen came out and Ana was gritting her teeth with impatience to leave, the flutter kept building. It was almost a full wingbeat now, but still, there were doubts

What would Jesse think, being a father of another child so many years after his own daughters had grown up? Would he be displeased? She wouldn't have thought so, but...

Jesse still hadn't contacted her.

That was what really was keeping her thoughts whirling around like a rickety carnival ride. She perked up like a dog hearing a squirrel at every pair of footsteps that walked by her door, and she felt so silly every time it wasn't him.

In his silence, Jesse had made it painfully clear he wanted nothing to do with her. But she couldn't escape needing to talk to him. Her predicament was a joint affair, equally his responsibility as it was hers—and it was equally their excitement, too. At least...she hoped that would be the case.

The nerves she'd been attempting to soothe all day slithered back into her stomach and chest. Ana breathed in deeply, still a little strenuous from her healing lung, but it calmed her enough for the nerves to go away. Until she thought about Jesse again, that is.

Ana debated whether to call him now or after she left the hospital. If he visited her here, she could tell him the news. If he had any questions, he could ask the doctors. Then again, if the conversation went badly, Ana wasn't keen on crying in front of strangers; she barely enjoyed doing so in front of those she loved.

Clapping her hands together, she knew she had to make a decision, unpleasant or not.

Ana had to talk to him. She *had* to.

She stretched for her phone on the small rolling table. It was fully charged. She expanded her sore lungs once more, then swiped it open. Just as she was about to bring his name up to text, her mother stopped her with a quick, "Wait!"

Ana furrowed her brow. She hadn't even realized her mother was there, but when she glanced at the time on her phone, her eyes widened. It was much later than she thought, around the usual time her parents visited.

"Why?" she asked.

The thin lips and frustration overtaking her mother were not what Ana was expecting to see; she leaned back, more in confusion than anything, when her mother moved forward to grab the phone. But Ana removed the device from her reach with a raised eyebrow.

"Mother, what are you doing?"

"I'm trying to take the phone."

"Yes, but *why*?"

Mary took a couple of steps back, crossing her arms. Ana frowned when she didn't answer.

"Mama, I don't understand. What's the matter?"

Ana knew her mother was considering something from the way she was biting her cheek. It took a few more seconds before the irritation left her as she breathed a long and weary sigh.

"I just…want to make sure you're not making a mistake."

"A mistake…?"

Ana's eyes widened, then drifted to the phone in her hand.

"You said you called him," she said, her voice barely above a whisper. If she spoke too loudly, she feared how true the words would be. "I thought you changed your mind when you said that. But you said a *mistake*."

Her mother didn't say anything and trained her gaze to the wall behind Ana's bed.

"Mother," Ana said, voice grave, "did you contact Jesse?"

Finally, her mother's eyes—the same shade as Ana's—locked on to hers, and the two stared at each other. Ana didn't dare look away, not when the answer to her question was so imperative.

Mary's jaw clenched, then it released when she answered, "No."

Though it was what Ana suspected, the blunt reply created an uncomfortable, painful lurch in her stomach.

"You didn't call him. You didn't call him when I was in surgery, or when I was unconscious. He has had *no idea* where I've been for a *week*?"

"It's better this way," her mother said, using the same words as Jesse had spoken before the accident. Every ounce of repressed anger at the unresolved situation flared up, exacerbated by her mother's attempt at a soothing, reasonable tone.

"It's not *better*," Ana seethed, fury pulsing under her skin. "Nothing about this is *better*."

"It is when you make unreasonable choices, Ana." She gestured to the phone like it was some sort of immoral torture device. "Not that I had much to worry about. That was silly of me."

"What do you mean?"

A thought came to her, and her heart dropped. Ana searched through her phone, scrolling frantically down to the Js in her contact list. Jesse's name was gone. Her hand shook, her grip tight against the case.

"I can't believe you," she said in a voice harsh and rough next to the smooth, tidy lines of the hospital room. "I cannot believe you!"

Mary stepped forward. "I'm trying to make the best choice for you, Ana!"

"No, you're being controlling! As always! You took my phone and deleted his name. What, did you delete messages and calls from him too? I wouldn't be surprised." At Mary's pinched expression, Ana gaped. "Oh my god, you *did*. What would possess you?"

"I'm trying to protect you!"

"*Protect* from what?"

"From—from that man! Who got you *pregnant*! You're not even married!"

Ana's temper flared, and she clenched her fists at her side. "His name is Jesse, Mother, and like it or not, I love him. And I *am* pregnant with his child. *Our* child."

"No," her mother snapped. "He is no good for you, too old, and you will *not* contact him."

Ana stared, disbelieving and disgusted.

The moment seemed cavernous in the way it sucked the rest of the world into its maw to leave just the two of them to decide how the next should proceed.

But Ana decided.

She fingered the bead at the end of her braid, something she had for as long as she could remember. Even after all this time, it was smooth; it came out easier than she expected.

Ana heard her mother gasp, but she wasn't looking at her, only at the bead in her palm. It weighed less than she remembered.

All the memories swirled in her head, the many times her mother had woven the bead into her hair, the pictures of her grandmother with the same braid, they all came to mind. As did her mother's lie.

The clack as it hit the floor seemed to echo, and the resulting sound shattered the bubble surrounding them. As loud as it seemed, the din of the hospital as well as the people within it drowned out the sound.

Only one thing remained in her hair, and she fingered it with a gentle touch. The museum charm Jesse had given her.

After a moment of stunned silence, her mother practically fell to her knees in a desperate lunge for the bead. Mary stared at the blue orb she cupped into her palms with both hands.

"A-Ana," she gasped like she could barely comprehend what her daughter had done. Ana felt a moment of regret, but she didn't even need to actively squash it before the anger flared once more at how her mother didn't seem to be regretful in the slightest.

"I don't want it anymore," Ana said, voice sure. "And I don't need your approval *or* your permission for my choices." She pressed her lips together as she stared down at her mother. I'm not a child anymore, Mother, and you can't control who I allow into my life. *I* decide that. *Not* you. I can't believe you would honestly deny the father of this child, the man I love, an opportunity to at least know that I'm pregnant. All because you think you know what is best."

Finally, her mother's expression saddened, and she appeared as though she might speak, but Ana didn't want to hear anything she had to say, especially if it was more excuses or even an apology. What she wanted was to contact Jesse.

Without another word, Ana gingerly got out of bed and turned away from Mary, who was still crouched on the floor. She exited into the hallway, where she made her way to the hospital's café.

With phone in hand, her movements were automatic as they sought Jesse's contact information, but she quickly remembered her mother had deleted him. Thankfully, Jesse had been old-fashioned concerning the exchange of their numbers, and he'd scrawled it onto a paper coaster from work. Until she'd spilled water on it, and the ink numbers bled into each other. Still, the coaster had remained on her coffee table, and she'd become familiar with the digits.

She typed them in to the message app and didn't think twice before sending her message.

I'm in the hospital. Please call me.

Chapter Twenty-Three

Within a minute of Ana's text, her ringtone echoed through the cafe. She answered immediately, not even checking the caller ID — not that she needed to. It was Jesse.

"Ana," he breathed out.

"Jesse," she answered in kind, feeling as though their names meshed and coiled into each other over the line.

"You're in the hospital? Are you okay? What happened?" His questions were rapid and panicked; before he could worry himself anymore, she cut him off.

"I'm okay."

A sigh escaped through the speaker, and she could hear the relief in it.

"Good," he said. "Good." A moment went by before he asked, quieter this time, "What happened?"

"After...after you left my apartment, on my way to the hotel, a car hit the taxi." She heard him gasp. "I had surgery, and I was unconscious for a while. But I'm alright now."

"I—" His voice cracked. "I can't believe it."

"I know," she whispered. "It all happened so fast."

"And you're—you're *really* okay?"

Her heart warmed at the ongoing worry, so she reassured him, and once more he let out a breath. The sigh was so long Ana could almost feel his anxieties releasing with it.

Silence overtook the line, and Ana bit her lip. She was tempted, very tempted, to blurt out what the doctor had told her, but she didn't want that to be the reason they talked. She didn't want the news to overshadow what they needed to discuss first.

Besides, it wasn't something to tell him over the phone.

Instead, she licked her lips, debating on what she should say first. There had been so many things she'd wanted to tell him over the last couple of days, but they simultaneously felt like the most and least important. Why mention her feelings about the breakup when she could talk about her family? Why mention her family when she could say how much she missed him?

The conversation she'd imagined developed like a painting, everything in order from background to foreground, but what she was actually experiencing was a series of doodles on a blank page. A wolf in a corner, a star in the middle, a scarecrow on the bottom, and none more important or prominent than the next. She didn't know where to start.

"I want to apologize."

Ana was startled when he spoke, but she stayed silent while Jesse continued.

"You were right," he said. "I gave up. I was...a coward, and I shouldn't have taken the easy route, breaking up. We should've figured out our family situation together. So, I'm sorry, Ana. I'm sorry I made the decision for us and didn't even talk to you." As he spoke, his voice grew quieter until it was almost a whisper when he asked, "Do you think you could forgive me?"

Her answer was immediate. "Of course, Jesse. I was hurt by what you had done, but... after the accident, I realized all of it—the pressures and the fight and our family's opinions—it doesn't matter. As long as I love you and you still love me, that is all that matters to me."

"Yes—yes, I love you," he said, quick to reassure her, though she admitted to not being very worried, especially after she found out how much he'd tried to contact her.

"Then that's all we need."

His voice was soft, and it caressed her ear like a feather. "Yeah. Yeah, it is."

Her throat tightened—out of happiness, for once—and all the worry and agony of the last few days whistled away in the breeze of his voice.

"Can we be together again?" Ana asked, and she didn't care if he heard the hitch in her voice. Not if it was Jesse.

"Ana," he said, "I would like nothing more. As long as you'll have me, I'm yours."

Her exhale was jovial, as close to a laugh as a single breath could be, and it was thick with her cresting emotions. "Then I'm yours, too."

"I wish I was with you right now." Ana heard the longing and felt it in her own chest. "I want to hold you in my arms again."

"Yes, please," she said.

"When can I? Are you being released from the hospital?"

"Tonight I can leave."

"Do you want me to pick you up?"

Ana shook her head but repeated the sentiment aloud, her lip pulling up at the edge. "As much as I want to see you, I think I love the thought of my own bed even more."

Jesse laughed. "Fair enough. You should get your rest anyway. Even though they're releasing you, I'm sure you're still exhausted."

"I am." Her words were almost like tired sighs.

"Then how about I see you later this week?"

"Tomorrow afternoon," she countered.

"That soon? Are you sure?"

"Absolutely positive. Besides, I can easily bring you home with me if I am tired still."

"Bring me home? I take it you have somewhere in mind to meet that isn't your apartment."

Ana smiled. "Where we always meet, of course."

There was a pause before she heard him speak again, and it was with a grin clear in his voice. "Why, of course. *Lebada Pod* it is, my lady."

"Perfect." Ana licked her lips and hesitated, placing one hand on her stomach. It was quickly becoming a habit, the fastest one she'd ever formed. "And...I have some news for tomorrow. Good news," she reassured quickly. "Very good news, but I thought I would let you know."

"I'm looking forward to it."

Ana beamed. "Me too. I'm so glad we could talk."

He hummed his agreement. They quieted, but Ana didn't mind. It was reassuring just hearing his breaths against the speaker after so long without him being near. She felt a little clingy thinking like that, but she found she didn't care. She enjoyed his company. She was content to sit with him in a hospital café, while she imagined him in his hotel room. Probably the bed; his chair would be littered with his clothes, folded or otherwise.

Ana closed her eyes. This was the first time she'd been able to *relax*. From the moment she woke up in the hospital, it was oxygen, breathing tests, and visits with her parents. Being away from the room she had been contained in was freeing in a very simple way.

"Hey, Ana?" Jesse asked, disturbing the silence with a soft voice.

"Yes?"

"I'm glad you're alright."

Her eyes opened, and she smiled, trying to imagine the expression on his face.

"I'm glad too," she said.

Shortly after, they hung up, and Ana couldn't describe how light, how strong, how *happy* she felt. It was an amazing relief. The worry she had about the baby barely existed anymore. If truly nothing mattered to them but their love for each other, she didn't think Jesse would be upset at all.

Her steps on the way back could be considered jolly with how much spring there was in them. Perhaps she was overexerting herself, but she hardly cared, not realizing until that moment how riddled with negative emotions she had been. Talking to Jesse was like someone using an eraser on the angry graphite lines running up and down her body.

But her movement ceased as she stood in the doorway of her room. Her mother was waiting, sitting on the edge of the bed with her hands cradled in her lap. Her troubled expression, half hidden by her hair, deepened her wrinkles, and there was something so sad about seeing her mother look...old.

Ana traced the lines of gray in her loose bun with her eyes, then trailed them down to her hunched shoulders. She wondered if her mother had been waiting there since Ana left. Ana's mouth pulled down, thinking of how she'd stormed out of the room while her mother was on her knees on the floor. She bit the inside of her cheek when she imagined how long her mother stayed down there.

Movement in Mary's lap caught Ana's attention, and her eyes found blue. Her mother rolled the bead in her fingers. Ana stared at it.

She stepped into the room. "Mom," Ana said.

Her mother's head whipped up to reveal wide, red-rimmed eyes.

Her face crumpled. "Oh, Ana," she said, and the small sniffle cracked any lingering hurt Ana felt toward her mother. Ana strode forward, sitting next to Mary.

Ana sighed, "What you did...It really hurt me, Mama."

"I know." Mary wiped at her eyes. "I know."

Ana didn't know what to say. She had been so consumed by what she'd say to *Jesse* that any other conversation seemed negligible in comparison. As much as her heart hurt seeing her mother look so downtrodden, Ana was still shocked and betrayed by her actions. Perhaps it was pride, or merely the principle of the argument, but Ana didn't want to be the next one to speak.

They sat in silence long enough for Ana to wonder if her mother would really bend. Finally, the older woman shifted, turning herself so she fully faced her daughter. Mary breathed deeply.

"You're right."

Though that was exactly what Ana wanted to hear, the experience still made her mouth part in surprise.

"I—I should've have..." Mary shook her head. "Not contacting...*Jesse* was a mistake."

Ana graciously ignored how she grimaced at Jesse's name. "Then *why*?"

Her mother lifted a hand to rest on Ana's cheek. "Because you're my baby girl." She sighed. "And I suppose I forget you're not a baby anymore. You'll…have your own soon."

Ana gripped her mother's fingers. They held hands on the bed between them.

"I will," she said. "And Jesse will be there too because this child is his as well."

Mary sucked her lips in, a habit Ana noticed when she was thinking. Her mother squeezed her hand.

"I know," she said in a quiet voice. "I don't *like* it, but—"

Ana was already opening her mouth to argue, but her mother held up a hand, releasing Ana's.

"*But*," she stressed, "you've made it clear it doesn't matter what I think."

She said it sadly, but Ana couldn't find it in herself to feel the same.

"So, you are right." Her mother echoed her statement from earlier. "It was cruel of me. I know."

"It *was* cruel," Ana said. "And even after, you still didn't want me to contact him."

There was an implication of asking for more, asking *why* she had commanded such a thing.

Her mother rolled the bead in her hands again, and turned her eyes down at it.

"I didn't want to believe it," Mary said. "I didn't want to believe my daughter was pregnant—and from someone so much *older*. You were supposed to meet someone nice in your coffee shop and settle down and *then* have a child. It was supposed to be *different*."

"Mom, Jesse *is* nice, and I don't want it to be different. I'm…I'm happy as I am, right now."

Mary locked her eyes onto Ana's and held them there for a second less than uncomfortable. "Are you? Happy?"

"I am."

Her mother considered her, then she sighed. "What did he say?"

"About…?"

Mary tutted. "The *pregnancy*."

Ana shifted on the bed. "I didn't tell him yet."

"What?" Mary frowned. "All that fuss, and you didn't tell him?"

"*Mom*, that's not something you say over the phone!"

She crossed her arms. "Well, why not? You'll say the exact same thing either way."

Ana sputtered. "I-I mean, sure, *technically*, but—"

"If you were talking that long, what did you say then? I was waiting here a while."

Ana pinched the bridge of her nose, secretly pleased her mother was back to normal.

"I told him about the accident—since *someone* neglected to do so."

A slight dusting of pink appeared on her mother's cheeks. "I *am* sorry about that."

Ana softened. "I know you are, Mom, but you can't do anything like it again. You're also going to have to get used to the idea of Jesse being around."

"Will I?" Mary licked her lips. "Are you sure he'll be okay with all this?"

"Jesse won't abandon me." Ana was completely confident in that. Whether he was disappointed or uncomfortable with the idea was another matter, but even with those opinions, she still knew he would never leave her to deal with the child on her own.

"If you're sure."

"I am."

Mary narrowed her eyes. Ana didn't look away, keeping her own gaze on her mother for yet another bout of scrutiny—but Ana didn't mind. She knew her mother wouldn't find anything concerning.

"Alright," her mother sighed. "I'll leave it alone, and I will...*try*. I will try—for you."

Ana leaned forward to wrap her arms around her mother's shoulders, who returned the gesture in turn.

"Thank you, Mama," she said.

"You're welcome."

Being in her mother's arms was nice, and Ana realized she hadn't hugged her mom for weeks. *So long*, she thought, as she considered the two of them hugged every time they visited.

When they separated, Mary's smile was soft, but Ana raised an eyebrow when it shifted to quirk into something teasing.

"If he's not as nice as you seem to think, please tell him I will eviscerate him if he hurts you."

"Mom!" she scolded, but her lips tugged up anyway.

"Just pass the message along."

Ana chuckled. "Okay, I will."

"And..." her mother trailed off, biting her lip.

"Mom...?"

Without words, Mary lifted Ana's hand, rotating it so her palm was face up. She placed the bead reverently in the middle. Ana's eyes widened, then lifted to see her mother's vulnerable expression, eyebrows tilted and mouth pulled to the side.

Ana her attention back down to the bead.

How dramatic it had been of her to chuck it on the floor. She didn't regret it—not exactly—because it got her point across, and it made the gesture of her mother placing it gently back into her hand feel magnanimous.

With both of their hands curled over the tradition of their family, it felt like forgiveness; it felt like moving forward.

Ana closed her hand around it.

"Maybe you could give it to her?" her mother said, gesturing to Ana's stomach.

"What makes you think they're a girl?"

"Only that I've always wanted a granddaughter."

"What if you get a grandson?"

Ana laughed at the way her mom pursed her lips. "I suppose that would be fine. And that's a style, isn't it? Men wear long hair sometimes. The little one could still have it."

"Very true."

Ana felt the pressure of the bead against her palm, and she bit her lip before extending the bauble to her mother.

"Can you…?"

Mary's expression gentled as she took the bead. Ana scooted close and brushed her hair—sans the braid—out of the way. She felt more than saw her mother run the pad of her finger down the length, then she paused at the end.

"A museum charm?" she asked.

Ana hummed in agreement as her mother undid the strand.

"Jesse got it for me."

Mary didn't answer, she only stared at it.

"For Christmas," Ana replied.

"I see."

Her mother held it in her hand, running her thumb over it.

"I've missed a lot, haven't I?"

"Jesse knows me very well."

Mary shook her head. "No, no; not just that." She transferred the charm to her palm, presenting it to Ana. The overly bright lights of the hospital room illuminated it so well it was difficult to see the dips and grooves; without any shadows, the delicate contours were nearly erased. "This means enough to you that you would put it in your hair. Your dreams…" Her face flashed a grimace for such a brief moment that Ana almost missed it. "You want this more than anything, don't you?"

For a reason she didn't understand, Ana's heart beat harshly against her ribs. She knew it was a silly reaction—it wasn't as though her mother was accusing her of anything. But Ana had gotten so used to avoiding the subject of her dreams after her father got sick, when she needed to help out and be near her parents. Ana never wanted either of them to feel guilty that she was somewhere she didn't want to be. Besides, Ana really did enjoy working at the café; she had met Elaine, she had met *Jesse*, and for so many years, she had the pleasure of being so close to her family. She wouldn't trade anything for that.

When presented to her this time, though, the option to say what she wanted, she found she couldn't stay quiet. Knowing she'd already revealed what she wanted to Jesse made it easier; she'd already said it before.

"I want it so much, Mama," she said as her eyes filled with tears, but Ana managed not to burst into hysterics. She'd done enough of that in front of her mother lately; she wasn't keen to act so again.

Not that it mattered to Mary. She made a little sound, that sympathetic coo every mother seemed to make, and kissed Ana on the forehead.

"Well," Mary said, voice a little raspy, "better start, then. I think I can handle the sewing myself."

"Are you sure?"

"Absolutely. Don't you worry about your mother. Worry about yourself." She straightened herself and grabbed the strand of hair. "Now, shush, you're distracting me."

Ana laughed, wiping her eyes. They fell into silence, but it was a comfortable one. From the corner of her eye, Ana watched her mother skillfully separate her hair into three even strands before braiding: three over two, one over three, two over one. Ana imagined sometime in the future, Mary cooing and running her fingers through the dark hair of a child with crystal green or maybe stormy blue eyes, and her heart felt practically ready to burst through her chest. Ana was so very glad she had patched everything up with her mother. She wanted the image to become reality and give her child grandparents to dote on them.

Mary hummed, a lullaby she used to sing Ana as a child, and as the notes delicately plucked at her heartstrings, Ana realized it was likely what *she* would sing once the baby was born. Another tradition, she mused. She wondered if Jesse had any lullabies he sang to his children.

"There," her mother said, patting the braid overtop of Ana's shirt. "All done."

Ana touched her hand to it. It was, of course, perfect; as many times as Mary had braided Ana's hair, there was no doubt it wouldn't be.

When Ana's fingers reached the end, her eyes widened. The charm was there, too. Ana didn't know why she didn't expect it to be there, but feeling it next to the bead her mother had clasped onto the end, a new feeling of warmth blossomed, and she went to hug her mother once more.

"I love you," she said.

"I love you, too, Ana."

This hug was longer, and when they separated, Mary stood.

"Now, back to bed. You need a little more rest before they release you tonight."

Reluctantly, Ana agreed, sliding up the sheets to lay sitting up. Her mother pressed one more kiss to her head, then left, but she paused at the door and cleared her throat.

"I assume you're seeing him tomorrow?"

Ana nodded.

"Then...say, uh. Say hello for me."

Ana's grin couldn't be contained. "I will, Mom."

"Good." Mary looked distinctly uncomfortable, but she nodded anyway. With one last wave, her mother left, and Ana was alone in her room. Thankfully, the atmosphere in the room had shifted from what felt like the heated core of a volcano to clear and light, like a room after a cool breeze filtered through from an open window.

Ana settled into the blankets and closed her eyes. Only one more day until she could see Jesse. Her lips tugged up. Only one more day.

Chapter Twenty-Four

Taking one, two, three steps onto the bridge, Jesse was reminded of the urgency and hope he felt when he first returned from America, when he and Ana first said they loved each other. He almost skipped to his destination then too.

At the thought of her, his heart throbbed in a combination of anticipation. Jesse tempered his excitement and the overwhelming feeling of seeing Ana after so much had happened with a few deep breaths. Though she wouldn't be there for a few more minutes, it was hard to not think of her and how much the day felt like a new beginning.

When he'd broken up with her, Jesse hadn't expected to see her again, convicted as he was in his decision, but he was infinitely grateful that wasn't the case. In only ten minutes, he'd see her again. Maybe she would be wearing her favorite peacoat. Of course, the weather that week had been warm—he could already hear the creak and crash of ice cracking and moving along the unfrozen parts of the river—so maybe she'd moved on to something lighter.

Jesse cast his gaze around his surroundings. Despite the warming temperatures, he didn't spot many people, which surprised him. The only other folks taking advantage of the melting snow were a mother and her son playing a card game next to the river.

He used to play cards with Sarah. Euchre was one of her favorite games, and he and his daughters usually teamed up during the holidays to play together—at least, when Jake wasn't underfoot. He enjoyed cards as well, and Jesse was happy to teach him Go Fish and War, but he tended to announce the cards in his hand, including those of the person he was sitting next to, so euchre wasn't typically one they played if Jake needed to be entertained.

A long time ago, before the military, when Jesse was still in middle school, he actually wanted to be a teacher. For extra cash, he babysat, and he'd always loved it, especially when he could teach the kids a new game.

Sometimes, Jesse wondered what his life would've been like if he'd chosen that profession instead. After the military had taken up so much of his career, it was hard to imagine, but he still thought he might like it.

But taking care of Jake was enjoyment enough, though he was getting bigger every day. Kids grew so fast. It seemed like only a month ago he was a mewling baby, red-cheeked and gurgling. Jesse missed all the rattles and diapers and chubby, awkward clapping. He missed being able to hold a little baby in his arms.

Jesse sighed. He'd have to wait until one of his other daughters had a kid, but that didn't seem likely anytime soon. Maybe Sarah would have another child, though with how busy she and her husband were this year, he figured it wouldn't be until at least next year that they even thought about it.

A thought, unbidden, came to his mind, but he dismissed it quickly. It was unlikely—highly so. But the image flashed in his brain—

Ana, hair curled back away from her shoulder, stood with an airy, summery dress which curved over a protruding stomach. Her hands gently rested overtop, and Jesse could picture himself placing his palm near hers and feeling a small kick.

Ever since their conversation in the hospital, he had been thinking of him and Ana together and how much he wanted *everything* with her. He wanted wedding bells, living together, and small feet padding across the wood floor.

He shook his head. Very unlikely—at least the last one. Besides, Jesse wasn't sure how Ana felt about having children of her own. She had always seemed interested in stories of his own kids, but she'd never posited her opinion on the matter during their many talks. That probably meant she didn't want them, which was admittedly a little disappointing, but he would be happy as long as she was.

He would be even happier once Ana officially met Sarah. Jesse and his daughter had been talking more lately.

"I want to meet her," Sarah said to him yesterday after he had explained why Ana hadn't been answering.

"W-What?" Hope sparked in him. "Really? You mean that?"

"Yeah," she said. "You were obviously upset being apart. And you—love her." He appreciated how much Sarah was trying, despite the pain that statement seemed to cause her. "And if she's going to be in your life, and if I want to still see you, I'm going to have to…get used to it."

"I'd really like that, Sarah."

"Maybe, you could call while she's with you?"

Emotion swelled up in him, and he fought off the urge to tear up. Her suggestion meant the world to Jesse.

"Yeah, yeah," he said gruffly, speaking through a tight throat, "we can do that. I can't tell you what this means to me, Sarah, you wanting to meet Ana. I really do think you'll like her."

There was a pause, a bracing breath, then Sarah continued, "Dad, I promise I will make her feel welcome. I can't guarantee the same with Kaylee and Monica, but I know how happy she makes you, so I'll make sure she doesn't feel unwanted when she visits. And Jake won't care," she ended with a note of amusement. "He'll play with anyone."

Jesse laughed. "Yes, he will. That poor delivery man couldn't get away."

Sarah giggled in response, and in that moment with Sarah's promise echoing in his head, everything felt like it was going to be alright. Jesse didn't have to worry about dividing his time between his family and Ana if she came with him back to America. Sarah was willing to bring Ana into their circle, and Jesse was infinitely grateful for that. It wasn't only because he didn't want to be estranged from his daughters, but he didn't want to deny either Ana or his girls from either part of his life. Both his daughters and Ana were what made him whole, and he was who he was because of them.

He wanted to give Ana the chance to put a face to a name and give Sarah the opportunity to meet someone who was already so central in his life. The thought of seeing them together, sitting on his sofa, brought a warmth to his chest that he didn't think anything else could.

All those times he'd imagine Ana's presence in his house were becoming increasingly close to reality, which sent a thrill down his spine. At the moment, he didn't have high hopes for Monica and Kaylee, not when they hadn't spoken to him since his visit there, but Sarah had bolstered his confidence. The world seemed all the brighter, and Ana and Jesse were going to be together again.

His smile probably looked goofy to any onlooker, but he didn't care. Jesse couldn't even describe how happy he was, joy more potent than any triple espresso.

Jesse was already imagining all the different places he could go with her, all the new vacations to take and meals to eat. He could cheer her on when she got a position at the museum, and they would try to soften her parents and his daughters to the idea of them being together. The issue seemed negligible now. They would come around eventually, or they wouldn't. Jesse and Ana weren't willing to give up their happiness for the sake of avoiding disapproval. And they *would* be happy. He knew they would be very happy.

A loud splash caught his attention. His eyes flicked up, not seeing what made the noise at first—until he heard the shriek. And there, a hand grasping out from the water before it slipped underneath the surface. Panic shot through him when he realized how *small* that hand was.

From the shore, the mother screamed for her son, but he was already swept up by the current, going too fast to grasp at anything; even if he could, the rocks were far too slippery for him to find purchase.

Jesse sprinted off the bridge, keeping an eye out for where the frightened splashing was. The arms poking out were short and clothed in red. The color stamped into his brain like a brand in hot wax. He thought he saw dinosaurs on the sleeves, too.

"I just bought him a new coat, and it's adorable. It's red with a couple dinosaurs on the front. You'd love it."

He jumped in the water.

Jesse stopped himself from sucking in at the jarring cold that immediately constricted his body. He swam toward the flailing child, but Jesse could tell he was tiring. He heard a cry of relief from the bank when he made it to the boy, and Jesse braced himself for the clawing and thrashing of the kid desperately trying to search for safety. He slipped below the water's surface to get a hold of the boy before his heavy clothes pulled him further down. A leg hit his stomach, which caused Jesse to take in a gulp of water and forced him back up to the surface, coughing and choking. Plan B, then.

He got a hand around the boy's arm and strained to drag him upward to get his head above the water. Relief crashed over Jesse when the boy's face appeared, and he sputtered weakly.

There would be time to check on him back on shore. Jesse shifted so the boy was on his back with his arms hooked loosely around Jesse neck.

"Hold on tight, okay?"

Once Jesse finally glanced up toward the park, his eyes widened. The current had shoved them farther down than he thought it would, and for a second, he was consumed with panic. But with the boy settled around his back, he had to push forward.

Jesse's breaststrokes were quick and steady as he kicked as hard as he could to make it to the side, but his skin was starting to burn from the cold, and his clothing was heavy. The boy was heavy on his back. Jesse wished he had thrown off his sweatshirt before he'd jumped in; the freeze would manageable it if he could drop twenty pounds of water-laden weight.

The current was so strong, too strong, and it felt like Jesse wasn't making any headway at all as the river rushed so quickly it erased all of his progress.

Fear—in cahoots with the freezing water—started to seize his lungs, but he stamped it down. He would make it. He *would*.

With that determination, he pushed as much strength into his limbs as possible, making sure the little boy was still with him.

The current, now that the ice was melting, sliced between the banks of the river with a freedom it hadn't had in weeks. Every ounce of water surged away from the captivity of winter.

Jesse swam.

And swam.

And swam.

The physical motions were all he thought of as he pumped his legs because if he thought of anything else, he would falter and sink both him and the boy.

He swam.

Voices were calling him from the bank, but he couldn't make them out over the roaring water. Every second, he was pulled or pushed back under, reminding him of not only his heavy layers and passenger, but the swift current that seemed to get stronger and stronger.

Then he saw a hand, and he thrust his arm out to clasped an exhausted hand around theirs. He was desperate for the rescue to be over and desperate to catch his breath, but the fingers in his started to slip. Any momentary relief he found got swept away with the river as the person was losing their grip on him. Jesse didn't have enough strength left to swim the rest of the way. He knew he didn't. His movements were already slowing, getting sloppy. He could feel the little arms around him, and he knew there wasn't much time left.

Jesse's hand slid a little farther out of their savior's.

There were a few moments in his life where he'd resigned himself to whatever his fate may be. In this moment, he knew exactly what it would be as the unrelenting waves of water pushed against his limbs. And though he tried not to think of it—he still had the little boy on his back to worry about—his family came to mind. The person at the top of the list was Ana and the image of her pregnant and in a summer dress.

He never got to see the bridge with her in summer.

He never got to see the little swan babies in spring.

He never got to marry her.

He wouldn't see Sarah again.

He wouldn't get to make up with Monica or Kaylee, and that was one of the most painful regrets he was tallying in the time he had left.

Jesse marveled at how his mind could distance itself from the situation to reflect, but he supposed that was what made the brain such a fascinating thing to many. He was grateful for it. He could see his daughters and little Jake and Ana's smile filter across his waterlogged vision even as his limbs wobbled and his lungs ached.

Only his fingertips were holding on now.

What would Ana think when she got to the park? She was due to arrive at any minute. Would she think he didn't come? Jesse hoped not. Ana was one of the best things that had happened to him, and he wished they had gotten more time together.

Jesse wished many things as his legs pumped fruitlessly. He wished he could've proposed to her. He wished he could've brought her to his home. He wished he would've told her at least fifty more times that he loved her—so much.

Jesse just wished.

The river pulled him away from the hand. Jesse instinctively tried grabbing for it again, but he was already careening away. If he could've seen it more clearly through the water splashing in his face, the release of his grip probably would've been dramatic and slow.

Instead, he swallowed more water without the extra hand keeping him afloat, and felt small arms tighten around him.

His foot hit a rock.

Jesse had never felt his body move so quickly. Both feet pushed against the rock, then in as many motions as he could spare, he grabbed the boy from his back and pushed him, tossed him, did whatever he could and hoped those hands, which had given him the gift of a few more seconds, would catch him. Even if he only shoved him forward a foot, Jesse prayed it was close enough.

Jesse didn't get to see if they did, for as soon as the boy left his arms, his muscles stopped, his feet stopped kicking, and his body followed where the river took it, down, down, down below.

He thought about *Swan Lake*, how Ana told him the prince drowned in one of the endings. That was his least favorite, he recalled. He preferred the happier one, where Siegfried and Odette stood triumphant over the evil wizard and lived happily ever after. He bet that version of Odette looked like Ana. He could even imagine Ana as Odette, graceful like a swan and just as enchanting.

Jesse wondered if the glittering darkness around him was what Siegfried saw when he jumped into the lake. Like moonlight dappling against the misty town of Heidelberg, that galaxy drawn down to earth. The changes in color made it less frightening, he decided, like the soft moment in the morning before waking, when the sun would warm the back of his eyelids, making them glow.

If he kept his eyes closed, he could go back to bed. Ana was there beside him, snuggled into his back like the sandy floor of an ocean beach, warm and light with her lips against his skin.

Just a few more minutes, he promised, then he would wake up.

The glow upon his eyelids faded, consuming them in full darkness.

Just a few more minutes…

Chapter Twenty-Five

The walk comfortable, and one Ana missed dearly. She remembered the first time she walked to the park after work to meet Jesse. She'd waited on the bridge for him, kids shrieking with laughter in the background. Ana was intrigued by him above all else, this man who so quickly became a regular in not only the coffee shop but her life as well.

It was strange, she thought, how far away that day seemed, how much older she felt. Looking back on that day was like reminiscing about childhood.

Though Jesse and Ana hadn't even been dating a year, it felt like so much longer. There was a certain heaviness to experience, and she supposed that was a fine definition of the relationship she and Jesse had. They'd loved, laughed, fought, broken up, gotten back together, and were now expecting a child.

There were many parts of the relationship she didn't want to ever change, but she could admit to a few moments she wished they'd approached differently. Mainly, their families. From the start, they knew how important they were to each other. His daughters were Jesse's life, which wasn't surprising given how much he'd sacrificed as a widowed father, and Ana was attached to her parents. Perhaps more than others, but she knew they were so close because they were *home*—the tradition and culture and identity of her country she had left.

Despite all that, they should've talked about what they'd do if they got the reactions they did. Instead, Ana and Jesse presumed they'd receive the blessings of those they loved, and both were horribly, painfully disappointed when the opposite was true.

Honestly, it was most of what happened since his last trip to America that she wished she could tweak.

But it wasn't to be. And, though it had taken longer than intended, Ana and Jesse had ended up where she wanted them to be: together.

It would be a little out of order, though. Most people tended to marry before they became pregnant, and Ana had assumed she would be in that majority. Of course, it was unlikely Jesse wouldn't propose after finding out. Ana knew he wouldn't abandon her; that much was certain. The only portion that wasn't was how excited he may or not be about the concept of another child so late in life. Regardless, she knew he was there to stay, which was a relief to her.

Approaching the entrance of the park, Ana fanned herself. The day was a little warmer, and she'd overdressed. She'd received so many conflicting accounts of pregnancy from friends—one was always warm while the other was always freezing—so she thought she'd play it safe and layer, but she was regretting that.

It was a gorgeous day, though. Ana was looking forward to meeting Jesse again for walks along the paths. She missed them during her stay in the hospital and throughout the harsher weather. They'd made such a ritual of it before that it was difficult for her to imagine going without their park visits.

With a smile tugging at her lips, she wondered if they would bring their child here. Ana could imagine it: a black-haired, blue-eyed little baby with their father's chin and her cheeks. Maybe a boy who would love theater or a girl who would collect business merchandise. Ana laughed at the image. Hopefully they wouldn't dress in sweatshirts—neither the boy or girl. If there was one aspect of childrearing Ana was unconditionally excited for, it was being able to buy clothing for them, and she figured Jesse wouldn't be too much help in that department.

She wondered what he bought for his daughters when they were young. Ana hoped something presentable; from the pictures she'd seen of them as adults, they certainly dressed better than their father, thankfully. Ana was sure he would look at them just the same if they did, though, that proud expression on his face.

It was endearing, the way his face would soften in a completely different way than how it did around her. There was a particular expression that all parents had, it seemed, and she wondered what hers would look like. She was thankful she would have someone quite experienced with raising children to help her along the way.

Ana didn't know what kind of mother she would be. It was something she hadn't considered to be so tangible, not for many years. Ana typically only had thoughts of marriage and baby showers and cribs when she had been dating someone a while, and for a few years, there hadn't been anyone she could even start to picture that with.

Then Jesse surprised her, and she was left a little anxious, not having prepared for the type of life she had unknowingly signed up for. In hindsight, their relationship did develop quickly. After all, she was already *pregnant*—a thought she still had trouble processing.

But even though she was fearful about bringing up an entire life from infancy to adulthood, Ana was excited. And she was looking forward to doing it with Jesse.

A splash and a shrill shriek pierced the air and startled her, and she squinted to see what the noise was up river. Someone had fallen in, she saw—and someone just jumped in after them. Ana started moving forward toward the commotion, but she cursed her weak body, unable to move as fast as she wanted. Though she was cleared to leave the hospital, her lung was still healing; she wasn't supposed to strain it. At least she entered the park in the opposite entrance, so she was in position to see what tumbled downstream.

The two were approaching quickly; Ana hurried closer, almost stumbling when she got a closer look at the man in the...sweatshirt?

Was that...?

Her eyes widened, and she gasped, her feet moving forward before she even thought consciously to do so. Though it had been years, she used to run the hundred-meter dash when she was a teen back at her school; speed burst from her limbs as if she was running in a race.

The soles of her feet ached in her loafers, but she pushed forward to make it to the edge of the river. Her heart lurched and spasmed when Jesse's face broke the water.

Ana lunged forward, stretching on her belly until she could reach them, and relief washed over her when she felt his hand in hers, so strong she almost lost her grip—but her hand tightened at the last second.

She yelped as his weight dragged her forward, but she managed to claw her hands around a jagged rock before she was pulled in too. She couldn't hold for long, her arm already shook from the strain and the sharp edges of rocks digging into her broken ribs was blindingly painful.

Her whimper was lost in the sound of the rushing water as his hand slid further from hers. Soon enough, only their fingertips would be clinging on to each other, and she couldn't bear the thought of what would come next. Her fist tightened.

When not squeezed from the pain and effort, her eyes would lock on to his body to make sure he was still there. He was treading water, and his eyes scrunched up with effort, or maybe from the water splashing into his face as it rushed by. He probably couldn't see her, she thought.

The wires sparking in her veins alerted her nerves and injected her insides with adrenaline; she was immediately aware of the way the hand suctioned to the rock lost some of its grip. Her heart consumed her senses with its incessant throbbing, pitching her veins with more energy with every beat.

Her head whirled back to Jesse, and she noticed his movements changed. Ana didn't know what it was about them that was different, only that his swimming had shifted into something else, something more tired.

His fingers loosened.

"No!" she shrieked, attempting to hold on—*just a little longer*! There was bound to be someone along who could help bring him to safety, him and the child.

His fingers loosened further, and a sob wrenched from her throat. Ana tried shifting her body so she could find more purchase, but one move would release either the hand on the rock or the one around Jesse. And both were failing.

Tears streamed down her face when it was only their fingertips desperately trying to hold on to each other.

"No, Jesse! Please no!" she cried, her eyes blurring with tears.

The next seconds were excruciatingly slow, and Ana could track every movement like the written cues for a play. Jesse's fingers released, released until Ana was grasping at the ghost of their presence. She swatted and clawed at air as guttural, raw shriek tore out of her throat.

Watching his hand drift away was like grasping at the moon when she was young. It looked so close, close enough to touch, but when she tried to envelop it in her small hand, she was always disappointed when she only caught air.

Ana kept grasping only air, over and over and over, grasping for a hand that was too far away from her, but she tried anyway, again and again—

Her eyes widened when she grabbed something, and she stretched forward to hold the moon in her palm, and her fingers tightened around it.

Blinking the water out of her eyes, she saw her hand was around a little red coat, just a tiny bit of a sleeve. She'd grabbed the little boy, who was struggling to make it to her, wheezing and coughing and crying silent tears.

Ana quickly dragged him up toward her, and he clung to her as soon as he made it onto the rock next to her. His hair was matted to his head and in his eyes, and there was a tear in his jacket on the torso; the red stuffing seeped out like blood. Ana smacked his back, helping him expel and hack up the last of the water.

Her eyes didn't want to look back up to the river, but like a morbidly curious onlooker to a disaster, she turned them up.

Jesse was gone.

Cold seeped into her very being, and her motions against the boy's back were mechanical. She didn't know if she could do anything else if she tried.

Her eyes didn't leave the river, but the area wasn't empty; her mind played back what had happened in miniscule, negligible steps that combined to the moment Jesse was pulled under and away.

There was nothing for her to grab when their fingers were ripped from one another's. But with a heart-wrenching lurch, she realized Jesse must've somehow thrown the boy to safety. She didn't know how, but he had.

A woman collapsed in front of the boy as voice cracked with relieved sobs. The mother, Ana figured. The older woman tried talking to Ana, but her sounds didn't register as words. She didn't understand, and she didn't really care to.

At some point, the two left her, and her arm felt heavy now that its purpose had been taken away. It flopped onto the rock, lifeless.

The water rushed by her.

A handful of stray leaves tumbled by in the river, and Ana stared as they went.

Ana didn't move, not for a long while.

Chapter Twenty-Six

When Ana was a girl, she remembered a storm torrential enough to keep the whole town indoors. Inches of rain and monstrous thunder. Unlike some kids, she was never afraid of thunderstorms. Instead, she was fascinated by the sounds, and she loved to close her eyes and listen when the rain hit

For one particular storm, she wanted to be as close to the cacophony as she could be, so she huddled on a window seat and pressed her cheek against the glass. She closed her eyes.

The sound at once dulled and echoed in her skull, skittering a distant sound of discord across her ears. The thunder, the rain—it was all a mass of muffled noise.

As Ana stood next to the river, empty-handed and alone, she vaguely recalled the memory. The world around her was distant, like the storm was barricading her body from everything, and her brain felt muffled as did her arms, blinks, and feet. Ana herself was the glass, and the rain raked along her brain, trickling down her spine into the rest of her limbs to waterlog them.

In her periphery, the flash of emergency vehicles glowed over her eyes, but she didn't have the energy to look fully at them. Her eyes were centered on the river, just past the rock she'd lunged for when she went to grab Jesse, to pull him to safety, to her.

But instead of Jesse in her arms, there had been a child, crying and coughing and shivering. He was gone now. She didn't remember when the boy left, only when she blinked down to see nothing. She didn't remember when the vehicles came, either, nor when men in unforms decided to poke sticks into the river to look for...

She didn't know how long she had been sitting there.

Everything felt so far away, yet ridiculously close—looking through a binocular lens in one eye and out to the horizon in the other. There was something nagging at her mind to pay attention to, but all she did was stare. It enveloped her gaze so much that everything but the river faded, and she was tempted to say she was floating down it.

Ana wondered if she would find Jesse if she was—not like the men with poles, though. Actually find him, and watch him break through the water and claw his way to the bank. He'd gasp in air, but he would still be able to pull himself up. In fact, he'd wait until he was on his feet before shucking the heavy material off only to be left with what she assumed was his plain cotton T-shirt underneath.

And what would Ana do? Would she leap onto him and cling to him like a sloth to a tree branch, or would she whirl around to him, cursing his recklessness but thanking everything in the world that he was alive?

Alive.

A pitiful whimper escaped her throat, and she swallowed it down. She curled herself around her bent knees and buried her head in her legs.

In this new position, she realized something hurt. When that thought flickered in front of her, her awareness centered on it. Something *did* hurt. A physical hurt.

Her stomach.

As soon as the pain registered, the world bombarded her with lights and sounds. A blanket over her shoulders scratched her cheek, voices spoke over each other; it was cold, it was *really* cold, and *her stomach hurt*.

With a gasp, she brought her hands up and cradled her flat stomach. Her breath quickened, and her heart hammered in her chest. Time warbled again, and Ana had no idea how long it took her to find her feet as she breathed and breathed and breathed too fast. But she finally did—they carried her to the flashing lights she'd seen earlier, only a stone's throw away from her. There was even a paramedic standing outside, and as soon as she saw Ana coming, the woman met her, bracing her with an arm on her bicep.

"Ma'am," she said, "tell me what's wrong."

"I-I-I—" Ana's breaths were still rapid and uncomfortable, and she didn't know how to breathe normally anymore. All that was in her head was *her stomach hurt*.

The woman directed Ana to sit on the back of the ambulance, and the cold of the metal against her legs coincided with the sharp intake of air. She could feel the cool air expand against her lungs, and the sensation brought focus to her. She breathed in again, then again.

"Good," the paramedic said with an encouraging smile. "Now what's wrong? Are you hurt?"

Ana swallowed then said, "M-My stomach. It hurts. M-My baby."

Understanding softened the woman's gaze, and she directed Ana into the back of the vehicle, where Ana sat on the cot. Ana attempted to answer all of her questions; no cramping, no burning, no nausea. After a few more, the woman nodded.

"Do you mind lifting your shirt up for me?"

Ana did as told, and she shivered at her warm skin coming in contact with the chilling air. With gloves on, the paramedic did a quick exam of her stomach, gently pressing her way around until she made it to right underneath her bellybutton, and Ana winced.

"You can put your shirt down," the woman said as she removed her gloves.

"Is everything okay?" Ana placed her hands over her stomach again.

"You and the baby will be just fine."

Ana sagged in relief like a waterfall crashing over her chest, cleansing it of worry.

"You have a bruise," she continued. "It'll probably start darkening this evening. Nothing to worry about."

"So just a bruise."

"Just a bruise." She stood from the tiny stool she had been sitting on. "Probably hit it on the rocks when…"

Guilt flickered over the woman's face as she trailed off, looking quite uncomfortable with her explanation, and Ana pressed her lips together. She could only nod, tightening her hand around the fabric of her blouse.

The woman was kind enough to lead her out of the truck. Ana didn't know if she'd be able to find her footing with how shaky she felt now, but she refused to wear the blanket again. She'd already made her statement, not that she fully remembered doing it, and she…she just wanted to leave.

Ana's trip back slogged like she was on a looping children's ride—slow and ready for it to end. She just wanted to be back home. That was all. It became a mantra on the way back, a less enchanting mimicry of Dorothy from *Wizard of Oz*.

She wasn't counting how many times she repeated it in her head, but she imagined it was the hundredth by the time the cab finally stopped fully.

Her apartment building.

She'd stayed at her parents after being released from the hospital the night before, but as she stepped out of the car, her apartment building looked different to her than it had when she left. Ana couldn't place what feature seemed out of place; only that it was *different*. The drive back was, too, as were the stairs when she bypassed the elevator. The thought of standing alone in an enclosed space made her stomach roil, so although she wanted to collapse on the floor, she took the stairs.

The last stairs felt mountainous, but Ana hauled her body up, up, up until she finally made it to her door. There were packages outside of it. She didn't know where they came from, but she didn't have the frame of mind or patience to deal with them in the middle of the hallway. She opened up her apartment door and unceremoniously shoved them inside.

Moving the packages into her arms, she ambled to the kitchen, and set them all down on the tabletop. She plopped down on a chair at with a heavy sigh and pushed the handful of packages away from her elbow room. She wondered why there were so many. She didn't remember ordering anything.

The curiosity that sparked in her was so noticeable after absence of feeling and then the overabundance of it Ana had felt within the last couple of hours, that she was glad to feel something so mundane. She pulled one to her and—

A whimper escaped her lips, and she raised a hand to cover her mouth.

It was from *Jesse*.

Ana clawed at the others, desperate to see the name attached, and her hands shook as her fingers pressed into the identical name on each. All of them were from Jesse. A card. A cardboard package. A vase of flowers.

She touched weak fingers to the flower petals. They were daylilies.

The others—she had no hesitation in opening them, not even to hold off on the harsh ache that would only spread, not when something from Jesse was right in front of her. The card she opened, and she laughed, wobbly as it was. It was a pun, both inside and out, with the message written: "To help with those strange English phrases, and to ask your forgiveness."

She held it to her chest for many moments, fighting off another set of tears. When the urge finally passed, she gently set it down and turned to the package. There was something about the size that tickled her brain, but she couldn't place why it would be important. Instead, she sliced delicately through the tape and folded back the sides of the box.

When the last flap cleared, she was met with green, swirly wrapping paper tucked sloppily around a rectangular object. With slow movements, she nestled it in her hands.

It felt familiar, so familiar that the paper merged into one blurry color through the building of her tears. She blinked, and the droplets escaped downward. With three swift movements, she tore through the paper and pulled the gift out.

Her drawing. The one she'd made for Jesse.

Swan Bridge was penciled on the page, the work that had reignited her passion for her own artwork again. And there it was, clutched between her palms in the same frame—no. Ana moved her left hand out of the way. It wasn't quite the original frame.

Jesse added to it.

"JA," it said in the corner, carved into the wood. The letters weren't precise, not like a laser or machine would do it. They were hand carved.

The ever-present clench around her ribs, an aching rawness that could only be grief, tightened. The only way she could release the pressure was through the already torn throat she could barely speak with.

Ana sobbed.

She sobbed and cried and whimpered her pain with the drawing clutched to her chest in cement-steady hands. As had been the case for the entirety of the day as it bled into night, Ana had no idea how long she stayed in her chair. Her every muscle rigid with static movement. All she knew was that she sat there until she could barely open her eyes and her insides were scraped clean.

The ensuing silence prickled against her senses, but she couldn't think of any sound she wanted to hear.

Except Jesse's voice.

Soundlessly, she padded across the floor to her bedroom. The frame was still in her hands, and she crawled into her bed and shut the door behind her. She left the lights off and cradled the picture to her chest with one hand, while the other rested on her stomach as she nuzzled her head into his pillow. Her lip wobbled when she smelled it. She had washed it earlier that day before their fight. It didn't smell like him anymore.

"Take care of you," she whispered to the picture, a raw sound that didn't even sound like her voice. She imagined the way Jesse's eyes crinkled in amusement at her strange turn of phrase, repeating it back to her anyway.

Then the next she directed toward her baby, and she almost sobbed again but held it in long enough to say, "Take care of you." This time, she meant it as a promise, in the way it actually meant. She *would* take care of this child. Everything that was on this bed was what was left of dear Jesse, and she would protect them at all costs.

She repeated it as many times as she was able, as many times as she could.

"Take care of you."

Both of them, Ana would.

About the Author

Jesse Myrow is a US Army veteran who always dreamed of writing a novel.

In doing so, his goal is to share some of the sights he experienced during his years of traveling as well as add a little love and a drop of drama to create *The Bridge* that links everything together.

Born and raised in Texas, Jesse always enjoyed the outdoors and loved adventures; his mind would run wild as he could only imagine places he'd never been and people he never knew.

But, all that changed when Jesse joined the Army—he realized dreams do come true and life really is one great big adventure.

Jesse Myrow

Made in the USA
Columbia, SC
31 October 2021